Know the enemy, know yourself; your victory will never be endangered.
Know the ground, know the weather; your victory will then be total.

Sun Tzu

ROBERT L RUSSELL

THOR'S JOURNEYMEN

Bohannon Hall Press

Illustrations © by Emelia Ann Designs
Cover Art © by Emelia Ann Designs

Library of Congress Control Number: 2024900796

Publisher's Cataloging-in-Publication Data

Russell, Robert L, 1963-
    Thor's Journeymen / by Robert L Russell ; illustrated by Emelia Ann Designs.
    Niceville, FL: Bohannon Hall Press, 2024.
    266 p.: 18 illustrations ; 23 cm.
    First edition.

1.   Science Fiction, American. 2. Weather Control—Fiction 3. Meteorologist—Fiction. I. Title. II. Russell, Emelia Ann, 1977- III. Mcleod, Bob (fictitious character)
PS3618.U77T463 2024   2024900796

ISBN 979-8-9850298-9-5 (softcover)

Published by Bohannon Hall Press

Thank you to all the family, friends and fans who invested some of their precious time and treasure to support me by taking a chance on Thor's Apprentice. Your investment in me is what inspired my commitment to following that effort with Thor's Journeymen. I truly hope you enjoy this work because it was done for you.

Acknowledgements

A special shout out to all those who serve our Nation in the Armed Forces, law enforcement, as well as, federal, state, and local government service. These are hard jobs. It requires personal sacrifice to do these jobs well, and we all benefit when those who choose a life of service succeed in their assigned work.

Thank you to all those with whom I have had the privilege of serving with in my 27 years of military service. To my brothers and sisters in arms, you inspired me to write this book, and shaped in my mind many of the characters and situations in this story.

Finally, a tip of the hat to my publisher and friend, Rip Coleman, and the folks at Bohannon Hall Press, without whom *Thor's Apprentice* would still be a stack of papers on my desk and a few files on my computer and *Thor's Journeymen* would never have happened.

TABLE OF CONTENTS

CHAPTER ONE

WHERE ARE WE NOW?

The morning was anything but typical for everyone, but especially for those in the National security apparatus of the United States. "Yesterday's revelations were seismic in their impact on the status quo of global power, and that is neither hyperbole nor exaggeration," began the Secretary of Defense in his unscheduled but urgent testimony to the Senate Armed Services committee. Accustomed to holding the attention of those in a room when he spoke, Secretary Fitzgerald was particularly pleased to see this morning he had the undivided attention of every Senator in the chamber as he continued.

"All the claims that controlling the weather is now a reality are true. But they are also incomplete. The Chairman of the Joint Chiefs of Staff, General Charles, and I have both seen first-hand this technology demonstrated in person. It is frighteningly fast, relatively scalable, and the device used is small and easily man portable," he continued. "Dutch and I immediately took this knowledge to the President, and while we believed we had a viable containment strategy in place to better understand and daylight this capability, the events of the past few days have made clear that is no longer the case.

"The person who showed this to us was the same person you saw on the press releases, and who the President appointed as the lead US scientist assisting the United Nations efforts, Professor Robert 'Bob' Mcleod. The good news is that Mcleod is a good man, a patriot, who wants this technology to be used for the benefit of all. That's also the bad news," he added.

"We had several months with Professor Mcleod at our advanced technology research center, and many of our brightest minds in the Department of Defense have had time to study and learn about the technology, how the devices are built, a little bit about operating them and the science behind what makes them work. That too is good news, we have a head start on the rest of the world in understanding this technology and how to employ it, and perhaps defend against it. But that good news also has a bad news flip side to it."

The Secretary took a deep breath before he continued, in part for effect and in part to steel himself for what he would say next, "It also appears that two of the four 'Thor's Hammer' devices that Professor Mcleod turned over as part of his deal with the President, have gone missing from the weapons storage facility at the underground research bunker. It also appears that the director of that facility and its operations whom you all know as Zach, has also been unaccounted for the past nine days. We have reason to believe these disappearances are related, and that it is possible, I say again POSSIBLE, that the catastrophic weather events in India are the direct result of his unsanctioned actions." Well, that was harder to say than he thought it would be as he reached for the water glass to his right on the table between himself and General Charles.

As the Chair of the Committee attempted to gavel the Senators back to order, Secretary Fitzgerald tapped the microphone a couple of times and continued his remarks which quieted the chamber almost immediately, "The threats to our nation are several right now. First, we have half of our working weather modification devices missing. Second, we have the potential of a rogue US government official using that technology in an offensive action against the government and civilian population of another nation, which is an act of war. Third, we have an international media engaged in support of a United Nation's effort to develop a safe and effective fielding strategy and implementation plan being led by the one person who knows almost everything about our botched effort to keep this technology hidden from the world's view."

"Finally, we have confirmed the Chinese weather modification program was much further along than we had originally believed. We knew they were monitoring and occasionally hacked into the systems at the advanced research labs, but until recently, we were not aware that they possessed a shadow system enabling them to see and copy all the camera feeds within the underground facility. They not only have all the computer files which we were careful to keep compartmented, but they also have video of the labs, fabrication and manufacturing areas which basically gives them a how-to-build-it-video of everything we have developed there. We must assume they have not only the knowledge of how to build our Thor's Hammers, but that they likely copied and made some of their own. They will likely work to undermine or even stop the United Nations efforts and blame us. We could be blamed for the events in India, as well as for their actions to undermine the UN efforts while they are advancing their own interests at the expense of ours. I think that is about enough for us to have to consider this morning. This concludes my remarks. Dutch and I will do our best to answer your questions, but please understand this is a dynamic and evolving situation and we know little more than what I have already shared with you this morning," he concluded with a glance over to the Chairman to ensure he was ready to take some of the questions.

As the Senators each took their allotted time to question, chastise, praise or request clarifications from the two men testifying before the committee, the thing that everyone was taking from the room was what General Charles said in response to the Minority Leader's question to characterize the level of threat that weather modification technology represented to the nation. Dutch's response was crisp and clear, "Senator, if I may use a comparison. The threat from climate change is like the boogeyman under the bed in your kid's room. It is slow, vague, and hard to see so you reassure your kid, pull the covers up, turn on a night light, leave them in their room, then you go to bed and sleep soundly in the next room. This on-demand weather modification is like a carjacking at gunpoint where the carjackers shoot you, pull you out of the car, leave you bleeding in the street and drive off with your kid still in the backseat. It is fast, is designed for immediate impact, goes where you go, is up close and personal and nearly impossible to defend against or recover from in time to protect against the next attack. Look at our national response to climate change, and use that to gauge what you think should be on the table for this."

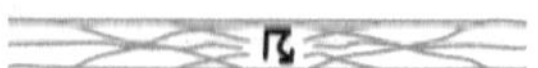

Betty was collecting the remaining checked baggage when the airport porter arrived with a luggage cart to help her. "Welcome to New York Ma'am, by the looks of all the boxes you must be moving here? Can I help you with these?" he offered.

"Yes, please! I could use the help with the boxes, but these are files and I doubt I'd get along very well living here. Pretty set in my ways; there are too many lights and concrete buildings and not enough trees for me. That said, I am excited to visit. I am also going to need some transportation for myself and these boxes to get to my hotel. Can you help me get all this stuff to the right spot to make that happen? I will make it worth your while," she smiled as she asked.

"Of course! You are in good hands ma'am; I got you," he grinned back, as he loaded the boxes onto two luggage carts, led them and her to the hotel shuttle area, flagged down the vehicle with the correct name scrolled onto the doors, and helped the driver load the precious cargo. Betty thanked him and slipped a couple of one-hundred-dollar bills into his hand as she boarded the shuttle. It felt good being able to generously reward someone for their initiative, positive attitude, and doing good work that produced the desired outcome. No job too big, no job too small she thought and wondered when and why the old rules stopped applying to jobs today. Hard and noble work seems to be paid a pittance when compared to some of today's so-called jobs that get exorbitant salaries for playing games, participating in sports, pretending to be someone else, or doing things that are so undefined that assigning a value seems arbitrary.

The noise of the city and the hurried movements of vehicles, people, flashing lights all quickly pulled Betty out of her thoughts and into the bustle of New York as she dialed Bob's cell phone to let him know she was about fifteen minutes out from their hotel.

"What do you mean? Why didn't you call earlier, I would have come to get you?" Bob questioned her.

"Stop telling me what to do and what not to do! You paid me a lot of money to do this stuff for you and I am doing it. Don't you dare presume to tell me *how* to do my job Bob! I am delivering a bunch of boxes to a room, if you don't think I can handle that then you better rethink why you brought me up here to help you. I just need you to tell me what room you want these to go to, so you can tell me on the phone now, or you can show me when I get there. Either way, you better get ready because I am almost there; I am tired, hungry and could probably use a drink and a hug. I sure hope Ann is there!" and the line went dead as she hung up and returned her focus to the drive. She was a great practitioner of the saying, never be so busy getting where you are going that you forget to be where you are, and right now she was in a hotel shuttle with a bunch of boxes in New York City after a very long flight.

As the shuttle pulled up to the hotel entrance, she could see Bob and Ann waiting inside near the revolving door watching intently as the few other passengers filed off ahead of her. Betty was giving instructions to the driver and the doorman about loading her parcels and luggage to be brought to a yet to be specified room when Ann climbed aboard and interrupted her with a hug and warm welcoming words that made them both appreciate the sense of family they had developed in the short time they had known each other.

Bob provided the doorman the room numbers for the boxes and Betty's luggage respectively, and then joined in welcoming Betty to New York and began to explain what was going on, including her role in their newly developing situation.

"Well Bob, what have you gotten us all into?" Betty asked as they rode in the elevator up to the floor that would be their new home for the foreseeable future. Bob had secured all the necessary rooms: a suite for himself and Ann, a connecting series of rooms that would serve as a makeshift office and meeting room, bedrooms for Betty and Father Gannon, and a guest room for whomever may be coming and going to help them get this effort up and running.

"How about you first get settled in, freshen up, change or whatever you do after a long flight and we can all get together in an hour in our room to talk, get something to eat or drink and plan the near future? I will answer all your questions and whatever else you want to talk about then. For now, thank you for what you have done so far. It is important that we have these files here and, most importantly, it is just nice to see you. Especially all fired up, I have been missing that side of you for a while now; so, it's nice to see you like that again! See you in an hour." Bob headed out of the elevator ahead of them toward the room with the door open as the boxes were being delivered from the baggage carts and pointed Ann and Betty toward Betty's room so she could get settled in.

"Well, he hasn't changed much with all of this has he?" Betty said, as if to herself but knowing Ann was walking next to her.

"You've known him longer than I have, so I will take your word for it. I love him just the way he is, so I hope whatever changes this whole situation brings about are small because I want him the way he is right now!" Ann confided as she and Betty entered the room and put the luggage in the designated area.

"Wow, this room is bigger and nicer than my house. What a beautiful and expensive place! I don't need anything this nice, is there another…" Ann interrupted her, and explained that Bob wanted them all close together for lots of reasons, and this was the only configuration in the hotel, or any other nearby that could accommodate them right now. Ann also explained the cost of the room was covered for as long as she was here, and it was not her bill to pay. Bob insisted that we be well taken care of because he had no idea what, or who would be coming in and out of our lives in the near term and wanted us to enjoy some of the finer things while we can. No telling how long that would be, as Bob was not confident in the President's promise to deliver the balance of his five billion dollars. If he did, Bob expected him to freeze those assets almost immediately to leverage Bob's newly approved efforts leading the newly announced collaboration with the United Nations.

As Bob surveyed the boxes of files, he was confident that all the items he needed were indeed present. Betty had always taken better care of him than he thought he deserved, and once again she had done precisely what Bob asked for, and also the things he had forgotten to ask for, to make sure that he got what he needed. Proof positive that she was the best.

The past couple of days had been quite busy for Father Gannon. Since he had been the one who brought Thor's Hammer to the UN and initially described its origins and capabilities, he was doing double duty as the face of the UN effort and the media's primary target for interviews, statements and appearances to describe Doc Auster and how this technology came to exist. As one might imagine, there was nonstop media demand on his time and energy, so the reprieve into the room with Bob, Ann and Betty was a welcome port in the storm that had become Father Gannon's current pace.

As Bob began reading from his notes, he said "Ok everyone, as near as I can tell, here is where we are…"

- The world knows "we" have the technology and devices to control the weather.
- The UN will be leading a multinational effort to field that technology in a fair and benevolent way for all.
- The technology was developed by Doc Jim Auster and delivered by Father Gannon.
- The President of the United States has agreed to join the UN effort and has appointed me to lead the US technical contribution to that effort.
- For now, I still have my fortune accessible and intact.

- The emergency stash at Ann's Dad's shop is safe and sound.
- Someone used Thor's Hammer to impact an agricultural region of India causing catastrophic damage. The President swears he did not conduct or order that operation and does not know who did.
- The US military, government, and law enforcement agencies all are aware of this technology and should be assumed to be examining it to some degree or another...everyone is watching or doing something related to this right now.
- The Pope has not yet been successful in his attempt to get a video call with Father Gannon, who has been very busy with the press.
- Neither the DoD nor any law enforcement has made any new contact with any of us to this point
- Dr. Hugh Durbin was probably not having a good time hosting the University's Board of Director's meeting today without Betty, and with the President's personal pick and premier subject matter expert on weather modification no longer on the University staff but very much in the international headlines.
- The first of a series of meetings with top national leaders will take place at the UN Headquarters in just a couple of days, and everyone in this room will play an important part in setting their objectives into motion at that meeting.

As Bob wrapped up his summary and began to discuss the next few things that needed to be done, he was unaware of the similar-in-function but different-in-content briefing the Secretary of Defense had just wrapped up for the Senate Committee. And neither of them was aware of what was transpiring in India as they were busy with their tasks in New York and Washington.

Zach contemplated the ramifications of the recent turn of events back in New York where the United Nations Secretary General had just outed the secret technology that Zach had just contemplated in India. As he sat at a small table outside the café in the little town, he wondered why this relatively small agricultural community town would be so popular with the tourists. Every day since he arrived, he saw busloads of what appeared to be Chinese tourists getting on and off buses and wandering in and out of shops and eateries. What people traveled that far to see was a mystery to Zach as he looked around wondering what was the attraction for all these tourists to come here?

As he finished his coffee and began to depart the outdoor sitting area of the small café, Zach was frustrated by the group of rude tourists pushing their way into and through the small space that he was trying to exit through. As he turned sideways and shuffled through the group toward the street Zach suddenly realized that he was surrounded and being quickly pushed and carried toward the street and the open door of the charter bus parked at the curb. Recognizing the situation, but too late to adequately respond he found himself on the bus being supported by several burly Chinese tourists as the door closed behind them and the bus began to move. Behind the commonly tinted windows and plain aluminum exterior walls of the bus, the interior did not have the rows of seating found on a typical charter bus. There was instead a large open space, a small table with a couple of captain's chairs and racks of computers, radios and other electronics. As he began to surveil his new surroundings, he felt the pat downs and searches being conducted as the men and electronics chattered in Chinese. And just like that, once again Zach's plans were about to change without him being in on the planning.

It was then he saw the man standing near the front of the bus, someone he recognized from numerous conversations and computer network security meetings at the research center. Zach felt a sudden return of calm and confidence as he waited to see what would happen next. The man who had already paid him millions of dollars over the past two years to look the other way began to approach the small group that just shuffled into the bus. As they made eye contact, Zach smiled at the familiar face, but the gesture was met with a stern look and a subtle but clear east-west shake of the head as he closed the distance between them.

"Mr. Zach" the man began, "you have done some very bad things recently. Bad for India, bad for the United States, bad for us…and most of all, it seems very bad for you. Why would you take such a drastic action? To use the Thor's Hammers on India is a very serious problem for us all.

Who directed this action and when? The order, the fielding was not done in the normal channels, there was no communications between you and your bosses. There was no elaborate cover story to unravel. No money trails to follow through the normal institutions and dummy corporations. And most disturbingly, this was not something that my bosses, our party has any direct role or involvement that we are aware of. This can only mean one of three things my friend…that is, if we still are friends?

"First, it could mean that you are playing both sides well. That your government does not trust you enough to do this in a typical fashion, and that your operation was sanctioned by your government but tasked in a new and very innovative way which eluded every established capability we have to monitor the activities of your government and its industry leaders. We believe this is the least likely because we see and correlate everything.

"Second, it could mean that I have not been paying you enough to sate your appetite for nice things and power. That you are now a weather mercenary and are already working for someone else who is or will be paying you much more than I have been to let us look through the windows and behind the doors of your technology development activities. But to do this without at least giving us the courtesy of making a counteroffer seems both foolish and unlikely given the damage we could do to your credibility by exposing our previous arrangement. Or we could simply un-alive you for such a slight. No, I continue to believe that you are smarter than that despite the protests of my less-patient colleagues.

"Finally, and I believe most likely, you decided to go rogue and search for the best deal before the United Nations destroyed the value of the commodity of which you currently hold forty percent of the known global supply. I think that you are someone who can be a great servant, but who would prefer to be served. I know you can be bought, but I believe you prefer to do the buying which is why you work where you work. I believe you like being surrounded by and having access to those with your nation's highest power…but I also believe your thirst for power has now switched to gathering it to yourself and not so much for your

President and those around him. Am I correct Mr. Zach, have you gone out on your own with Thor's Hammers?

"Either way, you have created a situation that very much disrupts my country's plans and ongoing strategy for this technology. We were in the final stages of testing and readying to field our own version in a much different way when you began this whole India debacle. Now Mcleod is known to all, the UN is not only involved but they are leading an effort to field this in a way that benefits the many not the few. The potential returns on our investments in this have plummeted so we will need to, as you say, pivot to a new plan which now must cost more talented people their lives. All because you decided to be greedy and free-lance with potentially the greatest weaponry that has ever been fielded by humans?

"My Zach, which of the three is it? How is it that you are here in India and responsible for the greatest eco-terrorist attack in history?" he finally concluded and stopped long enough for Zach to reply.

Recognizing that he was not in a good position, but still had considerable leverage Zach's response was calculated but clearly subordinate to his captors. "Well, it appears you did not get my postcards," he began hoping a joke might offset the threatening tone of the conversation, which it did not. "As usual, you are perceptive and read the situation clearly. I am here in India waiting for a potential partner in the weather modification business. My country and its feckless leaders have clearly lost an early competitive advantage, and I am seeking a mutually beneficial opportunity to market this limited resource, and to keep it limited in order to retain its value. The facts that I am standing in this bus with you all, nobody else has been following me or contacting me, or, as it appears even knows I am here, indicate to me that you are indeed the best partner for this new enterprise. It would appear our only competition right now, is the UN. So, what kind of deal are you offering?" He waited patiently for a smile in response, which took much longer than he had expected but when it arrived it was both broad and sincere.

"I think we can come to a mutually beneficial arrangement. But that will have to be done in another place, with people more powerful than I. You and your two devices will accompany us to a facility much like the one you used to run for the United States. We will begin our travels immediately," he said and on cue, the bus lurched forward and began to roll toward its newly announced destination. "Relax, Mr. Zach, we have a long journey ahead of us. If you will excuse me, I have some calls to make. The staff will see to it that you are comfortable for the journey, please let them wine and dine you along the way. We certainly want you to be in a good mood and well rested for the journey and work we have ahead of us. Your actions have forced a very accelerated timeline which we were not well positioned for, but with your help all that will change soon."

As he watched the man disappear into a small cubicle near the front of the bus, Zach settled into the seating area his host had motioned him to. He was handed a small tablet with a drink and food menu and was instructed to simply make his choices whenever he was inclined, and the selections would be brought to him. As he sat there wondering how long and how far the bus trip would be, he reached over and patted the case containing the two Thor's Hammers. He wondered how long they had been surveilling him before they were sure he and the devices were together, but it didn't really matter at this point. They had him, they had both devices and they could produce proof of his past deeds. What they did *not* yet have was the book of recipes. That knowledge is what determined whether these devices were just a fun parlor trick or a weapon of mass destruction. That is what made Zach valuable; that is the leverage he had that made them willing to deal, for now. That can be the only reason he is still alive.

CHAPTER TWO

WHERE ARE WE GOING?

As they climbed into the shuttle it remained clear that, at best, their plan was dependent on what they found upon their arrival at the UN now that Bob and Father Gannon were not leading anything. Ann and Betty would stay close to Bob and provide support for whatever direction the evolving situation warranted. Father Gannon was the only one with a specific itinerary. He and the Public Information Officer, known as "the PIO" had a detailed and synchronized string of briefings, interviews and events that stretched deep into the evening. Being the face of this technology was far more burdensome than any of them anticipated, it was worthy work as Jim Auster was becoming a household name across the globe for his creation. Father Gannon was equally thrust into celebrity as the narrator of this great story that had captured a global audience. It was unclear at this point whether Bob would be drawn into that same popularity vortex or if he would succeed in maintaining the relative obscurity he was hoping to keep.

As they pulled up to the entrance, the paparazzi were the most on scene thus far, and as they spilled out of the van with the now familiar priest their faces also appeared in video clips and photos worldwide. This was not the way to keep a low profile, and Bob began to accept the notion there was no possibility that he would be fading into obscurity any time soon.

This was just a beginning, not an ending, so that just needed to be part of the program for him but it need not be for Ann and Betty if they so chose. As they approached the security screening area the now famous Father Gannon was greeted and whisked away with the PIO, circumventing the scanners and line awaiting entry to the tightly controlled main entrance leaving the rest of the group to fend for themselves. Making their way through the short line, Bob introduced himself "I am Professor Robert Mcleod, the United States lead scientist for the weather modification strategy meetings, and these are my associates," gesturing toward Ann and Betty.

"You are on the list. Good morning, Professor. You may proceed through the screening stalls and then follow the signs. Unfortunately, your associates are not on our list. It is a very short list sir. They will need to return to the lobby area they came through." The security guard motioned them back down the hallway which they had just come up.

"I am very sorry to hear that, but that sounds like a you-problem and not a me-problem. Call whomever you need to call to get them on your list. We will all stay right here until all three of us proceed to the meeting we are here to participate in. We are here at the invitation of the Secretary General to provide important information and advice to him and whomever else he wants us to advise. To save some time, you might just start with calling him directly." Bob's response was calm, measured and almost kind because he knew the man was simply doing his job, and doing it correctly. After only a few minutes, the security guard returned and asked Ann and Betty to produce their driver's licenses which he then scanned into a handheld device and excused himself once more.

A few minutes later they were all led to the screening and scanning areas, and once cleared they each received a lanyard with a staff badge denoting areas where they were allowed unescorted access and others which would require an escort. Once they were clear of the security area and walking toward "the pit," which is the large conference room used by the Secretary General for top level discussions, Bob broke the tension of the past fifteen minutes by saying "Well that was much easier than I expected it to be. Now we know not only how much they want the US here for this effort, we also know how much they specifically want me here for this. That is a relief for us all. Let's go see what we have gotten ourselves in for, shall we?"

They arrived and were surprised to see how informal the session appeared to be shaping up. There were no printed name plates designating who was to sit where. The appearance of those in the room ranged from gray haired men in expensive Italian suits to college aged dudes in cargo pants and dry fit tee shirts. Of the fifty or so in the room when they arrived, you could count the women on one hand, and two of them were with Bob. It wasn't long after they arrived that the room began to quiet down, people began to take seats and the Secretary General strolled in from a side entrance and began to mingle and greet some of those in the room as the settling in began. As Bob and his associates were surveying the seating for a place they could sit together, the Secretary General locked eyes with Ann and started across the group directly toward her and did not divert until he was stretching his hand out in greeting.

"Hello, you must be Ann? It is my great pleasure to meet the woman who is the love of Professor Mcleod's life. Congratulations on your engagement, and welcome to our solution session on the challenge I have no doubt you were instrumental in bringing us," and without missing a beat he turned to his left and continued, "And you must be Betty?" he continued as she smiled at the recognition. "I am equally pleased to meet you my dear. I would be fascinated to hear about your front row seat to Doctor Auster and Professor Mcleod's amazing story when we all meet for dinner this evening. What a best-selling book that will be! Please promise me an advance copy with a personal note before it hits the bookstores?"

"Of course," was all Betty could muster in response, as he turned to address Bob.

"So good to see you again Bob and thank you for bringing some beauty into this room with you today. Please trust that I also recognize the brain power, dedication and ability at your sides. The best of both worlds! You are either very lucky, very good or both. My money is on both. Let's go prove me right to everyone else. Please follow me to our seats. By the way, sorry about the little delay at security this morning, it was a test which you passed with flying colors. Thank you for that." He led them to three empty seats which he motioned them to take, as he remained standing and began to bring the meeting and the room to order.

"Thank you all for taking time from what I know is a very busy time to be here for this strategy session," he began as everyone settled in to listen intently to the designated leader of this historic effort. "The purpose of this meeting is to discuss the challenge at hand, define our success criteria, assess our range of options to address them and walk away with an agreed upon strategy to get there. That is why we have assembled a small and select group, as the people in this room will largely make decisions that will affect everyone on the planet going forward. Make no mistake, whatever we decide will be criticized and second guessed for all time to come. Whatever we decide, there will be those who will say we got it wrong. They will likely be more correct than we will be here today. That is because they will have the benefit of two things we *do not* have today. They will have more information than we do, and they will have the benefit of hindsight to make visible the actual outcomes that we can only imagine or hope for. We will be measured by what did happen, not what we expected to happen, nor the outcomes we hoped to achieve.

"Now that we understand that we need to also accept that the path to failure is trying to please everyone. That is, while admirable, not possible. What we will endeavor to achieve is a strategy with the best likelihood of a most favorable outcome; one that can stand the test of time and the scrutiny of historians. And in order to gain as much hindsight of our own to help us produce the best approach we can with what we have…I would like to introduce you all to the people primarily responsible for us being in this room today.

"You have all seen Father Gannon on the news and ongoing interviews. While he won't be here for this, or subsequent meetings like this one, I would like you all to meet our three primary US delegates and the authors of this story thus far. To my right, please stand and be recognized, is Professor Bob Mcleod, his lovely and brilliant fiancé Ann, and their behind-the-scenes facilitator of the details that need attending, Betty. Today they will tell us in detail their stories of how we got here, and they will answer your questions. They have been cleared by the US government to tell us all they know in support of our efforts to get this as right as we can going forward. Everyone in this room has signed non-disclosure statements, agreed to and created compartmented classified programs and know the ramifications of breaking any of these agreements and protocols. It could cost people's lives in one or many ways. In addition, the US has provided complete immunity to our three participants, as well as advance pardon for any actions up to today's meeting that may have been near to or illegal under US law. So, what I would like to do now is take a short five-minute break for Bob, Ann and Betty to review and sign the documents I have described, and then we will settle in to hear their stories so we are all starting from the same page with as much of the same data as possible," he concluded, and then turned to the three still standing to be recognized and led them to the side entrance and a small office where the papers he had just discussed were spread out for their examination.

Once all were inside, and with the door closed, he continued speaking to the three of them as a group, "I do apologize for having to spring that on you in that manner, but it was necessary. These are valid offers but are not effective until each of you has signed your own, identical agreement. I couldn't do this until I knew who, and how much from your response at the security entrance this morning. I assure you these are legit, I have your President by the short and curlies right now, but that won't last long, so I took the liberty of negotiating on your behalf while I was negotiating on my own behalf still from a position of strength. You already have all the money you need, so I figured "get-out-of-jail-free-cards" were your next best thing. He wouldn't go for a pardon for something you might do in the future, nobody would, but I asked anyway…made it easier to get us here. What do you say? I will let you keep the pens if that makes it easier for you to decide."

Bob was the first to respond, "Wow! This means we get to move forward and help bring this technology to the world with all the shackles removed...legally and legitimately. Thank you, while I can only speak for myself, I'm in. I leave the lady's decisions to them."

Without missing a beat, they each reached for a pen, scanned and signed the documents, and returned through the same passageway they had exited through a few short moments ago. As they entered the room and resettled, Bob remained standing this time. He provided a short personal introduction of himself, Ann and Betty, then began to tell the story of how they all came to be in the room, inviting Ann and Betty to chime in and share their details along the chronology of events. All in the room agreed to hold their questions until the historic narrative was complete. Three and a half hours later, it was time for questions and the real work to begin. The ask from one of the youngest and most casually attired men in the room would prove to be immensely important. He wanted to know from Bob, "Based on what you know, combined with what your gut tells you, how many of these Thor's Hammers do you think are out there right now? And who do you think has them?"

Bob's response was, "I'd like to respond in reverse order if you will allow me. It is my belief that the United States government has at least one safely in storage somewhere. I am almost certain that the man who, in our discussions, ran the lab where Ann and I met—he is known to us as Zach—has at least two or more and has used them to cause the recently devastating weather events in India. We, this UN group, have the one Father Gannon brought to you. As for what I believe, what my gut tells me? ... Zach either has already sold, or soon will be selling the technology ... or he has already made or is in the process of making more to sell to the highest bidders."

"Most of the components are available in some version. Locking these key components down or tracking who is buying them will be the best way to determine who has, or who has interest in getting or selling their own version or replica of a Thor's Hammer. One of the decisions for the strategy we select is whether we choose to proliferate this capability quickly or choose a slower more deliberate fielding. To do that we must be confident in our counterproliferation ability. Candidly, given what I know right now, I don't think we can have any confidence in anything except the fact that we are too late to seriously consider counterproliferation. It already appears that it's being used for nefarious gains, I must think Zach has taken that strategy off the table for us, and we need to focus on proliferating this as soon and safely as we can in an overt and transparent way to highlight and expose anything that is an outside effort. That means everyone knows everything we are doing as soon as we decide to do it. That will make it harder and easier at the same time."

"Damn. I was afraid you were going to say that," the young man replied softly, but loud enough to be heard by those around him. "Well, do you suppose inviting this guy Zach to join our team might be something he would consider? My people can be very persuasive, some say they are excellent motivational speakers and put on great training seminars. Do you know where we might find him to gauge his interest in our effort instead of his own?"

Bob pondered the question, as he examined the young man for clues to who he was, who he represented, and what his primary expertise was although his questions made the latter a bit obvious. His response surprised even Bob himself, "Zach might consider joining us under the right conditions. He is a genius, proven to be capable of great evil, but also has a sporting, competitive, even soft spot for underdogs and love. Those are two things I have personally witnessed him deviate from his plans to accommodate to some degree. He just might again if we find a way to tap into something akin to it. That said, I have no clue where he is now. But I bet I know where he was last week. He and his Thor's Hammers were in India, and probably in or very near the agricultural belt that experienced the devastating flooding. He needed to be close because he does not yet know the outer limits of the range of these devices. Now that he has used them and seen the results from these settings, he has a better idea. Better than we do because he has this one to learn from, but we don't. We have several reasons to have a long talk with Zach about a lot of things we care about," Bob concluded.

Across the globe, Zach had been listening to the hum of the bus tires taking him and his new Chinese travel companions to a destination unknown. Had he heard Bob's request for a sit-down discussion with the UN group, he would have accepted readily in trade for his current situation. While that idea was not exactly top of mind for Zach, he was in fact wondering what the UN and Bob Mcleod would decide to do on their current undertaking of bringing on-demand weather modification to the world. While they were not enemies per se in this enterprise, they were not working on the same team for the same goals so Zach had to keep one eye on his own efforts and the other on Bob and his. Right now, the slowing bus averted his mind and both eyes to the area the bus was slowing down in order to enter through what looked like a well-guarded gate a short distance from a road to nowhere, out in the middle of nowhere India.

As the bus cleared the gate, it drove into the open side of a small building and immediately the front of the bus dipped downhill as it began a long low spiral down in a slow sweeping left turn for several minutes until it leveled out onto a parking area near a series of large steel doors that appeared to be the entrance to a deep, large, well-hidden and well defended underground bunker. "Seriously? You got to be kidding me!" Zach said as he obeyed the motion from the armed man signaling him to stand and exit the bus. "This should be interesting," Zach said loudly and plainly in Chinese as he began walking with the group toward the bunker security screening entrance which looked quite familiar to him. "I bet it looks just like the one I used to work at on the inside too. You guys copy everything, but don't create shit of your own," he said in English this time.

"Imitation is the greatest form of flattery," said a voice he did not recognize coming from the back of the group. It seems now Zach has someone else who oversees something he might be able to negotiate with, after all Chinese and English are just languages to exchange ideas. Tone, tenor and money are languages all their own, and far more important in negotiations than what words are being said. Let's see what's inside this place, who is inside this place and what we get to do next. Might as well settle in for what comes next because it took us a long time to get to the middle of nowhere; but to everyone here right now, nowhere is exactly the place to be for whatever is coming next.

Meanwhile, back in the midwestern United States, at the federal courthouse in room 3B, the Judge took the papers from the bailiff. She stated, "In this filing of State University vs. Robert Mcleod. State University is seeking damages for breach of contract, theft of property, intellectual property, defamation, actual damages, and lost income potential due to theft of property and intellectual property. This case has standing and is filed in federal court, because the intellectual property at issue is the on-demand weather modification technology in and resultant of Thor's Hammer which the University claims is the result of University research and is the actual and intellectual property of the University and not its former student and employee, Robert Mcleod, as he stated. He has acted in bad faith with the US Government and misrepresented University property as his own.

"I have reviewed the initial documents and evidence, and the motion is accepted and so filed in Federal District Court. Clerk, please see that it is appropriately filed, annotated and the parties are duly served and noticed. We will have the initial hearing, discovery motions and statements heard in ninety days. It is so ordered. Next case please."

Hugh Durbin's smile stretched from ear to ear as he slapped the attorney closest to him on the back and said "Thank you Johnny! I cannot wait to wipe the smug look off Mcleod's face and mop up his blood with it. That man messed with the wrong guy when he decided to go toe to toe with me. Let's go kick his ass, take his money and put him in jail where he belongs."

"Ok, whatever Hugh, I've got another case in half an hour and you're an asshole so…see you when I see you." Johnny was a great lawyer, a great judge of character and a pretty decent human being. He just might be one of the good lawyers that gives the rest of them a bad name.

In a similar but less legal proceeding as they headed back to the Pentagon after the Senate Armed Services Committee meeting, the Secretary of Defense asked his friend Dutch Charles to delay his anticipated retirement in light of these ongoing events. General Charles had already served what would be considered a typical tenure of a successful Chairman of the Joint Chiefs of Staff. The CJCS, as it's known, is the pinnacle joint assignment for any flag officer in every Service. The position is rotational by design to keep momentum, variety and a dynamic perspective at the forefront of military advice to the Commander in Chief. With that in mind, the ask from Secretary Fitzgerald came with a Presidential endorsement. The President had been pushed into a corner by the UN Secretary General and he did not like that one bit. Granting immunity to Bob Mcleod and giving up details on and from the most classified research and development teams in our nation was not high on his list of things to do during his second term as President.

The man thought highly of Dutch, and appreciated his intellect, his audacity, his broad knowledge and experience, but most appreciated was his ability to speak truth to power. Dutch had a knack for being able to see a line, walk right up to it, say or do what was needed and lean over the line to make sure it was understood without ever stepping over it. He would not back away from the line until a decision was made, and whatever the President decided, Dutch would back him knowing that his input had been considered in the President's deliberations. That was all he could ask, after all he was the Chairman and not the President. He was counsel to the decision maker, and even though the CJCS is not accountable for the President's decisions, Dutch felt that same accountability for every issue on which he advised the President.

When the President asked him about Bob Mcleod, what he thought since he had spent some time with him in this weather modification evolution, and what he thought about whether to accept the UN Secretary General's terms, Dutch replied candidly. "This guy Mcleod is trying to do the right thing. He may not be doing everything right, but he is trying to do right by the Doc who invented it. He did right by Frank and the weather guys at the base that got rung up a few times by what he did. He made good on the farmers that lost their crops while he was figuring out what he could do with this thing. He even gave his IRS buddy his dog when he got attached to it while we had the guy in custody for months.

"I know saying you two did not hit it off would be an understatement. But looking at the position he was in, what choice did he have? We boxed him in, and he figured a way out, he took it, and then made lemonade out of the lemons we left him holding. On top of that, he got a damn fine fiancé to boot. She saw something in the man along the way, too. She didn't know he had just become a billionaire. If we are picking teams here Mr. President, and I think that is exactly what we are doing, then I want to have this guy playing for our side not the opposition. If you want me to run alongside him for a while, I will do that. Much rather go up with him than go up against him. He has been thrust into the big leagues from nowhere, and already has some victories without really knowing much. Imagine what he might be capable of with the right team and the right coaches. Give him a fresh start. Point him in the right direction, tell him how far to run, and turn him loose. My money says he gets there."

"The SECDEF and CJCS share the same opinion about this guy," the President conceded. "Alright, give the Secretary General what he wants but tell him to kiss my ass and, if Mcleod shits in my bed, I expect the Secretary General himself to personally lead the laundry brigade to clean up the mess. And to bring cigars for us to enjoy while we watch," he instructed his Ambassador to the UN. "And by the way, I expect you to keep an eye on all this, but from a safe distance so if it goes bad you have some room to maneuver so we can get in and save the day without too much collateral damage on our end. Mcleod can lead the way, but that makes him the first one to bite the dust if it goes bad."

That was the discussion earlier in the day, and now Dutch was being asked to extend his tenure and delay his retirement to help implement the earlier discussions and their resultant actions.

"OK Mr. Secretary, I will give you and the President another six months with me as Chairman. That should be plenty of time for us to have this well on its way, and then I will be too. What do you need from me on this?" Dutch concluded.

"Thank you Dutch, I am happy to hear that. And I am glad you asked," Fitzgerald said, with a grin.

CHAPTER THREE

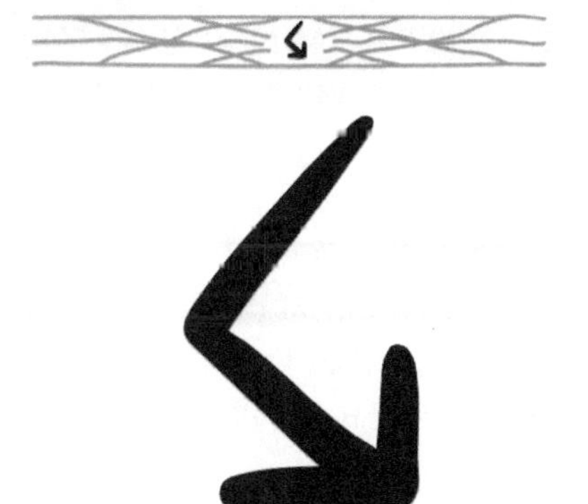

HOW DO WE GET THERE?

Dinner was an understatement Betty thought, as she observed the variety of food and drinks set out for their group as they were ushered into another room at the UN building. It had been quite a day thus far, and it appeared the conversation and the work would continue while they were dining. As promised, the Secretary General approached her and reminded, "You promised to tell me all about your experiences with Doc Auster and Bob, from the very beginning. I will be holding a chair for you so we can have that conversation over dinner if you would be so kind to join me once you have made your selections?"

"Of course," Betty smiled, curious but cautious at his seemingly misplaced interest in her while there were so many other important people at today's gathering that he had yet to even personally greet. She was flattered but not naïve enough to think that he didn't want something for his time and attention. Betty might be new to this world of international whatever this is, but she was not at all new to human behavior and it was clear the charm sent her way was both intentional and in hopes of producing something. As she finished her pass through the buffet style spread of culinary wonders, she walked gracefully to the empty seat as requested and joined the small group already seated with the Secretary General.

They all rose from their seats as she joined them, chivalry and good manners were alive and well in such settings and she smiled and thanked them as she settled in. It did not take long for the conversation to expose the heart of their curiosity, they wanted to hear the prequel of this story. What did she know, and when did she know it? She was the inside link between Auster, Mcleod, the University and whomever else was involved on the ground floor of the Thor's Hammer concept and development. He … no, all of them were confident there was a little more to the story than had been revealed thus far. They had isolated Betty from her colleagues who were each center of attention at a different table in the room dining with new and curious colleagues of their own.

"Surely the university was providing some research monies or objectives for modifying the weather. How did this program come to be?" asked her dinner host.

"It really was nothing like that, certainly as far as I know anyway, and I have been there a very long time. In fact, you knew about this weather modification before I did. You got a personal demonstration, I had to learn about it from the TV news," she smiled, but appeared sincerely hurt by that truth as she continued. "A couple of months after Doc's passing, I knew something wasn't right with Bob. He was missing work, not checking in, short tempered and tired. He even seemed to be unconcerned about the Dean's extra attention on him. You see, Bob and Dean Durbin have some history and do not get along very well. Bob was dedicated to doing whatever it took to finish that PhD and the Dean would delight at any reason he could find to threaten that goal. It didn't seem to be as important for some reason after Doc was gone. I thought one might have something to do with the other, but I had no idea this is what connected the two." She paused to take a bite of something that looked delicious but was still curiously unidentifiable.

"How can it be that Doctor Auster's program, his time, prototypes and testing were not funded by and tracked by the University? Surely, he had a sponsor for these efforts. Do you know who that was, after all we are all speaking freely now, and it's important we know who all the players are in this technology so we can make the right decisions for what comes next," pressed a man who had been silent until now.

"The one thing I do know about is the grant I had to track and bill. The only project that brought in any funding was the study to settle a dispute between the State and the charcoal companies that operated upstate. The University, well Doc was the researcher who set up the sensor lines and was doing the data collection to determine if the output and deposition from those plants was reaching, and impacting the downwind areas. The money came from the charcoal companies into a trust fund, the state was awarded in a lawsuit, then provided to the university for the research. That is where our program funds came from but it was not a blank check. It barely covered the effort but Doc was frugal, especially since Durbin threatened many a time to shut it down because it was not making money or headlines, it was just break-even science on what he considered a stupid argument in the first place.

"But Doc, he considered it worthy work to protect the people and the environment they lived in. These were his people, his state, and his job to determine if they were being harmed or not. How that turned into him developing and building a device capable of on-demand weather modification will be a mystery to me as long as it is to everyone else. I worked with the man for many years, and I can tell you he was kind, a creature of habit, and dedicated to his work. I now know about the fruits of that labor because of Bob, but before he brought me into what he and Ann were doing, I had no idea any of this was even possible let alone real. And to come from people I know and love, let me assure you I was just as pissed as I was proud when I learned about it all. No, I wish I had been a part of this effort earlier, but neither Doc nor Bob ever put me in that position. I know now it was to protect me, but that hurts as much as it makes me happy at the same time. And that, I believe is all I know about that. Does anyone know what this delicious dish is? I may need to go back for some more." She was finished, if not with dinner at least with the conversation for now.

The men at the table graciously followed her lead into the next discussion item. The Secretary General did not get the story he was hoping to hear about military sponsorship, but he had gotten a lead to chase down. State grant funding to a state university for a long-term atmospheric research grant to settle a standing dispute would be perfect cover story for exactly this kind of research and live testing in plain sight.

He had no doubt Betty was telling the truth about what she did and, more importantly, what she did not know. But what he did doubt was what Doc Auster knew, the authenticity of the dispute he was researching, the source of the funding, and now there was reason to doubt the cause and timing of his sudden death. There had to be more to this. It was too neat, too many consecutive miracles in a string of unlikely events to believe that it was not some government, or government agency which led the effort. One well intended old man trying to make his dead wife proud of him almost single handedly created a technology that will change the world? That he did it out of benevolence for mankind and not to get rich, and that he had it in his possession for some time but hadn't used it, and before he decided what to do with it, he was killed by a drunk driver while walking home? Seriously, was he supposed to believe there are still good, honest, hardworking successful people in the US who just want to make their families proud of them and make the world a better place? That was what he was being asked to believe and while he considered it possible, he thought it exceedingly improbable. That made him sad but also motivated to find out what version of the story was the truest.

"How ironic?" was the thing that kept popping in and out of Zach's mind as he walked with the group of men into the containment and decontamination areas at the entrance to the underground facility. They had been driving for a few days and he was glad to be off the bus, despite the lack of fresh air here. Although he was no expert in India's geography, he did know that he was driving east for most of the trip, with several northward legs. The last sign he recalled seeing was Assam. This is northeastern India, in difficult terrain, but near enough to the borders with China and Myanmar (Burma) to allow for some covert cross-border operations to make a hidden underground bunker on the India side as possible as it was desirable. So much so that what appeared to be the case to Zach was exactly what was revealed to be true as he was led deeper into the facility's maze of hallways, doorways and less than desirable artificial lighting. The more he was led around, intending to disorient the newcomer, the more he began to see what he expected to see from his past role at the covert US facility.

While not an exact replica, it was clearly a knock off from the US design where he had spent many of the past years of his life. He had a good understanding of the mechanical hubs, work areas, and command and control centers of this facility just based on what he had seen thus far. As they finally reached what appeared to be their destination—at least the first one—the group began to disperse, and Zach was instructed to take a seat in a fairly large conference room where several dozen people were already assembled.

As he sat and was settling in, a man came in and began to address the group, "Good day my esteemed colleagues. Today we have a most valuable and honored guest. Mr. Zach, it is my pleasure to welcome you to our ongoing weather modification program. We have not met. I am Mr. Wu. My job is to lead this operation and our fine group of experts conducting on-demand weather modification for the benefit and well-being of my countrymen. Your new job, for which you are being well compensated, I must say, is to help us succeed in very short order. I am very thankful that you have brought us these working devices from the United States, developed in collaboration and funding from the government of China. Our party leaders believe their generous investments in you and your US facility will produce great dividends in your continued work here with us. Let's all give Mr. Zach a warm and courteous welcome. While I am confident he is ready to get straight to work, I also recognize it has been a long journey, from which he must rest and use today to get settled into his accommodations. We will begin our work in the morning. Thank you all and I am anxious for your speedy successes to be shared with all for the common good."

As Mr. Wu finished his comment, he gestured for Zach to rise, be acknowledged by the assembled staff, and then follow behind him out of the conference room into an office down the hall. Once inside, the last man closed the door as Mr. Wu invited Zach to please take a seat. Seeing that the three men near the door were not moving beyond their assigned security position, Zach understood now was the time to listen and learn, to negotiate terms, but not the time to go hands on with the three armed bad-asses who seemed to only be there to protect Mr. Wu.

"So, what is it you want from me, and what is it you will give me in exchange for what you want?" Zach opened, which he liked to do so that he could control the conversation at least somewhat.

"Well Mr. Zach, before we get to that let us make sure we are starting from the same place, if I may. Over the past several years, my government, through an intermediary has already paid you millions of dollars. We have brought you safely across much of India after you have caused, what some have already estimated as high as two and a half billion dollars in damage to the crops, homes and businesses of India's farmers. And you are still alive after all that. I believe, we have already paid you generously with treasure and your life. Let's both start there," Mr. Wu hissed at him.

Zach was trying to take the man as seriously as the situation he found himself in, but the best he could muster was a twenty second string of chuckles and giggles that he failed to conceal. That failure actually angered Zach into a harsh, venomous reply which forced him down a path to which he had not quite yet fully committed himself. But the game was now on.

"Screw you, Mr. Wu!" Zach fumed as he laughed out loud and smiled at the man. "I bet you get that rhyme a lot huh? Look, you paid me before, but for things I have already delivered. Monies in the past were for access to things…in the past! You got to snoop and steal from our expensive R&D efforts with relative impunity while I made sure my IT folks were looking for something else, in a different direction. You got and saved billions worth of return on the small number of millions you paid me. I am both well-travelled and alive because you need things from me.

Things you will pay me handsomely for or you will not get. This is not my first rodeo, and what you need will not, and I repeat *will not*, be cheap and they most certainly will not be free.

"The man who made a deal with the US President for these devices was paid five billion dollars. Billion, with a 'B' Mr. Wu. Now stop insulting me. Stop threatening me. Do not even begin to patronize me. Do not tell me you don't have the authority, because if you did not someone else would be speaking to me right now. So, the next things out of your mouth will be numbers and a timeline. Those are the only two things we are here to settle, and the longer this takes, the higher the final number will be. So, what say you, my good Mr. Wu?"

Zach knew he had both insulted and angered the man, both being personal attacks and not particularly good for a captive's well-being however he also knew this was his best negotiation path to get what he wanted in exchange for what they seemed to be needing.

"One billion. Six weeks and we release you at a place of our choosing. You will help us build and test replicas of the Thor's Hammer. We will keep your devices as part of our purchase price. You will not divulge our location nor our activities, nor our deal in any way. In fact, you will deny any connection to China, the CCP or any other entity you may be exposed to over this activity except those we choose to make. We will not have a written agreement of any kind, but rest assured we will have a swift and final penalty imposed upon you for any breach of these terms. That is my offer," Mr. Wu concluded.

"Thank you, that is most generous. And please accept my apology for my inconsiderate outburst, the confines of these places sometimes get the best of me. The long bus ride was very tiring as well. Tell you what sport, let's just wrap this up and get something to eat? What do you say to one point five billion, you get your six weeks, and you drop me off at a place of *my* choosing? All the rest works fine for me. We got a deal? I'm tired and hungry? Can we shake on this and go get something to eat now?" he asked as he extended an open and empty hand toward Mr. Wu as the three security guys all tensed and poised to respond at the advance toward their charge.

"I can live with that. I can recommend the steak and lobster. Kobe beef with the crustations fresh caught and flown in from Maine yesterday. We wanted you to feel at home," Mr. Wu smiled and grasped the outstretched hand. Both gripped firmly, locked eyes, shook vigorously three times then broke contact and took a step back and smiled. It seemed that these two sociopaths had their moment of mutual respect and were looking forward to gaining whatever insights could be gained over dinner and what Mr. Wu hoped would be way too much alcohol for Zach in celebration of his new wealth. As they walked down the corridor toward the dining area, Zach asked whether Wu was assigned to the facility or if he was brought in just for him.

"Oh Mr. Zach I am afraid neither of those options apply very well. I have been assigned to you since you first became our employee years ago. Since then, it has been my job to become the Chinese version of you. I do indeed work here at the facility, in the same capacity as you did at the US version that we replicated but improved upon here. I know so much about you already, but there are a few gaps I would like you to fill in for me over the next few weeks. I am excited to finally meet you in person, but I do feel like I know so much about you already.

"That said … oh and my English is pretty good right? I am particularly interested in how Thor's Hammers operated for you in India and what settings you used. I was struggling with getting our devices to do what we were trying to produce and for how long. Something gets lost in the translation. I hear this all the time but it seems to be especially true with these devices."

"So, you already have your own built then?" Zach wanted re-affirmation.

"Yes, of course. We built ours the same time you were building your copies with Professor Bob and his girlfriend Ann. We were watching and listening intently, but it appears we missed something very important. Small perhaps, but very important. Operating these things has proven much more difficult than building them," Wu continued. "Please don't be surprised at that Mr. Zach. Once you let us into your facility we never left, and why would we? How could we? With so many interesting people and projects going on there, it would have been irresponsible of us to allow your country to continue misusing and abusing some of the greatest creations of some of the greatest minds ever assembled. As you say, you make the cake, but we will put the icing on and serve it to our guests.

"There is little risk in me sharing all of this with you now that our deal is in place. I know I can trust you with keeping your word, and so you can trust me to keep mine. And just in case you need to grow into that, I will remind you of the cost of any breach of trust or discussion. I would hate for anything to ever happen to you. I have grown very fond of you over these past years, and I know I too would feel any pain we were forced to inflict upon you should you break that trust. No Zach, may I call you Zach without the Mr.? Thank you," he continued as Zach nodded. "Hurting you would be hurting myself; I know we can avoid that. It would be horrible for all of us if we could not. Let's eat, shall we? I took the liberty of ordering for both of us. Medium rare, butter and sour cream on the potato, melted butter on the side with the lobster, blue cheese dressing on the salad which we will eat after the entre rather than before. Bon' Appetit Zach. When you are ready, let's share some recipes. I would love to hear about the one for long duration heavy rains over a large area of fertile Indian cropland."

Damn! This is going to be an interesting six weeks Zach thought as he raised his glass to toast his dinner companion and newly revealed alter ego.

Back across the globe that same day, with their own glasses emptied and refilled several times after a working dinner and, with conversations about what next in full motion, Bob spied Father Gannon entering the room of small working groups. He was flanked by both Kevin Armstrong and his boss Mr. Dau who had essentially become Father Gannon's handler with daily press briefings, interviews and public speaking events both exposing and explaining this new technology and the unique role of the UN in its global fielding of this unprecedented power. Bob broke from his discussion to seize the opportunity to engage all three of them together for the first time in what seemed a lifetime despite it being measurable in days.

"You three look like you could all use a drink, and I'm buying so follow me! Long day?" he said as he smiled and continued walking toward the small unattended counter lined with bottles, labels, and liquids of all colors.

"What can I pour for you Mr. Dau...Padre...Kevin? And how was your day, what did you do and who did you do it to?" he said only half-jokingly as he poured out three drinks in the order of the responses to his questions.

"Sounds like you had a busy day! Who seems to be the most upset or concerned about our newfound ability to change the weather on-demand?" Bob asked the three men wo currently had him boxed in with an open bar to his back.

Mr. Dau, who was instrumental in getting this whole thing into and—for the time being—remaining in the hands of the UN responded quickly, "The President of the United States is at the top of the list, and everyone who works for him is tied for second place. When the Secretary General took it upon himself to renegotiate your deal and get you amnesty, I am afraid he may not have made it entirely clear that it was his idea and not yours. A little salt in the wound I am afraid. Shit, Bob, please tell me the Secretary General has already told you about that." He stopped and stared at Bob, who three drinks in could not resist saying with a widening grin as he spoke, "What are you talking about? Amnesty? Yeah, he mentioned that this morning as we got started. What I was really surprised about was the greenlight to talk about the research facility and share the goings on there with everyone here today. That was really helpful and liberating."

Bob was interrupted by Kevin Armstrong's observation, "Why was that a surprise, Bob? You and Ann are both fresh out of there with the most disruptive technology ever unveiled in the most wide-open display of up-yours any president has ever paid five billion dollars to have thrown in his face. That facility's existence and location were clearly burned and between the two of you, and their missing director of whatever he did, that was all damage control not a concession to the Secretary General." Armstrong took a sip from his iceless glass but before he could continue Bob shot back, "Wait, what?"

"I said it was damage control," Kevin replied.

"Not that, who's missing?" Bob pressed. "Is Zach missing? Is he the one who they can't' find? How long has he been gone?"

Mr. Dau responded in an even tone, "I don't know the details, but I believe it has been several weeks."

"We must know how long…no, no, no, no! Did he go missing before or after the flooding in India? No, no, no please say after, please say after…" Bob pleaded.

"If we said after, we would be wrong. It was at least a week before the flooding according to the classified report I may or may not have read …that may or may not have been the same one that may or may not have been flagging his disappearance to folks who may or may not care about such things related to such places," Armstrong concluded then drained his glass.

"It's him! It must be. Zach had access; he has the knowledge; he knows the Hammers. You remember how the President got so upset when we accused him of ordering the whole thing in India…well, he blew a gasket! I am not a murderer, the whole righteous indignation but I didn't buy it. What if he really didn't know? What if he really didn't order it? What if Zach went out on his own and did it to impress, or even blackmail the President? What if it was a demonstration to sell it to someone else, the United States already had it so the President wouldn't pay for it again, right? Would he?" Bob was rambling with the possibilities and Kevin pulled him back into the present.

"Bob, stop. You really think Zach could pull this off alone in such a short amount of time with the knowledge and resources at his disposal?"

"Yes, he absolutely could," Bob responded with certainty.

"More importantly, *why* would Zach pull this off alone in such a short amount of time with the knowledge and resources at his disposal?" Kevin continued.

"Because he could, and for recognition from his boss, and for profit. He felt under-appreciated there, he told me that when we were negotiating for Ann's release from her contract," Bob responded with concern.

"What does your gut tell you Bob…do you think Zach *did* that to India with Thor's Hammers unsanctioned?" Kevin pressed.

"Holy shit, it all makes perfect sense, I know he did! Oh, sorry Father," Bob said to the until now quiet Kevin Gannon who replied quickly.

"No problem, I'm getting used to it. This is bad, but now at least we know what we might be up against."

Mr. Dau thought for a moment and responded thoughtfully, "You understand, this changes everything if you're right? We are now in an arms race. This is no longer, 'What should we do?' This becomes a matter of how fast we can do what we must do before anyone else does it. We need to get some time with the Secretary General, and probably the US President in the same room at the same time. This won't be fun, but better be soon. Next time you offer to buy me a drink, Bob, please give me the opportunity to say no thank you and head for the door."

As he led the other three across the room toward the Secretary General and his group, Ann and Betty took the opportunity to join Bob and Father Gannon as they passed.

"How is my favorite man holding up? It's getting late," Ann whispered to Bob as they walked.

Bob was focused on the problem just discussed and the potential issues it presented, and his curt response to Ann was honest but cryptic, "I'm doing ok, but I think this day is about to become several weeks long." With that, the group stalled and hovered as the Secretary General leaned in to listen to Mr. Dau who always had license to interrupt the man with anything of importance.

"Would you excuse me please?" the Secretary General asked of the group he had been addressing. "And would you please follow me?" he asked of the group directly behind him. Once they were all inside the small but well-furnished office with the door closed, he asked for clarification from both Mr. Dau and Professor Mcleod.

"Give me a number! How certain are you this Zach did on his own in India what we, for all practical purposes accused the President of ordering someone to do?"

Mr. Dau was first to respond, "Sir, based on what I know, and what I have heard tonight but have not yet been able to corroborate myself, I have eighty percent confidence this was unsanctioned, and Zach is our rogue player."

Without missing a beat, Bob followed confidently with, "Mr. Secretary General I am devastated when I say my confidence level is much higher. One hundred percent it's Zach. I should have put it together sooner. I should have seen it coming a mile away; I should have believed the President when he said it wasn't him. If indeed Zach has checked out and Thor's Hammers are unaccounted for, it's him. We know without a doubt the weather events in India were unprecedented, and so was the damage. There is no longer such a thing as coincidence in the area of weather events. That's the problem with this capability. Even if it were a natural phenomenon, the very existence of Thor's Hammers makes the events attributable to those in possession of them.

"Right now, the known attribution can only be laid upon the one you have in your possession, and the four in the US possession. If we believe the President's claim that he knew nothing of it, and we believe the reporting that Zach is gone missing and perhaps Hammers with him? What other conclusion can we draw? Unless someone else has already duplicated and used what we just discovered, the odds are it's Zach. I spent enough time with him to know he could, and would go on his own if he thought it in his interest to do so…and how hard could it be to find something in his own interest with technology like this in his personal care? We should have seen this coming, well at least I should have, and I missed it big time. Right in front of me, right in front staring me in the face." Bob was crushed by his own words, but he was also enraged by what they represented. He saw what he expected to see rather than what was actually there.

The Secretary General responded in a calm voice that instilled confidence into those in the room, "Thank you both, that is enough for now. Mr. Dau, please make the calls to arrange an in-person meeting with the President. Sooner matters more than where. While I would love to have everyone here in attendance at that meeting, as well, I am afraid there are certain protocols that are outside my control so please understand and do not take offense if you are not invited to this important but limited discussion. Please do not judge your importance to this effort by your proximity to this one meeting. I greatly appreciate all you have done to get us this far, and I thank you in advance for all you will do in the coming days and weeks.

"With that said, it's been a long day, and tomorrow promises the same. Please everyone, have a good evening and I expect to see you tomorrow for more on this ongoing effort. It should be a lot simpler now that everyone has a badge to get in and out." He smiled as he left the room and everyone followed suit, headed straight for the elevator and departed the building.

As the group of four left together, like they arrived at the beginning of the same day that seemed almost a lifetime ago already, Ann broke the silence, "Well, that was a hard way to end an otherwise fun day. I suppose the good news is now we know where we are going and when we need to be there. That leaves only one question, what route do we take?"

Betty replied for everyone, "I guess that depends on what happens tomorrow. For today, I worked hard, ate well and learned a lot about a lot. I'm prepared, all I need now is a good night's sleep. I suggest the same for each of you. Especially you, Bob. I also suggest you let Ann pick your clothes for tomorrow, I expect you will be in the hotseat with someone whom I know you did not vote for. Better you than me, but I didn't vote for him either just in case you need to call in reinforcements."

With that the shuttle pulled up to the hotel entrance, they all piled out and walked through the lobby toward the elevator when they heard Bob's cell phone ringing and his responses, "Hello. Yes. I'll be ready, see you then. Goodnight." The call finished as quickly as it arrived, and once the elevator door closed, Bob revealed its entirety.

"Tomorrow 0530 at the hotel entrance. Ann and I will be picked up by a Secret Service detail who will bring us to the White House to join a meeting of the UN Secretary General and the President, and whomever else. After all, Ann has spent way more time with Zach than I have, and we both worked on Thor's Hammer with him. Father Gannon and Betty will go to the UN just like today, and we will meet you there. Heck, depending on how our meeting goes we may get there before you do. Questions?"

"Nope, sleep well. See you tomorrow," was the unanimous response. Funny, Bob thought. If I told my year-ago self about the events of today, I would be recommending serious psychiatric care. Hard to believe this new reality, yet it is ours to live and write. Let's hope we get it right he thought as he opened the door for himself and Ann. They'd be up again in a few short hours to make their assigned show time to meet in person with the leader of the free world…who was not a big fan of Bob's.

WAY OFF PLAN

The alarm clock rang way too early for Bob and Ann, who readied themselves quickly, fueled themselves with coffee, bacon, eggs and toast courtesy of the not yet busy room service and kitchen staffs. The conversation was more about what they thought their first time inside the White House together would be like than it was about the topic they would be discussing once they arrived. They wondered which principals would be there for this morning's discussion whether in person or dialed in from whatever remote location. They arrived at the designated pick up at 05:25 and were greeted by two Special Agents whose job it was this morning to get this lovely couple in front of the President of the United States at the designated time; whenever that might be was not on the table for discussion just yet.

They were ushered into a black Suburban, just like the ones Bob had spent a lot of time in recently, and began their journey. First the drive to the private terminal at LaGuardia, where they almost instantly boarded a small jet for the one-and-a-half-hour flight to the nations' capital. From National, a DC traffic-impaired drive to 1600 Pennsylvania Avenue and they found themselves screened through and waiting in an office near the Oval where they expected to soon meet the President of the United States and some number of others to talk about shaping the future of the world where on-demand weather modification by Thor's Hammers was now a reality that had not existed a few short days before.

As Bob and Ann were wondering when Mr Dau, the UN Secretary General, and the others would join them in the waiting area, the door opened, and they were informed "The President will see you now. Please follow me." As they had followed every instruction to the letter thus far, so too did they follow the gentleman who led them into the Office of the President of the United States.

There were only a few people in the Oval Office as they entered. They were greeted by the President as he walked toward them, "I understand congratulations are in order for your engagement. Please accept my best wishes to you both. Bob and Ann Mcleod, that has a nice ring to it, don't you agree? Please have a seat, we have much to discuss, and time is not on our side." As he motioned them to take a seat while he did the same. The unexpected courtesy and the absence of the UN members whom he expected to see had Bob off guard and Ann concerned, as well.

"How about some introductions before we get too far into our discussion? Bob I am sure you remember, and Ann I'd like to introduce you to Secretary of Defense Fitzgerald, Chairman of the Joint Chiefs of Staff General Charles, and one of my National Security Advisors, 'Tom'." Bob recognized him as the young khaki cargo pants question-asking young man from the UN sessions in New York yesterday, "…and you are probably wondering who else is going to join us this morning. Well, the answer is no one, at least not today while we sort this out as best we can with the people in the room. I hope you were told by the Secretary General last night to not be offended if you were left off the list for this meeting, and to not judge your importance to this effort by your proximity to this meeting. Well, that was for everyone to hear, but more for the UN staff to take to heart. We need them for the long game for sure, but right now we are playing the short game and I don't need them for that. Besides, after the Secretary General got you amnesty and both of you free and clear to talk about our classified R&D operations to everyone, I needed to take him down a peg or two, so that he doesn't make a habit of pushing too hard on us.

"So, for today it's just us, and we need to wrap our minds around this whole Zach thing. Mr. Dau, I love that guy! Wish he was working for us instead of that asshat running the UN, but anyway, Mr. Dau says you are one hundred percent sure that Zach did that weather over in India with your machines. Is that right?" he asked Bob. Given this was his first opportunity, Bob nodded a quick hello to everyone in the room as he began his reply to the Presidents' questions.

"Well Mr. President, yes Mr. Dau accurately conveyed my confidence that Zach used *your* Thor's Hammers to cause unprecedented weather events in India. One hundred percent," Bob paused.

The President smiled, paused and leaned back into his chair before he replied and nodded up and down as he spoke, "You're right Professor, your clarification is spot on, and I deserved the tone in which it was delivered. After all, we did not get off on the best foot with our last dealings, and now you have a fiancé to look out for, and I suspect that is what you are doing. I imagine I would do the same in your shoes, but right now my shoes mean I must do that very same thing for an entire nation. We both take our obligations seriously, yes?" Bob nodded acknowledging their commonality as the President continued, "So, we both need to put the past behind us. Chalk up our wins, learn from our losses and move on. I am willing to do that Bob and I hope you are willing and able to do that as well. You see we now have some common goals and a common enemy, or at least a common problem.

"Those goals being we want this weather modification thing to do good for us, and as many others as possible without doing damage to us. We want your friend Doc to get the credit and results he worked and hoped for. We want the UN to lead this effort to success, that way they can regain some of their squandered credibility, and we get credit for being their top backer and providing you as the expert on the field. Should that effort fail, heaven forbid, because honestly none of us wants that, but should it fail the UN has to eat that one not me. Which brings us to what could make this whole thing fail, and that is Zach.

"Bob, I agree with your assessment *if* it wasn't you who did that business in India. So, I must do my due diligence, look you in the eye in front of the woman you love and ask you man to man, was it you who did that catastrophe in India? You have clemency for when that happened, so if you did, I can't do anything to you for doing it, but I have to know with one hundred percent certainty if it was or was not you? Shoot straight with me champ; did you do it?"

Eyeball to eyeball the President waited for Bob's reply which came swiftly but measured, "No sir, it was not me. And I need to know the same, man to man, was it you?" Bob held his breath, did not blink or move until the President responded.

"No Professor, it was not me. Rule you and the UN out, rule me and mine out, that only leaves Zach gone rogue, right? Now we both are one hundred percent. Now what?" asked the leader of the free world.

"Ask Ann, she usually has a good idea when I got nothin'," Bob said as the tension in the room eased with soft laughter from everyone in the room except Ann.

"Alright Ann, now that we have all *that* out of the way please make some recommendations we can all put into motion to get what we're after," the President shifted to her.

"OK, so no pressure on the engineer, right?" she started nervously. "How many Hammers are missing; I mean how many can he have from the lab?" she pressed.

"Two are missing," Tom responded.

"So, he has to limit his actions to using or selling the two he has—*or*—he has to make some more to use or sell. Or both. Zach won't give up what he has until he is sure he can get or make more before he does.

"When we were doing the lab research there were a few components that were scarce, but commercially available expensive satellite components. Isolate these and see who bought them in the recent past, besides us, and who is trying to buy them now. We may not know where he is yet, but we do know what he needs, or is going to need very soon. I know what those parts are; for starters I can help with that," Ann offered.

"That's a damned good start Ann," Secretary Fitzgerald observed. "You sure you want to settle for this guy? You know you can do better, right?"

His calculated attempt at establishing some camaraderie in the room seemed to be working as Ann quipped back, "Yes, I know I can do better but this guy is already so far out of his league I didn't want anything else bad happening to him. I'll finish what I started, it's the least I can do. I am a woman of my word."

"OK, if you two are finished keeping me humble in the presence of greatness, what can we do to prevent Zach from using the Hammers again between now and when we find him?" Bob asked no one in particular.

Again, Tom was first to respond, "Probably nothing. He holds all the cards when it comes to when and where."

General Charles asked, "What if we help him play them? Why wait? Let's ask for something he is looking to get. Why not put the word out that we are looking for a demonstration to purchase one of our own Hammers before the UN makes them lose their value? We just pretend to be someone else when we are asking and offering to pay. Tom, I know you can help us with that. When he comes up to the bait, we will know who it is because we already know who it isn't. We set a time and place for the demo and we know where Zach will be."

"Two good ideas, three's the charm. Who's next? C'mon we are on a roll," the President encouraged.

Bob took a shot at the third idea with a contrarian point for the President to consider, as much to see if he was as ready to bury the hatchet as he claimed, "Sir, you said you don't need the UN for the short game, but what if we put them in play right now anyway? There is only one way for this effort to go given what we all know now, and that is fast. If we control the tempo, that keeps Zach in a reactive posture and maybe disrupts his agenda, maybe forces an error he otherwise would not make if he was controlling the clock.

"We are only here because the UN pulled you into what we figured out. Alienating them right now means we are fighting amongst ourselves and not synchronizing our efforts against Zach. Double coverage, blitz, whatever metaphor you want to use, we both need to be working our efforts for the same result. If we are trying to get Zach to pop up for a demonstration or a targeted event for hire, or a sale of a hammer we need to impact the market price by doing our own for the world to see.

"We can take the UN's Thor's Hammer on a dog and pony road show. Media blitz, look and see what we can do with this thing. Call it public outreach to show what it can do, and what will be coming your way soon as we operationalize and proliferate it to a jurisdiction near you. We whet everyone's appetite and make it clear, having your own will only give you a competitive advantage for a short amount of time. It will put pressure on Zach to sell whatever he is selling before there is no more value in what he is holding. His forty percent of the global capability is at the apex of its value bubble right now, and that number can only go down as time passes and more Hammers get made and fielded. The UN effort on full display, all gas and no brakes getting this out to the people for doing good things. It is the actual objective, and it complements the other two good ideas if we do them all concurrently." Bob sounded more confident than he actually was with this idea.

"Well Bob, I can't argue with your logic. It is sound, and it hides our objective in plain sight like a stolen car parked in a used car lot," the President agreed. "Dutch, what can your folks bring to the party once we have an idea of where Zach is, or is likely to be when all this works?"

"Whatever it takes to do whatever it is you want done. Meaning it depends whether you already know if you just want him brought back or want both him and the devices in good condition, if you want a smoking hole, or if you want to call an audible. The more advance notice we have the better, but we are a global power so I will have a range of options for you once I know what, when and where. In the meantime, I will put some units on alert and increase some key units and recce assets readiness posture." The Chairman's confidence was calming, and Bob recognized that the lack of specificity was anything but a non-answer to the Commander in Chief. It was the answer he needed to hear, once the President provides his desired result his forces would find a way to do it, or he would hear a range of alternatives.

"Thanks Dutch, I know you need more to go on than we have laid out here, but once we see what it is we need to do and where it needs doing, we won't have a lot of time. Be ready is all I can ask for now, because I don't yet know whether this global ecoterrorist murderer Zach needs a trial at the Hague, or to be vaporized in the name of global public health and safety. We've done worse to better for less than we believe he has done already. That is a pretty good start everyone, thank you. Do you all have enough to set this in motion, and, if not, what do you need from me that you don't have already?" the President challenged them more than he asked them.

After exchanging glances, SECDEF and CJCS said almost in unison, "We're good."

Tom was next to respond, "With your permission Mr. President I would like the Mcleods to accompany me back to New York on the company jet so we can plan how best to bring the UN into alignment on this effort without exposing too much of the what's next. I would also recommend a video teleconference with you, the ambassador and the Secretary General some time tomorrow evening to allow them to brief you on their idea to roll this out. I believe you will find it remarkably similar to the ideas described here today, but it will offer an opportunity to thank them for bringing the Zach thing to your attention, and for you to like their roll out plan.

"I am sure they will also appreciate your offer to provide support for that plan in the form of military transport aircraft, rotary wing support and a mix of uniformed and private security all under the command and control of the UN for the effort. This will give us eyes and boots on the ground and a good cover story for some of General Charles' advance force operators to be out and about in case Zach pops up nearby a UN-sponsored effort. It may be that he goes after the competition once he gets wind of these high visibility demos. If he wants to slow us down, to buy himself some time he might roll in on one of ours to blow up our game with his own. Did you ever put one of these machines against the other to see which one wins Professor?" Tom concluded and waited for a response from Bob, seemingly not at all concerned that the President had yet to agree to the meeting he had just suggested. Ann recognized immediately that Tom's request was taken as a de facto addition to the President's calendar and not a request for anything.

"We did some small-scale testing when we were at the R&D facility, but nothing on a large scale. Plainly, I don't know for sure what would happen if two or more of these were pitted against each other. We know for sure the recipe for a tornado works controllably, but if that device was put next to one programmed for a calm clear day. I don't know if we would get one, the other, both or something in between. We might be able to counter an event we ask Zach to do with his Hammer, and he might be able to disrupt our UN parlor tricks with one of his, but candidly I don't know how that works out, especially if and when there are more than two. Depending on the start time, this is all becoming very theoretical. Ann and I left once the technology transition was complete, but many of the field trials and testing was scheduled or done after we left. That was Zach's show at that point, so he knows more than either of us. If I had the test records that would help, but I imagine Zach took care to take all that with him once he left." Bob stopped once he realized he was thinking out loud but still hadn't provided anything meaningful that could not have been summarized with a simple I don't know.

"That sounds great, Tom, please make it happen. I will see you on the screen tomorrow with the UN team. Safe travels and thank you all for making the trip and for your time today. This was very helpful, and it was nice to meet with you both in person. I feel much better about you two now, let's see if you can walk this talk," the President concluded the meeting, stood up and was exiting the room at the same time the staffers magically appeared and escorted Tom, Bob and Ann in one direction as the SECDEF and CJCS followed out in a different direction. And just like that they were in another black Suburban on their way off the White House grounds enroute to Washington National and loaded into a government aircraft with no official markings other than the tail number and other FAA required safety markings. A short taxi out to the runway and they were airborne and enroute to New York and the UN with lots of details to work out with Tom before they landed.

Once everyone was settled in for the short flight back to New York, the young man who had brought them a beverage moved to the back of the craft to prepare their food requests. The two flying the small jet, and the cabin steward were the only others on the small but comfortable and well-equipped jet that Tom, Bob and Ann boarded. It was Ann who broke the silence.

"Tom, what can you tell us about yourself and what you can do for this effort as a National Security Advisor? Is that the same title you have when you are at the UN or is that something different but equally vague?" she asked politely but stared at him intently and did not blink until Tom's answer was well underway.

"Same title for both, but different responsibilities. Keeps it simpler. What I can bring to our coming efforts is whatever money and political influence can provide. What I cannot do is make things appear and disappear. On second thought I can do some of that too, but I'm not a genie or anything like that," he smiled charmingly.

"Ok well that might work on a lot of people, but it's not gonna work for us. We need to know what you can and what you cannot put into play for our UN effort to get Zach to pop his head up. What and where are your boundaries? What is your background and areas of expertise?

"When we come to you what is on or off the table and what are the lead times you need for which requests? This is not a game to us. Do not be coy if you want us to trust you, if you want to earn our trust. It's a short flight and we have a lot to cover if you want to help keep us working toward the same objective. We don't want to do this on our own, but, as you can see from our efforts this far, we are not afraid to do that if put in that position. Do you think your responses can be as plain as my questions, Tom?" Ann concluded as Bob sat there enjoying the view of his fiancé in the role of lioness.

"I can do that Ann, and if there's one thing I appreciate, it's candor. If you need information on a topic, a capability, a strength, weakness or vulnerability I can find it, or I can get it. Information, intelligence I can turn that quickly if we have it…not as quickly if we need to get it but it will still be in time if it is gettable.

"Communications are the same. You need someone to hear something, know something, or get asked something I can do that as fast as anyone on the planet. I can put what you want, where you want it, when you want it there almost as fast as you decide you want it…but within reason. If you provide me all four who, what, when and where. I cannot do that with Zach yet because I don't know the where nor the exact what and when yet.

"As far as capability, I can get you civilian or military resources or effects if they are within the law and under the direction of the Executive branch of our government. I cannot direct Congress or the Senate, nor the judiciary but, if the President can order it and I am doing what he asked me to do, he will order it. I have been doing this job successfully since early in his first term. He trusts me to deliver, to be discreet and above board and I have not failed him yet. Don't intend to start now. What have I not covered sufficiently?" Tom concluded without recognizing Bob even being on the plane during this exchange.

"Thank you, Tom, that is very helpful, and I appreciate your candor as well. Now what about Tom? You have not sufficiently covered anything about you. Who is Tom?" she asked softly but genuinely.

"Tom is not my real name, and my real name is not important. But I will tell you I am well educated, served in the military, was recruited into the intel community. I am fluent in more than English, good at math and science, as comfortable in a shithole with a weapon in my hands as I am wearing a twelve-thousand-dollar suit in a small room or restaurant with world leaders talking about stuff that nobody is supposed to hear. Not married, no kids. Patriot. I say what I mean and mean what I say. That's all the Tom you get. For now, and probably for as long as we know each other. I hope that's enough cause that's all you get." He smiled as the steward arrived and began to serve their food as if his actions were intended to transition the conversation to a lighter topic. Which they were. This was Tom's plane, with his hand-picked crew, they had been together for years and had conducted many meetings on this aircraft in that time. Tom was not one to leave anything to chance if there was something he could do to control the situation, and there was always something he could do.

"What and who, when we get back to the UN, Bob?" Tom transitioned the conversation and its participants as all three were chewing their food.

"I think Ann and I will find Mr. Dau and ask him to put together a very small meeting with the Secretary General to debrief our meeting with the President. See what and who he considers small. We tell him that we met, that we all believe Zach has used Hammers without the approval of the US government, and that the UN needs to do a full-on media blitz to show the world what is now possible and how it can be used in collaboration for the benefits of all rather than the few. The US has promised airlift, global communications and some security for that effort. We don't tell them everything, but we don't tell them anything that is untrue," Bob waited to gauge Tom's reaction before he continued.

"OK so far. How do we wrap this together?" Tom asked.

"Once Ann and I have UN buy in, we develop a gameplan of locations and what to demonstrate. You are the US lead for developing that gameplan and arranging for putting that in motion for the UN. That way you can help steer based on what we learn about Zach when we learn it without having to draw attention to any sudden changes. You make the aircraft unavailable for an engine swap or whatever you do to control the tempo of things you are already used to controlling. Ann and I will focus on the science, Hammer use and development, etc. It will look right because it is right. But it will be serving multiple purposes and we can work out and collaborate on the details as we go, as more information comes in." Bob was done now.

"That works for me. It enables us to have regular contact, but allows that to be event driven and responsive as the situation changes. Now what about Father Gannon?" Tom asked.

"What about him?" returned Bob.

In response, Tom offered, "We need to transition him out and you in. You have to be the face of this road show for this plan to work. We need to eliminate the gap between what and when we need it and his ability to deliver that or understand it from you. A middleman reduces flexibility and speed. We also need to remove him for what is already becoming competing priorities from his Church leadership. They are already unhappy with him for bringing his Hammer to the UN instead of the Vatican and are putting pressure on him to add the Church into the UN fielding plan. That cannot happen if we are to do what we agreed to in the Oval.

"Your small meeting with Dau and the Secretary General needs to include a comment about concerns regarding the Church's agenda. You have Father Gannon focus on telling the story of Doc Auster, Bob Mcleod and how these devices and capabilities came to be. That is where his role ends, that is his box and he needs to stay in it. He is not part of the demonstrations; he is not in the same place at the same time as the demo teams. These two wires don't cross. The Church can allow him to help tell the story, but it's the history and not the present nor the future. That is ours and the Church and Father Gannon needs to be free and clear of what is to come. They will get to play like everyone, at the time and place of the UN's choosing but they don't get a seat on the steering committee any more than the University you were working for when you guys came up with this stuff. Can you agree to that and make that happen?" Tom asked seeming to already know the answer.

Bob and Ann were both nodding in agreement as Bob replied, "Yes, and I don't think anyone will be happier about that than Father Gannon himself. He will be relieved is my sense, and the sooner he can get back to his parish the better. He never wanted to be a part of this but did so out of loyalty to Doc and us. It won't take us much to do that. I know his bosses won't be too happy about it, but it will take him out of the middle of their ambitions and that will be fine with all of us I believe."

Ann leaned back in her seat, "All settled then? Sounds like we have a good plan of action. Betty helps us move forward and Father Gannon retrogrades back to however normal his life can be after all of this.

"I don't know about you all, but I am going to close my eyes and try to get a power nap before we land. This has been quite an eventful day for me, and we have a lot still to try to set up after we land in twenty minutes if my math is correct. Let's do our best to get this right," Ann said as she closed her eyes while her two traveling companions did the same.

In what seemed like only a few minutes, they touched down in New York and taxied to parking. Once they unloaded, they were shuffled into another waiting Suburban and were headed to the UN building. There was little conversation as each of them were contemplating the many actions, reactions and potential roadblocks ahead of them.

It was Ann who broke the relative quiet of their ride, "Why don't we start with making it rain in a place where it usually doesn't, but some-where that would benefit from it? Why not start right where this all started? The first demo should be in the Midwest, right where Doc started it all. We could pick a family farm, with a big cornfield and give them a slow half inch of rain to help the corn take off. We could let Father Gannon head home from there and then do the next ones in whatever country on whichever continent gets us closer to Zach as that develops.

"We spread the word around the world in a two-week blitz by showing it works on each continent right out of the blocks. Everyone will be talking about it, but more importantly it will be seen everywhere and each of those spots will spread the word and confidence in what we are doing more than having them come to us. It also gives us good cover to respond to Zach whenever he comes up in response to our wide coverage and short timeline? What is the downside of this approach?" she concluded.

As Bob and Tom looked at each other shrugging their shoulders without saying anything aloud.

"OK, hearing none, it's settled then. First Demo will also be a home-coming of sorts for our team. Then we take the roadshow on a global circuit to areas where agriculture is a big deal, rinse and repeat. Zach will come out of his hole, or he won't. We still get the word out and increase confidence while the conversation about the potential of on-demand weather will be going on around the world. Father Gannon gets to find peace and return to a new normal. Betty gets the best of both worlds. Let's go do this," Ann concluded as the Suburban rolled slowly to a spot where they could exit the Suburban and enter the UN as unnoticed as was possible given the happenings.

Within seconds of their arrival inside, Mr. Dau appeared and took a track directly intersecting their path from the security check point. As he walked towards them, he spoke from a distance, "Welcome back! The Secretary General and the small team are assembled to hear and discuss the outcome of your trip. We are both excited and intrigued as to the content and decisions from your discussion with the President," he said as he walked them to the elevator and pressed the button and access code for the limited-access floor which was their destination.

Once they arrived and settled in, Bob and Ann relayed the take-aways of the discussion to those assembled. Tom was appropriately content in portraying his role as a "strap-hanger" in the entire affair, and only spoke in response to one question from Mr. Dau, "…and the US will provide the airlift, supplies, communications and lead the security for the entire world tour?" he queried Tom, who responded calmly, "That's why I'm here."

After a few affirmations of who had to be where to do what next, they all left the room continuing multiple conversations as the small group made their way out. That left Bob and Ann last in the room, looking at each other a bit surprised that they were alone in the wake of the busy leaders who had just been hanging on their every word.

"I don't know about you, but I am hungry, I'm tired and I need to pack. We need to find Betty and Father Gannon to make sure they know what's coming…or that what they get told matches what we think is going to be happening. And I am ready for a drink. This has been a day," Bob said as he looked at Ann and let out a hopeful sigh.

"Sounds good to me. Just please tell me this is what you want to do. I know once I started talking, it might have been hard for you to suggest something else. Are you really good with this idea, because if you are not you gotta say so. We can change whatever you think needs changing?" Ann asked sincerely.

"I wouldn't change a thing. Not about this, not about you, not about us. Let's take a deep breath, because I think this only gets harder before it gets better. Let's enjoy what we can, while we can. How about that drink now?" Bob smiled.

"I'm in. You're buying, and I am having doubles," Ann smiled as she took Bob by the hand and led him to the door that would take them to the elevator, the lobby, the exit, the waiting car, the hotel bar and the drinks they were headed out to enjoy.

CHAPTER FIVE

WHAT JUST HAPPENED?

They had just finished drink number one in the hotel lounge when Betty and Father Gannon walked in together and joined Bob and Ann at the quiet, dimly lit table at the side of the room. After everyone had given their drink orders, with some snacks to help absorb the alcohol, Betty and Father Gannon listened to Bob summarize the events, decision makers involved, and the path forward for each of them that would commence the following morning. As the news and the drinks began to sink in for each of them, it was Betty that broke the rather somber mood with a loud laugh which she tried unsuccessfully to control.

"What am I missing?" Ann asked cautiously.

"Well, it just occurred to me, this is a huge middle finger to Hugh Durbin. We are all flipping him the bird for how he treated Doc, and the rest of us. Maybe we should invite him and the University Chancellor to the event, after all they were part of the context at one time, but certainly not relevant to this story anymore. I would love to see the look on his face when we make it rain and he fully grasps what it is he is not involved in rolling out. Can we do that without looking like complete assholes? Sorry Father; was that over some line we shouldn't cross, because I know I would enjoy it?" Betty waited for someone to answer, not particularly caring who.

Ann spoke first, "That is not something I considered when I suggested we start back there. But if it's an added benefit for you all, I don't care how you decide to play it with Durbin and the University. You two are the ones who used to work there, or maybe still do. I am not sure where all that sits."

Bob smiled as he said, "Betty, as much as we both would probably enjoy rubbing Durbin's nose in it, I really think that would be kicking a man when he is already down and out. He got his already, and we must be looking forward with everything we have to get this out there so people can see and believe the potential greatness of this technology. I think we are all big enough to leave Durbin as a mere footnote in the story, which he is, and I don't want to add anything else next to his name. Can we live with that? Look ahead and not behind?" Bob said aloud, already knowing the heads nodding in agreement were aligned in their thinking.

"Alright, then. Let's finish up here. I don't know about you all, but I still gotta pack and we have an early start tomorrow. Don't worry about checking out or anything like that. I am keeping the block of rooms for as long as we are going back and forth to the UN, which as far as I can tell will be at least another month or more. We need to have something stable in this craziness up here." A little small talk continued as they made their way to the elevator, up to their rooms and bid each other good night.

As Bob and Ann packed what they thought they would need from what they had with them in the hotel room, Ann asked quietly, "Would it be okay if we invited my dad to come to this first event? Let him see what he helped us with already, and what we are going to be working on for a while? I haven't been able to spend much time with him since, well since you got me out early. And while I am so grateful for that, he was the reason I was there in the first place and I would like for him to see first-hand what this is, I want him to be proud of me, proud of us. After all we are going to be married, and I would prefer if you both were complementary instead of in competition for my time and attention. Especially this early. It's a lot for all of us, and I think he would come if we…if you invited him."

Bob smiled, "I think that's a great idea. You better be careful, if you keep having those, I'm going to start expecting them every time I ask you something."

Ann smiled, "Good. And it's cute that you think I'll only give you my great ideas when you ask for them. You do still have a lot to learn, Professor Mcleod."

The next morning as the four were assembling in the lobby to meet the UN arranged transportation for those in the hotel, Tom emerged from somewhere and addressed them all.

"Good morning, everyone. I trust you are all well rested and ready to go?" As they all looked a bit surprised to see him there, he continued without giving anyone the opportunity to respond, "Change number one today is you will be flying out with me this morning. We have a shuttle out front that will get us to our plane. Got everything? We are in a bit of a hurry if we are going to keep our timeline. Ladies, is there anything I can carry for you? Ok then, if we're good, please follow me." Without being asked, Tom picked up Betty's bag turned to lead the group to the door and led them to the waiting shuttle. He loaded the bags and once the four climbed aboard he followed, closing the door and loudly slapping it twice indicating to the driver that it was closed and ready to go. Before he was seated, the door closed behind him, and the shuttle was rolling toward the traffic they would disappear into on their way to whichever airport they were headed to this time.

As everyone was adjusting for the ride, Tom addressed them, "Sorry to spring this change on you, last minute, but as we spend more time together you will find that happens more frequently than any of us will like. We are staying on plan with our UN debut in your hometown farmer's field, but we have a couple of stops to make before we link up with Mr. Dau and the rest of the UN team. That is why we will be using our jet so we can keep our itinerary aligned with what is already laid in. First stop will be the regional airport, where we will drop Father Gannon off so he can get ready with the media team to talk about the pregame interviews, announcements, etc. with the group he was working with in

New York. The rest of you will stay aboard and we will make another couple of quick stops to grab a few others we will need but don't have yet for the demonstrations," he concluded.

As they smiled and soaked in the updates, Bob's voice interrupted their thoughts. "Hello, Steve? Good morning. It's Bob," He paused, then continued, "Bob Mcleod. Ann's fiancé, Bob Mcleod," he said shaking his head slowly left to right as he spoke slower and louder. "Yes, the guy who had you dig a big hole inside your shop so I could leave a bunch of my stuff there...Yes, I understand you can never be too careful...No, no Sir, everything is fine, Ann is fine...Yes, we are still engaged," he paused again, this time when Bob looked up, he could see by the smiles on everyone's faces that he had become the entertainment for the drive to the airport.

"Steve, I wanted to invite you to a big event that Ann and I will be doing in a couple of days...No, it's not the wedding, it's something else, it's work related. We are both working for the UN right now, and we are doing a very big demonstration. Big media event that we would like you to attend…Well, to be with us to see in person what we are working on. We would both love to have you there, we will cover whatever cost there is. All you have to bring is you and whatever you are most comfortable wearing...A couple of days at the most, then we will be flying out shortly after the event to our next location, which has not been set yet. You would head home whenever you like after the one here. Once we have all the details, Betty or someone will contact you to let you know where to be and when...That sounds great then...We are both looking forward to seeing you, too...Gotta run, and yes, I will. I will tell her. Thanks Steve, see you soon." Bob hung up and looked around the shuttle at all the smiling faces, stopping at Ann's he concluded with, "Your Dad says to tell you he loves you; he is proud of you and he will be there for you...and it's not too late to change your mind about me. If you do, he will certainly understand."

That brought out the laughter from everyone, and a conciliatory reply from Ann, "Thanks for inviting him. He must like you if he agreed to come; he does not like to travel."

Betty chimed in, "He's probably wanting to make sure his little girl is OK and that her fiancé is treating her right."

Tom smiled and added, "Sure let's go with that. It will play better than if it gets out that I called him earlier and told him we had someone to arrange his travel, give him an iron clad alibi, a priest to forgive him for whatever happens to said fiancé, and a guy who knows how to make the body disappear. Ann is with us; meet him wherever he asks you too."

They all smiled at what they were pretty sure was Tom's joke, but also recognized that many a truth was said in jest; that Tom put that line of thinking into a protective father joke at Bob's expense to give them all lots of room for their imaginations to run freely about what he was actually capable of pulling off. At the end of that exercise, nothing in his joke sounded out of the realm of the possible. Not likely but certainly possible.

Once airborne in the same small jet, with the same steward and two pilots that had flown them to DC to meet with the President, everyone chatted about the coming events, but mostly about all the details they did not yet know about their debut demonstration of Thor's Hammer. They did know it was likely to be in front of a global media, and whomever was not there in person would certainly be playing the footage from those who were present. The idea that you only get one chance to make a first impression was troubling the UN team pulling the details together, but it did not really linger in the minds of those in the small jet on short final to the regional airport. This group had already made first impressions of Thor's Hammer a few times already, and their track record was pretty good so far.

After taxiing to a stop and with engines still running, Father Gannon deplaned and the door closed as they rolled back to the active runway for their next destination.

"Sorry, but I could not give you all the rest of the story until we dropped off the good Padre," Tom began.

"It's not that he isn't trustworthy, but all this classified stuff mixed in with what we are doing in the open creates some seams we need to navigate carefully. Need to know, compartmented stuff sometimes requires some air gaps between individuals, so we know who is doing, or not doing what.

"It seems Father Gannon will have to spend a little time at the Vatican debriefing folks on what he knew, what he did and didn't do and the like. He can tell them everything he knew up until the doors closing just now. From this point on, you only get to share with Father Gannon those things you do with him in person. This is the fork in the road where we go off in our direction, and Father Gannon wraps up his involvement and goes back to being a parish priest. Does anyone have any questions about how or why this must work this way?" he paused.

"We can still talk, catch up, be friends and talk about everything that is in the open media or that we do with him, but we cannot tell him the what or why behind it if he wasn't there in person for it. Is that the gist of it?" Betty asked.

"Yes ma'am. That is the gist of it. And that is the gist of the papers I am going to need you to sign before we land," Tom added as the steward on cue handed Betty a folder with a stack of papers and a pen.

"It's what we call an NDA. A non-disclosure agreement. You already summed up in one sentence all the legalese it takes lawyers volumes to say. Bob and Ann have already signed the same documents relative to Thor's Hammer, this just catches you up to their agreements and let's us keep you next to them as we proceed through this," he assured her.

As Bob nodded, Betty quickly reviewed and signed the documents. "I am going to continue to trust that we are all in this together. Been that way since you came to see me about it, so I don't have any reason to change my mind now," she said as she handed the folder back to the steward who appeared next to her precisely when she extended her arm.

"Good. Thank you, Betty. Alright then this will be a short flight, in fact we are almost there," Tom said as he felt the aircraft slow and begin to descend in a sharp left turn that meant they were bleeding off the airspeed and altitude needed to make the odd approach into the short airfield at the military training area which was their next destination. A quick descent, a solid thump on touchdown, and a lot of brakes for a short and fast deceleration prior to the quick stop were clear signs that they were safely on the ground at a place Bob recognized once he looked out the window to his left. They were back at the military isolation facility where he had done some of his first demonstrations of Thor's Hammer. He could see his friend Frank walking toward the aircraft as the engines were winding down. It appeared they would be here longer than they were at the regional airport.

As the aircraft door opened and they began to exit, they were greeted by a familiar face in an olive-green flight suit. "Tom? I am Colonel Frank Lincoln, welcome and please follow me," he requested as he turned and led everyone inside the building closest to the flight line where they could better hear each other as the aircraft was being shut down, refueled and whatever else was needed.

Bob was pleased to see his new "old friend" and a few other familiar faces in the meeting room which also contained a lot of others he did not recognize. Some in, but most not in, military uniforms. "It's nice to see you, Frank!" he began. "You remember Ann, and this is my friend and make-it-happen lady, Betty." They both smiled and greeted the colonel who was doing his best to make them welcome and comfortable in the relatively austere conditions of the isolation facility at the remote airfield deep in the large military training area.

"Tom, we have your people here, and the few of my team that I think we need to cover what we talked about last night. If I can get you or your travelling companions anything please let me know, otherwise we are ready to begin when you are," Frank concluded, as Bob was reminded how intuitive the colonel could be when it came to understanding what needed doing, when it needed to be done and who should be doing it.

"Thank you, Frank." The response signaled to those in the room that Tom held at least the rank equivalent to colonel and likely higher given the uniformed colonel's deference to the seemingly much younger man in the room only known to anyone thus far as Tom.

"And thank you all for being here. This should not take long, but it is important that we all meet each other, understand what we are doing and why. This entire briefing and the people here are classified Top Secret, the special access program, also known as a SAP, is named THOR's JOURNEYMEN. Outside this room, there are less than a dozen others who are briefed into this and they are at the very highest levels of our government. If you have *not* signed an NDA for this SAP let me know right now so we can figure out what to do with you. Anyone?" Tom paused and scanned the faces all indicating their paperwork was in order, at the same time he indicated to Bob, Ann and Betty that the paperwork they had in place was more than sufficient for what was coming next.

During this short pause Bob was able to catch the eyes of both Captain Lessur and Sergeant Andies seated among the others. He was glad to see they had survived any potentially negative outcomes from their short but still memorable history. At least as far as Bob could tell, neither had been demoted since they were wearing the same rank as last time. Whether by reward, punishment or security necessity, they were among the few uniformed members of the trusted few currently read into THOR's JOURNEYMEN and Bob sincerely hoped it was a reward for them. He still felt bad about the credibility hit they took while he was still learning what the Thor's Hammers were and what they could do.

Confident that everyone in the room fit in the appropriate "who" category, Tom continued on to explain the "what, when, where, why and how" to those assembled and curious about who the other people in the room were and what they could bring to the operation. Tom was sharp, very sharp and if anyone had any doubts about him or his abilities when he started, by the time he was finished none remained.

First, he introduced every individual in the room by name, and briefly described where they worked, what they did there, and why they were seated in the room by explaining what areas of the operation they would oversee and what capabilities they would be expected to provide when called upon. It was a robust set of capabilities to be brought to bear by a small but seemingly capable group of individuals that were now key players on Tom's new team.

Next Tom provided a short intelligence update, which was the area of the operation he clearly intended to lead himself because there was no "Intel guy" in the room when introductions were complete. For a classified operation such as this, there's always an "Intel guy."

"Our objective is to find a man known to us as Zach. We know his real name, but nobody else of any importance does, so they will know him only as we do, Zach. He has at least two Thor's Hammers, which are the devices developed by Professor Mcleod and used to control or produce on-demand weather conditions. We are reasonably confident Zach has already used them for his own gain and is looking to sell them to the highest bidder, or someone he wants to get into business with. He is also likely capable of, and planning to make more of these devices to either use, sell or both. Zach's last known whereabouts were in India, but that was weeks ago. We don't know where he is now, or where he is likely to be, but we do know what he is likely to do and when.

"In the next few days, he and everyone else will hear about and see a publicity event put on by the UN demonstrating this new on-demand weather modification capability. They will also announce an aggressive schedule to demonstrate the capability on every continent within the next couple of weeks. This should put pressure on Zach to trigger or accelerate his next moves. We will try to utilize that to set up a meet to see them in action to confirm their ability and purchase the Thor's Hammers in his possession. Once we know where and when, or upon contact if we can confirm his location we will apprehend Zach, alive, if possible, in order to recover the two stolen devices and any other he may have made. Whether they are in his possession or not, if we have Zach, we should be able to get the information needed to also get the devices or their last known locations.

"I will need everyone in this room to be attached to the UN effort, present at the first event which will be in a local farm field, and available to travel with the UN road show. We will use marked US military aircraft to transport the UN teams and capabilities so there should be lots of room for us to maneuver back and forth between military and civilian expertise. Lots of cover room if we need it, which we likely will if we must conduct direct action OCONUS…outside the continental United States," he added for Betty's benefit, who at this point was feeling as exhilarated as she was completely out of her comfort zone. Tom proceeded.

"Whether we get Zach to pop his head up or not, the one thing we need to make sure does happen is the UN has a successful roll out of this new technology. I know the order of my briefing would indicate this is a secondary outcome but let me be clear. The UN must succeed on this Thor's Hammer roll out. That is both the national security objective and our priority, as well as, prerequisite for creating sufficient pressure on Zach to give us a shot at him. I mean that figuratively for now. Any questions for me at this point? You'll get another opportunity in five minutes." He paused while he scanned the room, trying to decide if he was that good a briefer or if nobody wanted to admit they needed additional information to do what had been asked thus far.

Sensing he had the right people in the room, he continued, "Seeing none, I will press on." He chose those words deliberately to signal to those who were wondering that he had in fact spent time in the military himself, or had been around enough of them to know how to effectively speak to them. "Zach is going to be looking, if he was not looking already, for someone who can spend a metric-shit-ton of money on these things. That means a near peer, or peer competitor nation, or a criminal cartel or terrorist organization…or group of them who can assemble a large sum of money and is seeking to benefit in the near term from that expenditure to quickly get a return on such a large investment. That means we are assembled here to keep some government or sophisticated group of bad guys from attacking us. It's not hyperbole to say if we fail, we may very well have failed to prevent a catastrophic event or even a

World War 3-scale attack on the United States. I need everyone here to bring their A-game. Do I have your commitment to do that?"

His challenge was met with a resounding mix of loud whoops, hollers, yes sirs and other signature affirmations that left no doubt that everyone in the room had just signed on to the mission at hand.

"You know what to do, now go make this happen," Tom said as he started toward the door, Frank fell into step right behind him and Bob did the same. Ann and Betty followed Tom, Frank and Bob like they were leaving behind a wedding party. Apparently, they were done here, but, as they climbed aboard the aircraft, they both seemed to wonder to themselves exactly what they just witnessed. How was what they talked about in general terms going to all come together in actions on a timeline? They were seeing first-hand what decentralized execution looks like. Everyone was on the same page, but clearly these folks were faster and better at reading the page than they were. Strangely that didn't bother either of them. They could tell from how it felt in the room, that they were now part of something they did not yet understand but did not fear. Confidence, perhaps better described as faith in those who do these things for our nation as their chosen profession, gave them a sense of ease as they settled back in the aircraft after about being in the same seats just an hour before.

As Bob waited at the stair to climb back into the small jet which was already spooling engines up, he shouted, "Good to see you again, Frank!" who smiled and responded. "You say that now, wait 'til we are elbow deep in this at some crappy airfield in the middle of the night at some god-forsaken place doing a demo for some rich and powerful people. You're gonna look at me and say, this was way easier and more fun the first time, Frank! Take care Bob, I'll be seeing you again soon enough." Frank helped close the door on the aircraft and headed back to the building and those waiting in it. He still had a lot to do, and not a lot of time to get it done. Things were normal despite how abnormal the day was for those on the aircraft taxiing toward the runway.

CHAPTER SIX

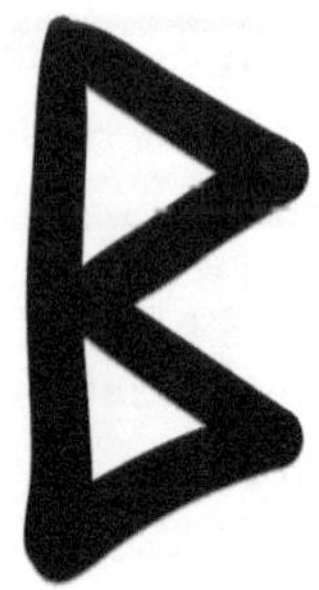

NOW WHAT?

The next couple of days after their small briefing at the airfield isolation facility were a blur for Bob and his small team. A seemingly endless string of meetings with Mr. Dau, Tom and a parade of both new and familiar faces had him, Ann, Betty and Father Gannon struggling to keep up with all the moving parts coalescing around the UN's first live demonstration of their Thor's Hammer. The news conference was just about to get underway, and they all took a deep breath before Mr. Dau gave the non-verbal cues that he was about to begin, and the small crowd began to quiet so they didn't miss a word he was there to share.

He stood before the cameras, microphones and colorful placards of many well-known and a few unknown news and media outlets and began to provide the details they had been patiently awaiting.

"Thank you all for being here today," he began and the silence was almost immediate. Mr. Dau was flanked by Father Gannon on one side, and Professor Mcleod on the other. It was the three of them who would make the announcements today laying out the upcoming events for the UN's debut of their new on-demand weather modification capabilities.

"You have all undoubtedly heard from Father Gannon the story of how Doctor Auster, Professor Mcleod and he brought this great technology to the world through the United Nations. And what a great story it is, and what great promise this new technology holds for us all.

"Today we are here to announce what comes next. Hearing a great story fills our hearts with promise and hope. But seeing firsthand, that is the fuel that fills the mind with ideas, potential applications. That is what suddenly makes the impossibilities of the past become the realities of the future. Transitioning the theoretical into the practical, taking a hypothesis and achieving measurable results is what we must do now. And what better place to begin doing that, than right here where it started not very long ago? So tomorrow afternoon we will conduct a live demonstration of this capability at a farm not far from this very spot. Professor Mcleod will personally demonstrate a few of the many capabilities of what is known as the Thor's Hammer. After that, in the next two weeks we will travel to each continent and conduct similar demonstrations to show the wide range of capabilities to an even wider range of audiences. This will help inform and enable the UN to select some of the most practical and beneficial initial controlled weather operations for the fielding of this amazing technology. At this time, I would like to thank Father Gannon for his tireless efforts to help tell this story for all of us, to all of you. And I will ask Professor Mcleod to take a few moments to describe to you all today, what you will have the pleasure of witnessing for yourselves tomorrow."

Mr. Dau smiled at the crowd as he stepped back to make room for Bob at a small podium covered in microphones, while at the same time reaching out to shake Father Gannon's hand and then began clapping for both men with whom he shared the stage. The crowd followed suit, and Bob paused to turn and applaud his friend who carried much of the weight in getting this story to the UN and far beyond. It was time for him to step back into the life from which Bob had pulled him without asking. Bob thought it both ironic and unfortunate that Father Gannon was also being benched without his consult or his consent. Bob felt like he was doing this to his friend instead of for his friend, but he was confident that Father Gannon was ready for a break regardless of how long this one would last.

Bob turned back to the small crowd and gave his full attention to delivering the prepared remarks describing what was to come.

"Tomorrow, around noon at a small family farm about twelve miles north on State Route B we will use the Thor's Hammer to demonstrate how we can change the weather. The current forecast calls for fair skies, light wind from the southwest and a temperature about sixty degrees. We will change the wind direction to come from a northeast direction at a steady twelve knots. Instead of its normal rise during the afternoon, we will drop the temperature to fifty degrees and hold it there. We will cover the sky in clouds and produce exactly one quarter inch of steady rain and then stop the rain and let those clouds clear out. Allow the temperature to rise back into its diurnal cycle and the winds to transition back to their southeasterly direction.

"I am telling you this in advance, so you know both what the weather is supposed to be if left to natural events, as well as knowing what we will change it to with the technology of the Thor's Hammer. I hope to see you all there. I also hope you will record what we do so you can share this first, and every future demonstration with all those around the globe who cannot be there in person. The United States is proud to assist the UN in this worthy endeavor, and I am personally proud to be able to continue this work which for me, started right here. It's nice to be back home for yet another new beginning for on-demand weather modification," Bob concluded as the flurry of questions came at him before he finished his statement.

After half a dozen or so canned responses to questions that may or may not have been among the ones shouted at Bob, Mr. Dau stepped up to the microphone, thanked everyone for coming and ushered the other two off the platform and onto the egress path back to the safety of the room where the rest of their core team was waiting for them.

"That went well," Tom said sincerely. "Thank you, Father Gannon. You've been a great asset to this effort. The President asked me to personally thank you on his behalf. If you will follow these two gentlemen, they will see you back to your parish. Your quarters, sorry your rectory, has been secured and a small security detail will remain in place until such time that you deem them unnecessary, or the Archdiocese or higher assigns someone to take over for my guys. We want to keep you safe. Get some rest, you earned it," he concluded as he reached out to shake the priest's hand and sent him on his way saying his goodbyes as he walked to the exit.

As the group was working out the few remaining details of tomorrow's gameplan Tom pulled Bob aside for a semiprivate discussion.

"So, my guys rolled up some local dipshit trying really hard to get an urgent message to you. Turns out he's here to serve you a subpoena. Do you know you are being sued by the University for stealing their intellectual property? They say you stole this weather modification stuff from them. The case has already been filed, it's real and they want to serve you with the suit, and of course then they want to depose you." Bob made it easy for Tom to read his non-verbal response, but his verbal left no doubts.

"You have got to be joking? You are joking right? That's Bullshit! But I will bet you it's Durbin's bullshit," Bob said loud enough to get the unwanted attention of almost everyone in the room.

"Not joking. And Durbin is one of the names on the court filing, so it looks like you got that one right. But here's the thing Bob, that case cannot get in the way of what we are doing. National security, your deal with the President, all that means even if you did steal it, even if they have a case it won't matter. You are already ironclad. I have a small army of lawyers on it already, they are filing so many motions and writs and all that lawyer stuff that it will be years before any of this gets anywhere even if the University wants to spend the fortune it will cost them just to get an initial hearing. You haven't been served, nor will you be anywhere in the next few weeks where that is going to happen. So now you know, but that is so you don't worry about any of it. Don't let it become a distraction, because that is the most it could ever become and right now, we don't need any distractions. Speaking of, have you seen your father-in-law to be yet? I know he made it in earlier."

"Not yet," Bob responded, happy to take the conversation in a new direction. Any topic was better than being troubled about or by someone named Durbin. It was increasingly comforting as Bob considered and understood that Tom really had that all covered for him. There was no need to worry about it, and there was also no need to be distracted by how much fun it might be to totally mess with Hugh Durbin over this. That might be some fun later, but there was serious business to take care of now. They needed to put on the best dog and pony show possible. You only get one chance to make a first impression, and theirs was tomorrow.

Tom and Bob wrapped up their final discussions, which was about the twelfth time they had gone through this in fine detail. They were ready, and Bob was ready to go. It had been a long day already, and he was looking forward to seeing Steve. Ann and Betty had gone together to meet him at the airport and bring him to their small house for the evening. It was fitting they were staying in the house in which Doc Auster labored so diligently to create this gift which they were lucky enough to deliver.

When Bob finally arrived, he was a little surprised to see Betty and Steve in the kitchen talking, laughing and cooking. Whatever it was, it smelled great and as Ann greeted Bob just inside the door, she was smiling ear to ear.

"You did great today. You looked great, sounded great, you were great!" she said as she kissed him quickly and kept talking.

"And speaking of great, those two have been getting along great. They haven't stopped talking since the airport. If I didn't know any better, I'd swear they dated in high school, haven't seen each other in forty years and are trying to catch up in one night. I'm not sure he even knows I'm still here. It'd be sickening if it weren't so cute. I hope you're as hungry as I am. Let's go in, say hi and see if they notice when we sit down and start eating." She was more than half serious and not quite half joking.

"Before we do, I have to tell you something and I am not sure whether to burden Betty with it just yet," Bob replied. Ann stopped and stared at him, well actually it was more of a look that silently but clearly communicated that she was already tired of waiting for him to tell her what it was.

"Tom told me that I am being sued by the University. Durbin is claiming that I stole the Thor's Hammer, and the technology from them. That Doc created it while he was working—no, while *we* were working—for the University, and it is their intellectual property. He also told me that because the Secretary General had taken the initiative to negotiate on my behalf and got my immunity deal that even if somehow, they could make a case that it wouldn't matter because my deal would protect both me and my money. He sicked some of his lawyers on the University and said they would tie it up for a long time. At best it will only be a distraction and that we should not take our eye off the ball for any of this. I believe him. I have the sense that if he says something, or someone, is going to disappear he is certainly capable of doing just that."

Ann interrupted him, "Good. I believe him, too. We need to focus on the effort to field this stuff and to stop Zach. The University and their lawsuit may or may not become a problem, but these demonstrations and Zach are problems. We need to focus all our attention on stopping him, and even that may not be enough to get it done. I agree with Tom, don't let it distract you. And by not telling Betty right now you won't have to concern yourself with her and maybe her reaction. You can pick a better time to share that with her if you decide to tell her, but for now let her enjoy time with my dad and focus on what we need to do. That's what I think," she said and waited for his response despite knowing that is what he wanted to hear whether she meant it or not.

"Thanks, me too. Let's eat!" he said with a smile as he walked into the kitchen to greet them both. After exchanging greetings, handshakes and hugs, they each filled a plate from the pots and pans still on the stove and took a seat at the small kitchen table to enjoy the fruits of their labors.

"I don't get it, Bob," Steve began between bites. "If I didn't see it with my own eyes, I wouldn't believe it but, seriously, it's very puzzling to me."

Bob replied as Steve was chewing his food, "It's a little complicated, but changing the weather is really based on some simple principles."

"No Bob, not that stuff I came up to see you all do tomorrow. I'm talking about you somehow having two of the greatest women in the world in your life. Loyal and willing to spend so much time with you and do so much on your behalf. They sure must know something I don't know yet." He eased into a wry smile, that Bob understood was intended to make him wonder if Steve was serious or joking. Pretty sure it was a little of both, Bob smiled back with a nervous laugh and tried to walk the thin line holding what he perceived as his safest response.

"Gotta agree with you Steve. Most days I don't know what I ever did to deserve having either one of these fine ladies in my life, let alone both. And at the same time? Luckiest man in the world right here."

As Betty rolled her eyes, she put a stop to it, "All right you two, we all know you are so far out of your league, that pity is likely the only explanation that makes any sense at all. I mean it's not like you're rich, famous, big hearted or handsome or…wait a minute, you are rich and famous, aren't you? Well Steve, I guess now you know. Can we move on to the next topic?" They all chuckled and as requested the conversation shifted to everything except the UN event that was one short sleep away. After what seemed like a Sunday family dinner, they all turned in, slept a few hours and were milling around the kitchen and its coffee pot way too early when the conversation finally landed on the logistics of the new day's events.

"We should all ride out together with Tom, when he and the UN security guys show up in a couple hours. At some point Ann and I will need to break off to get Thor's Hammer and head out for the demonstration area, get 'mic'd up' and all the show business stuff. If you two don't mind staying together and enjoying the show from the staff section, you will have a great view of everything, and you will be close enough to help should we need any," Bob addressed his comments to Betty and Steve.

"You mean I get to spend the day with Betty and still get to see you two doing your thing? Where do I sign up for that duty? Count me in," he said charmingly. Bob and Ann both shot each other a glance that said, "Did you see this coming because I sure didn't?"

"Betty, you good with all this or do I need to make something up for you to do back at the airfield instead?" Bob chided them both.

"No, Bob. Pretty sure I can handle this assignment but keep your phone handy just in case. I will text you if I need an out," Betty smiled.

They all chatted as they had coffee, breakfast and got themselves ready in plenty of time before their ride pulled up in front of the small house. It felt a little weird not having Father Gannon along with them, but Steve made for a good new fourth, especially since today his role was spectator.

They drove directly to the farm and joined the UN team under one of several large white, canvas-walled "circus tents." Their briefings completed, the media and a crowd of 'cleared-through-security' spectators assembled and witnessed a near flawless demonstration that produced exactly what Bob had described the day prior. The entire event went as planned, and they found themselves readying for their debrief in the same tent where they had briefed hours earlier.

Forty-five minutes later they were heading back to the vehicles to begin their drive back to the small house when Tom pivoted the conversation from what just occurred to what was coming next. "Alright, I hope you guys are packed because we are wheels up at 0530 tomorrow and we aren't going to be back home for a couple of weeks. Car will be out front at 0400 for the three of you. No offense Steve, but I wasn't planning on a fourth for this. That said, if you guys need him for this, I can still make that happen but I am gonna need to hear the why before I put that in motion."

Before anyone else could say anything, Steve had already begun to speak, "Not this time, Tom. You will need to start this without me. I need to get back to the shop and take care of some things I left undone to be here for this one. It was pretty short notice if you recall. You all don't get much sleep doing this stuff do you? Anyways, after what I saw today, if you need me to help do something to get this out where you need it, I will make it happen. This is some impressive, no, some amazing stuff with boundless potential. Just say the word and I will help where you need me."

"I appreciate that, Steve," Tom said what he and everyone else in the car was glad to hear. "We may very well take you up on that, after all, this is already a family affair. It is much easier and safer to trust family on things like this. Most people are careful to make sure they don't jeopardize their family. Keeps them smarter, tighter lipped and motivated when their loved ones are involved. People are looser when it's someone else's family members at risk instead of theirs. Until next time," Tom concluded as the car pulled to a stop in front of the now historic house where on-demand weather modification had its beginnings.

The four of them exited the car and bade farewell to Tom as they walked up to the front door and entered to settle in for what would prove to be a very short night. The television coverage of their earlier demonstration was massive. Every channel had some version of the day's events running and Bob's face and voice were streaming around the world as he explained what was happening, and what would come next. It was surreal to watch, and Bob couldn't help but compare this to a Vegas magic show on a live broadcast TV special. After packing a few bags, some conversations about and between the news clips and couple of drinks they wrapped up and turned in for what little sleep there was to be had. The next morning was a near repeat but shorter version of the previous one, except for their different destinations. Steve headed to the airport in one car, and the rest of them headed in another car to make a couple of stops before ending up in a different place at the same airfield.

The first event of the UN fielding plan was a great success. The word was getting out and seeing was believing. So it began, and just like that they were loading into a large military transport jet with some increasingly familiar faces and lots of pallets of stuff that weren't so familiar. Some of it covered, some in rolling bins, cargo boxes, and any number of containers with any number of unknown items that were important enough to warrant a spot on the same plane that was taking the core team and a few more to their next destination. It was unnervingly calm for them

Bob thought as Betty and Ann settled into their seats. They both seemed to take naturally to just doing what needed to be done without being phased by it. That was commendable Bob thought, as he considered how he felt right now, and at this point, he was far more familiar with this than either of them.

But familiar it became to all of them, and quickly. They repeated variations of the same basic performance on three continents in five days. It was as exhilarating as it was exhausting. Briefings, set up, do the thing, tear down, debriefings then head to the airport. Grab a meal and a nap when you could, try to stay hydrated and don't worry about what time zone you are in because there was always someone to tell you where to be and when to be there. Bob wondered for a moment if this was what it was like being in the military? He hadn't served but got the sense that what he was doing now was no different than any other mission for so many service members 24x7x365 around the world. He made a mental note to buy every military member he ever ran into a drink with a hearty thank you for what you do every day.

Shortly after takeoff to their fourth stop, Bob sought out Tom for a quick chat. "Have you heard anything about Zach yet? Seems like if this plan was going to work, someone should know or hear something by now," Bob asked as concerned as he could be given how tired he was now.

"We don't have a line on him yet," Tom started out. "But we did have more luck following the parts list Ann gave us. There were only a few places where the satellite components were made. A few weeks after you bought one piece, the other three were all bought on the same day. Three different purchasers, all LLCs. As we traced the LLCs and their officers, back and forth through some shell companies they all ended up having one thing in common. Wanna guess what that was?"

"No, but I want you to tell me," Bob shot back, his shortness showing as he fought to keep his eyes open but happy to have something perhaps worthy of hearing.

"OK," Tom continued. "Chinese. All three went to a Chinese business, that business to another business, and then delivered to a manufacturing facility that is owned and operated by the Chinese Communist Party. The CCP needs three of these obscure satellite parts delivered to a manufacturing facility location that just happens to also need key components of Thor's Hammers? They don't make anything at that facility. Not a coincidence. I do believe in Santa Clause, seriously I do, but I don't believe in coincidences. The Chinese are already working on, or already have Thor's Hammers. We don't yet know what Zach has in common with China, if he is courting them, already has courted them, or maybe they have him in their pocket already? We don't know yet, but we are narrowing the possibilities. I expect in the next couple of days we will hear from him or know why we haven't yet. Our next couple of stops are close to and in China so that should help expedite this treasure hunt."

"Ok Tom, that is helpful. The sooner we find him the better. Speaking of sooner and better, I am gonna curl up somewhere on this bird for a power nap. I need one." Seven minutes later he was lying atop one of the cargo net-covered pallets of bags, eyes closed and snoring. The aircraft ladened with its precious cargo of people and equipment glided through the sky toward its next destination which was about six hours away. Time enough for a good long nap, but not comfortable enough to make it very likely.

Meanwhile far below, but increasingly closer than ever, Zach's thoughts were interrupted by footsteps approaching his small but comfortably familiar room with its perpetual artificial lighting.

"What great news do you carry to brighten my day Mr. Wu?" Zach asked the man whom he hadn't seen in more than a day and a half.

"It seems that we must initiate a reunion with your friends Professor Mcleod and his lovely fiancée. They have done several demonstrations now, for the world to see. They are showing the world what a powerful and helpful tool the UN possesses. They are gaining momentum convincing those who will listen that their technology is safe, a tool for benevolent ends, and important for parity around the world. It is unfortunate that way of thinking is inconsistent with our own. It is also unfortunate for the UN and Professor Mcleod that we too have Thor's Hammers, and thus the ability to completely devastate that rising tide of optimism they are working so hard to build. It is time Mr. Zach, it is time to reveal the dangers of this tool now that everyone is looking. They are increasingly famous and wildly popular so it is time."

"OK, I'll bite," Zach said hesitantly. "What precisely does that look like, and just as importantly what do you believe is my role in all this?"

Mr. Wu continued, "We will be there at the UN's next demonstration. It is almost twenty hours from now, but it is only a two-hour flight from here. We will use our Hammers to create weather that is vastly different than what Mcleod and this team will announce prior to their show. It will be a disastrous result for them. Unexpected damage and death on their audience and their credibility, all at the same time and place. We will be the ones who will pick that exact time and place. We will decide what event to produce, and we will see with our own eyes the glory of our creation, the weather event that will destroy their credibility. We will ensure the fear and doubt of the masses we generate will be lasting. We will create the demand for careful certainty that only a strong, single entity can provide if, and when their device is ever used again. We will step in to fill that void. We will ensure the needs of the people are met with certainty by the party—the only ones truly capable and with the resources, discipline, and benevolence to care for the masses in a safe and equitable way.

"Every event without us, beginning with the next one will be an unmitigated disaster until there will be no appetite for another. It is then, we will step in and show that unlike the UN, the party can and will use this technology to achieve the intended results. Safely. Fairly. Efficiently. The world's trust will be ours. We will continue to disrupt and discredit any others who attempt to build and use their own devices. But we must begin with a success, and that is needed in short order my friend. Are you ready? We must begin preparations and depart in less than twelve hours Zach. What are your questions?" he concluded.

Absorbing these revelations and the looming timeline, Zach struggled to get far enough along in the myriad of variations to reach a final gameplan, but he began with the things that were common to all of his options.

"First thing I am going to need is a computer with digital terrain maps so I can determine the best disaster scenario for our location. And we will need both of the Hammers that you took from me, and any others you may have already made or mocked up if we are going to have to outgun Mcleod's Hammers. I will need a robust communications capability including HF, VHF and Satellite Communications so we can intercept their comms, and jammers for all their frequencies so whatever they might try in response we can shut down. Finally, I will need some maneuverable balloons with sufficient payloads for communications gear and the Hammers so we can get them into and keep them in position to both counter their event commands and still get the conditions we need to create the devastation needed. Your 'spy balloons' have already carried your test 'Hammers' so they should do nicely for this and be readily available. I think that covers everything, except my fee and the timely arrangement for my travel when this is done."

Mr. Wu smiled, pleased that he didn't have to convince Zach to do what was being told. It wasn't being asked. "Your fee we have already addressed, I should hope you are not looking to re-negotiate that. Your travel will be arranged once the desired outcome is achieved, which will not be from a single event. The faster the world looks to China to be the sole possessor and operator of this great power, the sooner the UN is out and we are in…the sooner your travel plans will be confirmed. For now, we must focus on our immediate travel to the coming demonstration…shall we?"

"Of course, the sooner the better for all of us. Let's go make this a reality," Zach said calmly as he took the first step toward the door, and Mr. Wu followed immediately behind, anxious to get started with his American counterpart.

CHAPTER SEVEN

CREDIBILITY CHECKS

Sleep was a luxury thus far for the UN team on their whirlwind tour. Bob's power nap was short-lived but helpful, and he felt a bit refreshed although he could use a shower like most of those onboard. As he moved toward the front of the aircraft to check on Ann and Betty, he was glad to see they were both asleep in two of the airline style seats that were available but in short supply on the airplane designed to carry cargo first, and people as an afterthought. Not wanting to disturb the two ladies, Bob approached Colonel Lincoln, Captain Lessur and Sergeant Andies who were busily discussing something that had them each concentrating on what the other was trying to convey over the perpetual noise that consumed the inside of every military aircraft when in-flight.

"Hey guys, what's on your minds? You look concerned about something," Bob asked the men, who by now he had gotten to know better and trust even more since their collaboration to show the abilities of Thor's Hammer to their own nation's most senior leaders. Doing something like that to the people of other nations and a bunch of cameras seemed much easier this time around.

"Hi Bob, how are you holding up?" Frank asked him, already knowing the answer but hoping Bob would spend a few of his own words to convince the three Airmen, and maybe himself, that he was better than he looked.

"Tired, but good," Bob smiled, "and how about you all?"

"Living the dream, seeing the world, and leaving a mark," Sergeant Andies chuckled. "What else can a man ask for?"

"Some better weather, that would be helpful," Captain Lessur offered. "We might need to use this thing just to get us where we are trying to go to show people what it can do. Which makes me wonder Bob, what if we used it in-flight? Would it work out ahead of us in time to make it better by the time we got there? I know that is some back-to-the-future kind of thinking, but seriously this is like a grade school math word problem. If Bob is on a C-17 flying at 450 knots, and he puts a recipe for clear skies and a 90-knot tailwind into his Thor's Hammer, how long will it take to get rid of the cold front and heavy rain that is directly in their path for the next 600 miles. Please show your work. For extra credit, how long will he be flying in clears skies with a 90-knot tailwind once he finds them? Again, please show your work."

Bob played along, "Funny Ron, funny but a good question that I don't know the answers to. I was only involved in testing where the time and distance were all from Thor's Hammers at fixed locations. That is how we tried to determine roughly how far the effective range of each recipe was. Ranges varied depending on the recipe we were testing, but I left with Ann before those tests were completed. The ground movement testing was to be next, and while we talked briefly about airborne testing, I wasn't aware that a test plan for that even existed during our time there. But I suspect they would have fleshed out each primary configuration, those being stationary, surface movement, airborne terrestrial, and finally on orbit. I'd say that having one in space this soon is highly unlikely but possible. However, doing at least some airborne testing already, now that would be very probable."

Frank was the one to verbalize the conclusion they had all come to, "That means whatever they tested, Zach surely knows about...which means he knows more about how to use these things than we do. At least for a while.

"I'd be lying if I said that part of me did not want to just fire up a Thor's Hammer and do a little in-flight testing while we are on these long flights. Can't do it, too much risk with so many people onboard and this being such a high visibility mission. If things got out of hand, it could quickly become catastrophic. Can't take that risk, especially since we aren't even halfway through our planned stops. At this point we need to get to our next one. That is where I need you guys to focus and find a way to pick through this weather as best you can to keep us on—or close to on—schedule."

"Yes, Sir, will do," the sergeant replied confidently, and it was a confidence that was well-earned. He was one of, if not *the* best weather forecasters in the Air Force which was in large part why he was on this flight today. As he examined the mass of squiggly lines, different colors and random looking numbers overlaid on colored geopolitical boundaries of countries, major roads and land features "the weather guy" was able to develop an understanding of what was happening in the atmosphere. With assistance from computerized numerical prediction models, he could then project that forward through time and space to envision what was going to happen along the time continuum. Rinse and repeat along a route and various destinations, and now you are getting the picture of Sergeant Andies' job. He could assimilate vast amounts of data into a few relevant pieces of information about the weather at any given point for a specific time. And just as importantly he was better than most explaining what that meant in terms of probabilities of both the positive and negative impacts on what you were trying to do at that spot at that time.

Andies and Lessur both understood that nobody really cares about the weather forecast. They really care about what that forecast is going to mean for whatever activity someone is trying to do at that location during that time. Both Air Force professionals were as knowledgeable about military operations and systems as they were about predicting the weather in the space and time they were being used. Knowledge of current and forecast weather conditions were "what" these two brought to the operation. The rare capability to collaborate and apply that "what" to explain the "so what" and help come up with the best "now what" is why they were among the best in this small but important Air Force skill code. With that in-flight weather assistance from Sergeant Andies, the aircrew was able to navigate through the layers of clouds, areas of falling precipitation, changing wind directions and speeds, aircraft icing levels and turbulent air and begin their descent into the airfield in Eastern India nearest the site of their next demonstration.

There always seems to be a flurry of activity aboard a military aircraft once that descent begins. Crew members begin to transition systems and equipment from focusing on in-flight to landing and unloading. Passengers begin to fidget for their belongings, hit the head before landing, fix their hair, hurry to finish that chapter in their book, the briefing on their laptop or the game on their tablet. While the flight has its own life, it is still just a means to an end. The work begins when the wheels touch down, the plane taxis to parking, the engines shut down, the tires are chocked, and the ramp and doors open. When the recirculated air from inside the plane meets the fresh air rushing in from the outside, that is when you know the clock has started and it is time to do whatever you flew in there to get done.

"Well Ann, this is the first time I've been in India. In fact, there have been so many firsts on this trip for me I can't count them all," Betty said as she stood to get some circulation back into her legs.

"Me too. Let's see what makes this place different than the last few we have been to." She smiled at Betty as they made their way off the aircraft amidst the others moving with purpose unlashing cargo and unloading in a prescribed but chaotic looking flurry of activity.

Bob, Frank and Tom were already huddled outside discussing what was next, and where, as Ann and Betty approached them and joined the nearby group of people who were responsible for the success of the demo tour.

Once the details of times, locations, transportation, food, lodging and logistics were all passed along to the group by the waiting ground team they climbed aboard the buses that would take them to their designated quarters or work areas. Bob, Ann and Betty were generally in the same place most of the time during these events and picked up the unofficial moniker of "Three Musketeers." Call signs were common for individuals, but this entire operation was anything but common, so it seemed appropriate to go a little outside the norm on this tradition as well.

The Three Musketeers loaded onto bus number two which was headed to a multi-story building with neatly organized floors of small but comfortable rooms that would house them for their brief stay. It was still dark when they arrived, and they agreed to try to nap, shower, rest or whatever for a few hours then meet for the 0800 shuttle back to the operations center for some food, a lot of briefings, and a demonstration that afternoon. At least the forecast was looking like a persistent stretch of cloudy and rainy conditions for the next couple of days which would make their options for the demonstration favorable.

The remainder of the night passed quickly and the three found themselves back on the bus and were pleased to see both Tom and Captain Lessur climbing up into the same shuttle in which they were already seated.

"Looks like we are going to get to use Thor's Hammer today to make the weather more pleasant for those attending our outdoor gathering. I really like it when we can give people conditions that make them feel better or get better. Spreading positivity and encouragement, now that fits into what Doc had envisioned for all this," Bob said to everyone on the small shuttle this morning. "Let's make this happen." As the windshield wipers on the shuttle continued to wave back and forth behind him in their ongoing chore of removing the water drops from the tempered glass.

Tom and Ron looked up from their conversation as Tom engaged the three, "Yes, the good captain was just confirming for me these dreary conditions are expected to persist for a few days. That is until we provide a few hours of temporary relief for our fans, take a bow and then let them settle back into the ongoing funk with everyone else. We will have given them a bright spot, and then we can move on to make the next crowd see and believe. This part of the plan is going very well thus far."

It was Ann who responded, "Yes, but there are other parts that aren't going very well, too, at least as far as I know. What can you tell us about Zach? Do you know where he is yet; do you know what he is planning to do or where?" Her concern showed both in her words and on her face.

"Not yet Ann. My best people are out there dangling carrots in the open and holding sticks in the shadows. There are tons of chatter and others asking some of the same questions we are about how and where to get their own hammers, but nobody is coming up to nibble on our offers. And every one of the top twenty-some baits out there with numbers on them are ours. Nothing yet, but in these circles money talks and eventually we will hear a voice. It's human nature," he said confidently.

"I hope that happens sooner than later. I know that man has the capacity for almost anything. He helped write our playbooks, so it wouldn't surprise me if he knows yours too. He plays chess not checkers, so I hope your guys are trying lots of things all at the same time," Ann encouraged as the shuttle rolled up to their designated off-load area. The ride was short as the quarters were always as close to the operations as could be to maximize their time on or off work while minimizing the time and distance between the two. Efficient and effective were the two main objectives of military planners, and this group was great at both so far.

The morning went smoothly for everyone, completing their assignments and coordinating the remaining ones. Arriving to start their final checks at the designated spot for today's demonstration, they were all struck by the magnitude of this one compared to the others. The crowd was by far the largest yet, and the strings of buses and other vehicles crowded into their designated loading and unloading areas gave a sense of scale to the groups of people huddled under jackets, and small plastic whatever's to help repel the cold light rain. It was clear it had taken some time to get them in place, and equally clear they would be there both during and after the planned demonstration. That further amplified everyone's sense of purpose. All these people were here to see with their own eyes the things they were there to make visible. A sea of people on hand, and myriad of cameras to stream out to those who couldn't be here in person.

As their vehicles rolled to a stop, the UN team members dutifully offloaded and went right to their tasks, making sure their parts of this event were ready, conducted on time and produced the intended results.

And just like that, it was time. As Bob walked with Mr. Dau toward "the spot" with its multitude of microphones and flashes from the cameras, the cheers from the large crowd drowned out every other noise. The magnitude of their response was overwhelming, and he knew they were impacting lives with their capability. He was there to give them the hope and assurance that better was achievable not only for them, but for everyone else working together to achieve a common good. Once the introductions were made, and Bob described the forecast and the briefly modified conditions the Thor's Hammer would produce for them. He then explained to the crowd how and when this would occur.

"Before coming to the stage, we entered the needed inputs to the device, and it is already performing the needed actions to achieve those results. The light rain that has been falling since well before you arrived will soon taper off and stop. The overcast clouds will begin to dissipate, rather quickly but only over a few dozen square miles. Elsewhere the cloudy rainy conditions will persist. Here, you will see clear skies and the sun for about a half hour to forty-five minutes before the clouds will move back in and the light steady rain will return. The temperature will rise three degrees with the sun coming in and then drop back two degrees as the clouds move back in to help our spot recover back to the natural conditions."

As he described what was touted as Doc Auster's vision for how this technology was to be used, and how the UN intended to bring that vision to life through these demonstrations and their collaborative international roll out plan, the rain had slowed to a stop and the clouds were beginning to thin just as he described earlier. The crowd began to recognize and respond to the noticeable changing conditions, and voices, cheers, eyes and arms all began to rise in anticipation of the sun breaking through. Bob stopped his remarks to allow the crowd, his team as well as himself to watch and enjoy the moment when the sun would peek through the first opening in the previously overcast sky. It was then that Bob felt the wind on his face, and the concern in the voice in his earpiece.

"Wind is coming up way too fast and it's not supposed to. It went from six to fourteen knots sustained in five minutes and is still trending up. It's not supposed to!" Captain Lessur was rightfully concerned and right to be letting everyone know. That said, nobody knew what they could or should do about what they were hearing, including him. As the wind continued to increase, the crowd noticed it too, as Ron called out another observation.

"Up to twenty-two knots now, still steady from the northwest" and two minutes later he called out, "Thirty-five knots everyone, and increasing, no gusts just straight-line wind." It was only a few minutes, but it seemed like hours. The sun was now breaking through as the clouds continued to dissipate as Bob explained, but now the increasing wind had everyone thinking this was a part of the demonstration. Bob knew he needed to get to the Hammer to see what was happening, but he also knew the crowd and the world were watching, looking for him to explain this surprise part of the demonstration. He needed to be in two places at once but knew he couldn't be in both. He turned to Mr. Dau and instructed him to leave the stage and get the Hammer to him as quickly as he could because something was very wrong.

Mr. Dau slipped off stage to do as instructed while Bob moved closer to the cameras at the front of the stage and began to speak again.

"Here comes the sun, everyone, the rain and clouds are gone for a little while and the winds will help dry things out a little bit until the clouds and rain come back in shortly." It was then Bob heard "Forty-five knots" in his earpiece and he knew this problem needed a different solution. He chose what he believed at that moment was the least bad option and addressed those assembled once more.

"These winds are stronger than we expected, please find some nearby cover if you can until they subside." There was an immediate and increasing threat to the crowd of people and almost no remaining time for them to respond in a meaningful way. The most visible and logical option for cover in the open area was the vehicles that had brought them. The crowds pushed towards the roped off parking areas to get either closer to, or inside the parked buses, trailers, and whatever else was available. At that point Bob heard sixty-five knots and increasing in his earpiece as he felt someone grab his arm to lead him off the stage toward safety and the Thor's Hammer that he asked to be brought to him. A minute later, still moving with the small security team, he heard Ron call out eighty knots. Bob was united with the device a minute later and began to look at the settings and consider what recipe to input when once again he heard the voice in his headset call out one hundred and seven knots! At that point, Bob and all those around him were on the ground huddled up tight and low and calling for Bob to do something as dirt, debris and hope were all flying past and swirling around them beckoning for something to make the winds stop.

Still gathering his wits and making the decisions about what to try, Ron's voice rang out "Seventy-five knots and decreasing fast." Bob realized that he had not yet entered any changes into the device, took a deep breath, and chose doing nothing as his decision. He consciously considered that might be the worst option, but he stuck with it because changing his device at this point might make it impossible to find and understand what went wrong. He hung onto it, kept the input screen locked and prayed for the outcome he hoped would result. "forty-five knots" Ron sighed into the radio over the next few minutes he called out twenty-five knots, fifteen, and finally light and steady at three knots.

The sun was still out, and the clouds sufficiently clear for all to see the results of the brief but intense windstorm. Debris was strewn all about, a number of taller profile vehicles had been blown over by the steady intense wind, and there were casualties as a result. People inside some of the flipped buses were injured during the roll overs, but the people outside huddled against them as a shield from the winds were crushed or trapped beneath the very makeshift shelters which they hoped would protect them. The devastation was palpable for those present as well as for those watching.

Chief among those watching from a safe, protected vantage point in the distance were Zach and Mr. Wu. As they began to pack up their Thor's Hammer and other equipment to evacuate their hide site as undetected as possible under the conditions.

Mr. Wu smiled with delight as he said, "Mr. Zach, that was as exhilarating as it was easy. You see we work smarter not harder. They fly around the world, spend much money, time and energy to build up expectations and credibility over time. We sit back, wait for them to come to us, and in a few hours, with just a few people, we get the results we want with very minor expenditures of resources or energy. But now our real work begins. We need to make the best of their misfortune and seize the opportunity we have created for ourselves. And we do this at their expense. We have put them down today, and soon comes the time to take them out. Let us go now, and finish what we have started."

At that moment, as Zach wrapped up what he was doing and joined the small team's departure he realized that no matter what they had in mind as their end game, Zach was a means to an end. He was not part of their long-term plan. Just as his involvement with the CCP was a means to the ends he sought and not a part of Zach's long-term plan. But today Mr. Wu made it clear to him that both their timelines needed to be changed drastically given the events of the day. On the drive out Zach began to reconsider what this new plan and timeline might include, and how best to distance himself from his captors. Meanwhile, across the valley, chaos continued to unfold.

The cameras were already rolling for the live demonstration, and they kept rolling to cover the unimagined catastrophe unfolding before them. To put this in perspective one hundred and seven knots, or nautical miles per hour is a straight-line wind speed of one hundred twenty-three miles per hour. In hurricane nomenclature using the Saffir-Simpson scale commonly referenced in the US, these winds were equivalent to a strong category three hurricane, only seven miles per hour shy of being a category four. While it was fortunate the location was fairly isolated as far as structures go, anything light and not secured was available to become an airborne projectile hurtling at or through the expansive crowd. The live videos from the scene showed people milling about dazed, confused, and many of them injured in some way from the event. Those who could were rendering first aid with what little they had to offer. Then there were groups of people desperately trying to right the overturned buses and other vehicles to free or recover those trapped beneath them. Desperation showed in their eyes and actions as they searched and toiled with the limited tools they had available for their worthy cause. Watching them was as maddeningly frustrating to the viewers as it was to those on the scene, there was nothing available to help with what needed to be done.

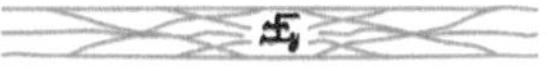

As the UN team at the demonstration site began to reassemble and account for themselves, the team members not at the site were coordinating action to extract their teammates and marshalling resources to render aid to those injured. Betty and Ann were close to the main stage area where Bob had been speaking, and it did not take them long to find each other and sigh with relief that each of them had emerged relatively unscathed from the wind and debris. The small security team was collecting and accounting for the UN staff members to get them all extracted sooner than later. It was human nature to move to help those in need around you, but these men also knew it was human nature to find blame when bad things happen. Right now, they were at the top of the blame list for anything and everything that went wrong today because it was them who brought everyone out here to witness the event. Now, instead of being spectators the crowd appeared to be victims, and every victim has someone who victimized them. The UN team needed some distance before the crowd turned their anger on them, and Bob Mcleod was the one name everyone in the crowd had heard. His face and voice were forefront on their minds as well as those of the security team. He needed to be disappeared from the site and the country as fast as humanly possible. That meant the Three Musketeers needed to be found and evacuated ASAP. The security team was halfway done as they stayed focused on their new mission.

Bob saw Tom approaching the three at brisk pace with five men who moved with purpose, scanning where they were as well as where they were going. The special mission security team enveloped the three as Tom said, "Stay close enough to hug me until I tell you not to. Do not stop moving and listen to these guys and do exactly what they say when they say it without hesitation or discussion. Are we clear?" His tone was anything but asking. Without missing a beat Tom led a six-person ring around the Three Musketeers moving toward the group of UN vehicles they had parked nearby for the demonstration. There were other UN staff members, some slightly injured but none appearing to be seriously hurt loading themselves and some sensitive equipment into shuttles and trucks intending to depart as soon as they were fully loaded. The temporary perimeter security fencing was gone but the jersey barriers installed by the UN team were still in place.

Tom and the team split into three small truck-like vehicles. Tom plus one and the Three Musketeers were piled into the second vehicle. Two each from the security team jumped into the lead and trail vehicles and all moved out together trying to not draw attention to their departure as they navigated through the maze of people and debris enroute to the airfield. As they rolled slowly past and through the confused crowd, the human toll of this mishap was in plain view just outside their windows and at eye level. There was no missing any of it as the skilled operators picked their way through the crowd with just enough empathy to avoid attention but the right amount of aggression to keep from ever stopping or having to use what they were driving as the 4,500-pound weapons they knew how to employ if the situation warranted.

As they approached the perimeter road of the designated crowd control area, the small convoy put the hammer down to get onto the paved roads that would lead them to the airfield. Tom was on his phone, at least two handheld radios, and whatever his earpiece was tuned into and seemed to be talking to everyone except those seated in the SUV with him. They heard him say, "Whichever one you can have fueled up and running the fastest damn it. We need to be wheels-up in fifteen minutes...

"No flight plan, we will get our Dip clearances (Diplomatic clearances for entry into or overflight of other nation's airspace) in the air, got five with me that will be our detail, get mission load-out kits on whatever plane we are leaving on. I need every trace of the Three Musketeers on board as well, anything and everything with their names or pictures. If it doesn't make the plane before we do, burn it. No trace except Bob's face and voice on the videos that any of them were ever here. Now get it done." Tom turned his attention inside the vehicle for the first time since he climbed into it. He pointed to the box at Bob's feet, "You better tell me you got both of the Thor's Hammers with you in that box."

"I do," Bob choked out the first words he had spoken, as he was in shock from the events unfolding around him, and possibly because of him.

"Bob, how in the hell did this happen?" Tom asked matter-of-factly. Not because he was not fazed by it, but because he needed as many facts as available and as fast as possible to determine what to do next and when.

"I am still trying to understand what just happened," Bob stammered.

Tom responded firmly, "OK. Let me catch you up. Halfway through our 'we-will-bring-you-sunshine-on-this-rainy-day' demo, to show everyone how good our technology is for the world…we blew their minds, but also their friends and families around the viewing area with a hundred knot wind that injured and killed a whole lot of people. We took this effort from *we will save the world* to *someone needs to save the world from us* in ten minutes flat. That is what just happened. Now how in-all-that-is-holy did it happen?"

Bob just stared at Tom. He had nothing to say, he couldn't say anything because he had no idea why, and that is what he finally responded with, "Tom, I have no idea. I don't. Those people…I don't know."

"Eight minutes boss, but we have an airfield checkpoint in three," the voice from the driver's seat boomed.

With that, Tom's attention shifted from Bob to the radio in his left hand. As he talked to what seemed like a dozen different people in a minute and a half, Tom instructed the lead vehicle, "Punch through the gate, then go back and play corporal noodlehead. 'So sorry, didn't see it, was on the radio what can I do to make it right.' Trail and precious cargo will proceed to the aircraft and roll out, make sure you are sincere enough to buy us the five minutes we will need to load and taxi. Thanks, and don't get yourselves or us shot up."

That got Ann and Betty's attention, and for the first time today they recognized that there might be some real danger mixed into the good they were doing for the world. This was not at all how they thought today would turn out. And just like that, the lead vehicle failed to stop at the airfield perimeter fencing and rolled through the clearly marked and manned gate. The driver skillfully angled the speeding vehicle toward the hinged side of the barrier to ensure that it would follow out of the path of the trailing vehicles upon impact with his. Once through the barriers a clear path was assured for the trailing two SUVs, and the first one turned the wheel sharply, fishtailing a little for the surprised guards then skidding to a stop. Both the driver and the passenger jumped out of the vehicle and immediately began arguing with each other about whose fault it was and who was going to be in the most trouble for this damaged vehicle and property. The sole guard on duty would have his hands and mind full just sorting out the two embattled gate crashers, their accountability issues and trying to get the now unsecured opening back into a protectable condition. It wasn't even clear whether he saw or remembered the two vehicles that continued driving through immediately after the first one failed to yield.

As they drove quickly to the parking ramp and its variety of immobile aircraft, Tom was again on one of his radios. "Got you. Two rolling, will be on your door in less than one mike. Be ready to roll out in three.

"OK people, the second this car stops moving, I want the right-side doors open, everyone gets out of the passenger side doors and directly up the steps into the airplane as fast as you can without falling down. Go as far back into the airplane as you can and get into an empty seat at the rear of the aircraft. Keep your heads down the whole way, until I tell you it's ok. Even after we take off. Wait till I tell you it's ok to sit up and relax. Hard part's over, but we gotta finish strong, ok? Bob, make sure that bag never leaves your hands. Get ready, and…GO!" Tom barked the last word as the rig rolled to a stop as close as was safe to the stairs leading into the small jet with its engines running. Following the fresh instructions from Tom, they were aboard quickly but recognized the interior of the jet as the same one they had flown on with Tom before despite the different paint job and tail number. The pilots and steward were the same people, but the looks on their faces as well as their weapons and body armor made it clear that greetings would have to wait.

On each seat was a vest with heavy ceramic plates held in place by Kevlar mesh. The steward barked some quick instructions as he pushed them each deeper into the small plane from near the open door, "Get to the back. Put on a vest. Sit in the seat. Keep your head down until I tell you. Don't talk, just listen." He too, made it clear he was not asking.

Everyone did as instructed. Tom plus the remaining three of the security team climbed aboard the plane and closed the door behind them. The plane was moving before the latches were closed and locked. As the plane began to roll, the steward took position at the front of the plane between the pilots with a clear view through the front windscreens. His weapon was pointed forward, low but ready in case it was needed at the nose of the aircraft. Tom and his SUV driver were armed, vested and poised at windows on the left side of the aircraft while the other two from the security team were similarly positioned on the right side. It was everyone's hope that nobody would need to do anything, but they were clearly ready and able for any unwanted call to action in response to their unannounced ground movement and departure from the controlled airfield.

Ignoring the radio calls from the tower, the small jet rolled hot onto the active runway, threw the throttles the rest of the way forward and lifted off as soon as they reached rotation speed. No radio calls from the aircraft before or after their departure. As they climbed through eight thousand feet without incident, and seeing no other aircraft approaching on the onboard radars, the steward walked to the rear of the aircraft and spoke with a demeanor now very inconsistent with his attire.

"Welcome back ladies, Professor Mcleod. Please sit up, relax and feel free to remove your vests for now. My apologies for how we began this flight, but your safety is paramount. Can I bring you a beverage or something to eat? I know this has been a trying day thus far, and I am afraid it will also prove to be a very long one."

"How about some water please? We should probably all start with some water and hydrate. Is that ok?" Betty asked for all of them.

"Of course, waters all around. I will return with them directly." As promised, less than a minute later he returned with a large, covered pitcher of water, three glasses which he handed out as he poured. He also left a basket with a variety of snack cakes, bags of chip, nuts and cookies for them to browse at their own pace. Today had already been a lot.

Tom walked back and inquired how they were holding up, "Everyone ok back here? Sorry about all the hurry up, but we need to get you across a border and out of India. Will let you know where we are going once we figure that out. The *where* and the *when* are far less important than the *what* for now. We need to understand *what* happened back there. *How* and *why* it happened are pretty important too, but first and foremost I have to know did you, rather did **we** mess this up? Or did someone mess this up for us? Bob, Ann, Betty the first thing, the thing that drives everything else must be a candid and honest assessment of that question. Accidents happen, and if this was an accident then so be it. We will figure it out and learn from it. I know that would suck, but it is what it is. But if someone did this to us, that is an entirely different thing. We absolutely need to know which of these two things just happened. I need you to focus on that right now and tell me what you come up with." And with that, Tom went to a seat right behind the cockpit and got back on the radios, phones, and computers that seemed to all have their lights blinking and buttons being pushed at the same time. Tom was both talking and listening to everyone important.

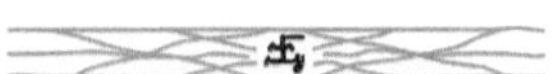

Well-below that aircraft, but not nearly as far away as either group imagined at that moment, Zach and Wu accompanied by a group of plain-clothed special military members of the CCP rolled across an unpaved road for nearly an hour and a half until they reached an expansive open area where the vehicles formed a semicircle and parked. As their occupants exited their transports, they quickly began setting up some small antennas, radios, and battery packs. One vehicle sped off and after a few stops, returned to the group which was now surrounded by a line of small strobe lights to help illuminate the center of the large field. It was then Zach noticed a slight buzz, which he did not recognize but it grew increasingly louder and more discernable until it was clear that something was headed toward the group from a considerable distance. It was then he saw movement in and out of the cloudy sky in the same direction the unmistakably manmade noise was coming from. So, this was how it was done? They were at the recovery site for the medium altitude balloon that carried the other Thor's Hammer for today's operation. While he understood how it was going to work, the clarity provided by seeing it in person was very helpful.

The balloon—a vertically oblong helium-filled elastic membrane—provided the lift for a suite of sensors, power supplies and communications modules in a carbon fiber framework contained within a modified cargo sling beneath the balloon. There were two powerful electric motors driving the propeller systems that provided the steering of the craft, as well as, assisting with controlling the speed of drift within the prevailing winds. There were two operators on the ground near Zach, one with his head and hands working what looked like a computer game controller who appeared to be flying the balloon. The other appeared to be operating one or more of the systems suspended below the craft that was being carried toward them by a combination of winds and the onboard spinning props. It seemed to Zach that these guys were pretty good at what they were doing, as the balloon and its payload appeared to be on the perfect vector and speed to land at the center of the lights that were put out not long before. Impressive, Zach thought as he observed the two men concentrating on bringing in the craft.

"Mr. Wu, as fascinating as flying balloons seems to be for these fine men why are we hanging out waiting for a bag of hot air and some cameras? Don't' we have better things to do with our time and expertise?" Zach asked impatiently.

"That may be true Mr. Zach, but this is an historic time, and should be cherished. You see everything has not gone quite according to plan. Or perhaps I should say, to be precise, everything did go as planned but not according to the plan you knew. Please allow me to both apologize and explain at the same time. You saw the results today, and they were exactly what we intended. But we didn't exactly get them how we discussed.

"You see, we had the Thor's Hammer at the ground site with us. And we put in the cook—I mean the recipe—to get the very high winds. But because we were not certain of your level of commitment to today's effort, we never actually activated those commands from the ground site systems at either location. We needed to be one hundred percent certain of today's result. And that was not possible because we could not be one hundred percent certain of you. But now we can be, because you did exactly what you had agreed to, and the effects we agreed to were achieved. You held up your end of the deal, so now we know you will again in the future. But because we did not know until today what you would do. So, we had a primary plan that did not include you nor the ground sites.

"That is why we are here. Your two Thor's Hammers were not used today at all. We used ones of our own. True they are exactly copied from yours. They were tested and proven to operate just as yours does. But, today was the first operational employment of Thor's Hammer from an airborne platform. That platform is our incoming balloon and slung below it is one of the devices responsible for today's hurricane force winds. An event created by us that will live forever thanks to the live video from the UN's failed demonstration.

"We have several great victories to celebrate today Mr. Zach. A successful flight and recovery of our Thor's Hammer. A successful offensive weather on-demand employment resulting in targeted destruction against an enemy of our state. The UN effort is now discredited. You have proven yourself loyal to our cause. And we have begun our strategic counteroffensive against the United States. This is a great day for us all Mr. Zach," he concluded.

"Well, Mr. Wu I am proud and humbled for my small part in these great successes. While I am disappointed that you did not trust me to do my part at the onset of this great campaign, I understand the need to prove myself and for you to mitigate the risk I could have presented, but clearly did not. What remains to be done for what comes next?" He genuinely wanted to know, but not for the reasons he implied. This was the opportunity he needed, a little bit of trust to gain a whole lot of distance from Mr. Wu.

"Let us finish up here, recover our important tools and then settle in to celebrate today and plan for the next action." Mr. Wu was quite pleased with today, and looked forward with great enthusiasm for what was yet to come.

After an hour or so of discussion, examination of the devices in Bob's bag and more soul searching than any of them had done in a very long time, it appeared they were ready to call Tom back to discuss his assignment. Ann watched him intently and waited until it appeared he was neither talking or actively listening to anyone then rose from her seat and began moving forward. She stopped when everyone at the front of the aircraft instinctively looked to the back of the airplane to evaluate whatever or whomever was moving behind them. She motioned for Tom to come back to join them, and he rose from his seat to oblige her.

"What have you come up with, or do you need something to get there?" he asked, very willing to help get what he needed from them.

"I don't think it was us, Tom. I can't be one hundred percent, but I don't see how it could have been us. The recipes input were correct. The wind direction and speed values are the original input and the numbers are right. There is not a wrong decimal point somewhere, or some other wrong buttons possibility here. They both match, and they are both correct. The keystrokes are recorded and the recordings are correct, and they match. It was set up correctly, and everything worked as commanded. The changes were on time, at the right location, the right conditions, as programmed and within the margins of error. Except the winds.

"The winds were the only thing, and there is no reasonable meteorological explanation for anything near that intensity. The short duration of those winds is also meteorologically unimaginable. That is not how wind works. That is not how winds naturally increase or decrease. I can say with certainty, that wind event was manmade. Well, at least, it was not a natural occurring event. What I can also say with near certainty is it wasn't us who did it. And that leaves me with near certainty that Zach, or someone who had dealings with Zach did this. Did this to us. Did this to those people at the demonstration. And that someone needs to pay for what they did. Right now, everyone agrees with me on that, but they think it's us who did it to them. Specifically, they think it's me who did that to them. To their families. We need to make this right. We need to find who did this and make them pay. I don't think it was us. I don't see how it could have been us." Bob's voice was shaking by the time he finished speaking.

"OK, Bob. Thanks. That's what I needed to know. Get some rest. You are gonna need it. We are all gonna need it," Tom said as he walked back to the seat behind the cockpit and picked up the headset, a phone, and a radio and began talking and listening at the same time again.

CHAPTER EIGHT

DAMAGE CONTROL

Very little else made it into the next twenty-four-hour news cycle since the devastating wind event occurred. There was so much live footage of the event, as well as, the recovery operations that the problem was what to cut out of the video clips and not show. The headlines were countless variations on a common theme, something akin to "UN's on-demand weather demonstration in India ends in disaster, hundreds injured or killed." The casualty counts continued to rise because everyone was not yet fully accounted for by family, friends and the authorities. The pictures and details of what happened were well documented, but the reason it happened was still an unresolved next topic in the global conversation. The UN had provided some very brief comments, expressing sympathy for those killed or injured and their families. Each time pointing toward prioritizing immediate actions to assist the ongoing rescue and recovery operations at the site.

As the UN spokespersons struggled to keep the focus on how much they were helping those on-site, there was tremendous effort underway behind the scenes to assess and understand what went wrong to help the Secretary General decide what to do next. Key to understanding what happened on-site was the UN team who had just lived through the very event they would now have to explain to their bosses. They in turn would tell their own version of the events they had not lived through but occurred on their watch only hours ago. Frank was on a video teleconference with what seemed like countless others in pages of small square thumbnail images of rooms and people he did not recognize nor know how much he could trust. But the secure video teleconference system they were using meant someone trusted them all enough to invite them, so either they needed to know what happened to help or to inform others who could help.

After providing a summary of the UN team's morning preparations, the events as they unfolded, and the ongoing operations to assist the local authorities, Frank paused. And with that pause, many hands went up and voices began asking a litany of questions. Colonel Lincoln was as cool as the other side of the pillow as he responded to the senior leader's questions and did his best to shield those around him from the barrage of incoming harpoons looking for someone to blame for this debacle and its aftermath. Finally, someone asked something specific enough about the weather conditions that Frank believed required some precision, so he deferred to his on-scene weather guys to add to his response.

"Sir, Captain Lessur here. The winds we experienced on-site were straight line winds. They were not convective, and there is no way they were a storm induced microburst. They ramped up quickly, they peaked, and they ramped down just as fast as they came up. They were consistently from the same direction the entire time. Windspeeds of this magnitude do occur naturally, but not on such a compressed timeline in such a persistent manner as these," Ron concluded, and hoped the next question would be for his colonel and not him. No such luck.

"So that means this was either a mistake of our making, or the device you are using has a flaw, some malfunction. Which do you believe it was—or most likely was?" A voice asked through the speaker from the sea of faces on the screen.

"It could be either, and at this point we do not have any evidence or indications that would favor one of those possibilities over the other. We will need to spend some time with Professor Mcleod and the device we used to gather any additional information to help us better assess what did or did not happen. We have not yet had the opportunity to do that," the captain concluded, not wanting to lean in either direction this early in the post incident assessment. As he inhaled, preparing for the next question, the voice he heard was a familiar one.

"Thank you, Captain, and if you don't mind, I believe now might be the time to address the third and most likely cause which you asked me to describe to the group," Sergeant Andies added. Both Colonel Lincoln and Captain Lessur had no idea what the seasoned weatherman was referring to, but they had great trust in the man and his ability. With the slightest detectable nod from Frank indicating it was ok with him but up to the captain, Ron replied without hesitation, "You were reading my mind Sergeant Andies. Please, by all means, this is the perfect time." The polite exchange gave the appearance of both knowledge and endorsement for what was about to be shared. While neither were actual, their trust in the non-commissioned officer was very real but, at the moment, still nerve racking. Frank and Ron listened more intently than anyone else on the call to be sure they understood what everyone was hearing for the first time.

"The weather at our site was exactly as prescribed and expected. Every element performed as expected. The clouds. The rain. The temperature and the dew point. The barometric pressure, even the wind. Especially the wind. Exactly what was supposed to happen did, and exactly when it was supposed to happen; all until the windspeed climbed up, spiked, then dropped back down. Then things continued exactly as we expected them to be. All of them were as planned except for those six minutes, and the only things that changed were the pressure gradients and temperatures which are what drives the wind speed.

"This means the only reasonably probable cause of a wind spike of that magnitude and duration was another weather event prescribed within our event. It was not part of, nor related to what we did. The most likely cause was someone else's on-demand short-term wind event transiting through our longer and much different event. Someone else, with the same technology, used it on us while we were demonstrating ours. They undermined our demonstration with a demonstration of their own.

"These were two events, and both worked perfectly. One we knew about, and one we did not. That is the third and most likely explanation for what just happened. Given the weather we experienced, there is no other plausible explanation. I am ninety nine percent certain of this, and we should proceed based on that assumption." With that, the sergeant muted his microphone as he figured he had nothing left to add. If the people hearing him couldn't figure out what that meant, they had no business being on that call. Of course, he was correct but he was also quick to be proven so as the follow up question was allowed.

"So, you think someone else has and used their own Thor's Hammer?" the voice asked seeking confirmation.

"No, Sir. I don't *think* that. I believe I just explained why there is no other plausible explanation," Andies reiterated with a tone that could have been considerably more professional but drove home the point that his was not a theory but the only explanation for what occurred.

Once they considered what Andies said, both Frank and Ron believed he had to be correct. They also knew, with near certainty, who was responsible for that second event, or who was responsible for enabling someone else if it wasn't Zach himself on-site making the killer wind event.

"OK, so who else has one of the things? Who else could have generated this wind event within your event? That must be a pretty short list?" asked an anonymous voice who was next in the moderator's queue for those important enough around the world who were being allowed to speak.

"That list is super short, and we have all our national systems and intelligence assets listening and looking for him right now. It won't take long, and we will find him. We will bring him in, and we will deal with him without hesitation once we do." That voice was clearly discernable and the President of the United States seemed to be keeping his word of late, at least for anything that had to do with Thor's Hammer.

That seemed like a great opportunity to request approval for his intended next steps, which would all require the UN team on-site to remain in place and work with the local forces and authorities to address their immediate needs. Frank believed, especially now with the new information Andies just dropped on everyone, that leaving any time soon would send the wrong signal for the effort and all its participants. The President approved Frank's request on the spot, bypassing everyone in the Chain of Command between the Commander in Chief and the Air Force colonel on scene.

"Frank, you do your best to fix this. If you need something you don't have, just say the word and we will make sure you get it. This is job number one for everybody. Do what it takes to make this right." And with that, the small squares with faces began to disappear as people dropped off the meeting until the host ended it for everyone with the push of a single button.

"Well, Andies, I gotta say, you know how to have a mic-drop moment don't you?" Colonel Lincoln chuckled. "It makes perfect sense. Now we must prove you're right, not just believe it. We need a smoking gun to do that. But I would much rather have this problem than the one we had before you opened that trap of yours. So, let's go prove you're right."

"I know where to start," Captain Lessur added. "If we were going to do to him, or them, what they did to us I would want to be there. I'd need to see that we did what we said we were going to do, and to see that what I was doing was working. See if I needed to make any adjustment during my op. You can watch from any of the channels and their live coverage, but this is weather. You need to feel it. A wind event like that, you are gonna want to be close enough to feel it but from a vantage point that you can be safe if something goes wrong. Or, in this case, safely see that it goes as planned.

"That would mean upwind, elevated, and close. That would be somewhere near this spot, and sometime before, during or after that six-minute window," Ron said as he pointed to the short ridgeline near the demonstration site. "We need to get every piece of whatever surveillance we had going in, out, at, above and below to find someone or something we can grab onto. See where it came from, where it was, and where it went. Andics, you just gave us the most likely haystack now we need some help to find the needle in it."

"Alright, then. That's why I have weather guys here; good work. I know who can help us with that the fastest, and it's past time to hear what they learned since the last time we talked." Colonel Lincoln, pulled a cellphone from the leg pocket of his flight suit, pushed some buttons, and a few seconds later the small group heard the familiar voice on speaker.

"It's Tom, what do you need?" He sounded rushed and the background noise made it easy to determine he was in the air somewhere.

"That depends on what you want to do about what I am about to tell you. Our weather guys, Lessur and Andies just told a video teleconference full of heavy hitters that the only plausible explanation for the winds at the demo was someone rolled a second Thor's Hammer event through the one we were doing. Our systems worked fine, but someone else punched a six-minute hurricane wind through ours. And we think we know right where they would have done that from. Does that thinking align with what you and Bob are doing wherever you are right now?" Frank paused to let the concept sink in.

"Shit! Shit! He was there and we missed him. And yes, that does align with our thinking. Bob and Ann went over our devices, and everything checks out. They didn't change anything, and it all looks right and did what they thought it would except for the wind. He cannot explain what did happen because it should not have happened. Your explanation fits perfectly inside what we have checked and rechecked. OK. I am buying what you are selling. Sounds like others have already done the same, too.

So back to my original question, what do you need?" Tom asked and listened to Frank explain what "everything" meant.

"OK I can put all that in motion, and what do you suggest we do in the meantime?" Tom asked looking over at Bob, Ann and Betty fidgeting in their seats. They were tired of flying, landing, refueling and flying again to stay as lost from the media as they could while this got sorted out.

"Well, our options are to stay here and make a stand, bring it to them where we know they were…and might still be. Or we see if anyone will let us go to the next spot and make him take his show on the road too. Maybe we get him enroute, or where we know he will need to be if he tries the same thing. Lots of cons to both, but I think the least bad option is to fix this right where we broke it. Let's take our punches right here, get back up and find these guys ,if we can, instead of exporting this somewhere else and risk an even worse outcome somewhere new. Let's give ourselves forty-eight hours here. If nothing shakes loose then reconsider taking it on the road and flushing him out of wherever he is hiding and try to grab him on the move."

Tom quickly considered the pros and cons and countless possible outcomes of the two options Frank just described. After a brief pause, he responded, "Alright. I am setting into motion from here everything you asked for, so that will happen either way. We will give ourselves two days, that is reasonable for any cover story or option we need to put in play. We will come back to you, and that will be about ten hours. And by we, I mean all of us. Have a spot we can work with as few people as possible knowing Bob is back on-site until we want or need them to know," Tom paused.

"Will do," Colonel Lincoln assured Tom, who added "and Frank, thanks. Tell Lessur and Andies thanks for seeing what we were missing. I should have seen it, or at least considered the possibility. Hiding in plain sight. He hit us with it, and we didn't realize we got what we were asking for."

"I will. And I gotta tell you, not only did Andies see it but he also put it out there in a way that took some real stones. Tell Bob, Andies gets the credit for this epiphany if it checks out. But if it turns out to be wrong then it's on me. I gave Andies a blind nod to speak his mind because I trust him, and yes, he is that good. In my gut I know he's right on this."

"I will do that. See you soon, I have a lot of calls to make," Tom concluded and the line went dead.

"Finally, some good news," Tom said loudly to get the attention of the three passengers as he rose to walk through the aircraft cabin toward them. "We are going back to India and rejoin the UN team. They know what happened, and that means the clock is ticking on Zach. Sergeant Andies figured it out. He claims Zach, or maybe someone else ran a single six-minute wind event from another Thor's Hammer right through the event we were doing with ours. That aligns with what you told me about everything working and being right about our devices except for the winds. What I need you three to do is wrap your heads around that, figure out what it means, and come up with some ideas about what to do now and how that might help us get this guy. Meanwhile, I need to do some things to get everything else in motion. We land back in India in about seven hours, and we will have a lot to do once we are there."

The news coverage of the event was still intense, but other stories were breaking and the intensity of negative coverage around the wind event was reducing slightly as each hour passed. That was a welcome trend, but it was short lived because one of the breaking stories was from a news conference in China that was as salacious as it was untimely for the ongoing UN effort. The Chinese official was making some eyepopping claims at the worst possible time from the UN perspective, which made it the best possible time from their perspective.

"This tragedy in India was preventable. It was the direct result of greed for both money and power. A nation that already has more than its fair share of both, pursued an agenda to gain even more. With no appreciation for others, or true concern beyond themselves the United States stole our technology and rushed to take credit under the guise of the United Nations. They leveraged their power to take credit for our breakthroughs in weather modification and rushed it to the world without adequately understanding the proper use, and the dangers of misusing these devices.

"The true innovators of this technology have been conducting extensive research, testing, and safe operations of these devices for some time. These are all Chinese in origin and practice. We can no longer stand by silently while others take credit for our advances and use them without regard for the safety of others. Given the events in India, we must now reluctantly speak out to bring this danger to an end. We must expose these untruths for what they are, and offer the services of China to the world. We will take the lead in openly bringing this technology safely to the forefront of global operations in a fair way. Clearly this is beyond the ability of the UN to accomplish. Our offers to assist them have been rejected time and again solely to protect the United States' deception and greed. Sadly, for the world, neither the United Nations nor the United States can be trusted in this endeavor. They have proven they cannot safely operate this capability and hundreds of innocent people have paid for this arrogance and greed with their lives. That must end now.

"China must, and now will, lead this effort. This should have been the case from the beginning. We will do that with our own demonstration of the safe Chinese version, which is the original technology others have stolen from us. We offer to begin in coordination with the Indian government at the very site of the UN's debacle. We will do whatever event is requested on whatever timeline the host nation requests. We will do this for them, not to them. But the results will be far different than the UN effort. The China demonstration will be upon request, it will be safe, and it will be for the benefit of all the people. Not for power and money for the few."

Mr. Wu swelled with pride as he listened to his countryman convey the message of his country across the airwaves to the world. He realized that soon he and his team would be called upon to put those words into action for all to see. Zach, standing nearby, came to the same realization. Rather than swelling with pride at the opportunity to serve his great nation as was Mr. Wu, Zach was considering the options he might pursue given this new revelation of upcoming events. He was hopeful the government of India would allow the Chinese team to conduct a demonstration as offered, and the sooner the better. The decisions he would make in the coming days would determine how he would spend the rest of his life, assuming he lived through the next few days.

"Mr. Zach, we have much to do to ensure our debut is perfect. Would you please join us in the conference room at the top of the hour? We will receive our orders from the Provincial Party Secretary and the participating National Leaders. These are the men who will give us specific direction and allocate the resources we need to accomplish our missions. They are also the men who will be paying off your contract once you have provided all that you promised. It would be wise to be respectful and confident in speaking with them. We want them to see how dedicated you are to delivering on your promises. Whether it is due to vengeance against the US, or Professor Mcleod, for the money, or for the good of the people and the party of China will not matter to them any more than it matters to me. What does matter, is that they see you are faithful to your words through your deeds. That you are strong, not intimidated by them or the UN team and that you are willing and able to use the Thor's Hammer as they describe. This is not merely transactional, rather a personal commitment to keeping your word. This will be important to them, and that makes it important to me. So, it must be vital to you Mr. Zach. We don't want any confusion, and we don't want any mistakes. There is too much at risk."

"I understand," Zach replied as he turned to walk away and mentally prepare for what lay ahead. He was still uncertain what he would do, but he knew exactly how he would act during the meeting. It was unclear whether they would be meeting in person, by video or a hybrid. Regardless, Zach needed to brush up a little on his Chinese to make sure he was pronouncing and annunciating correctly. After all, you only get one chance to make a first impression and he was very curious how high the level of participation would be for this meeting.

After too brief a time to prepare, Zach walked into the conference room exactly two minutes before the top of the hour. He was surprised to see the room packed to capacity, and several large screens with dozens of small video boxes indicating many remote participants. Hybrid meeting it is then he smiled to himself, realizing that not only would he be seen by lots of people offsite, but it was also almost certain that the entire event would be recorded by someone. That should mean a US intercept, and hopefully whoever was responsible for this sector would be on the ball. Either the presence of, or the words from an American intelligence operative addressing the key provincial leaders and the top tier CCP officials should get some attention.

Mr. Wu appeared from the crowd and grasped Zach's arm as he instructed him to follow toward their assigned seats. They were at the very front of the room just off the left-wing steps leading to the large stage which supported a podium with a microphone and several bright lights for the cameras. They settled into their seats and the speaker began precisely on the hour. His remarks were purely political, and seemed to be written for an eight-year-old, but Zach listened intently to the words he spoke. About fifteen minutes in, he began to thank Mr. Wu for his dedication and oversight of this project. Mr. Wu and his US counterpart were the keys to success of the previous operation and would be instrumental in those to come. They both rose from their seat, waived politely to the crowd as they acknowledged the recognition of their previous service and then took their seat to learn precisely what was to come.

As the meeting wrapped up Zach was disappointed to learn that standing to be recognized, politely smiling and waving to the other participants was his demonstration of respect and commitment to this cause. No questions, no answers, and no opportunity to speak. He was further disappointed to learn little more from this meeting than he already heard from the speech given by the party official which was now being carried by almost every press outlet. That same video had been played regularly on the many computer monitors throughout the underground facility where they had returned after their interference in the UN demonstration was complete.

Zach was disappointed to be sure, but there was also something said during the conference call that seemed a bit out of place, out of context that he was struggling to fit into the ongoing narrative. In his remarks, the CCP Provincial Secretary was pleased at the recent progress of this exceptional national effort. It might be nothing, but in Zach's mind everything about this on-demand weather modification was recent. The actions to disrupt and discredit the UN campaign were fresh, but for a country and a party known to take the long view it seemed odd to be calling one event a recent success. Calling an evolving new technology such as this an exceptional national effort? It might be nothing, but it might also be that others in the room were there to celebrate something he knew little or nothing about.

Aboard Tom's plane, just a couple hours from their destination back in India the passengers were all discussing the press videos the steward had urgently requested they review.

Bob was not in a good headspace already from seeing the carnage left behind after the wind event and this new revelation stacked right on top of what he was still struggling to understand.

"But it's crap! We all know how this came to be. What can they gain from claiming we stole it from them? And why now? One rational explanation is they did the second event during ours. Clearly, they want to take over the effort from the UN, but why put themselves out there like that? Why take that risk and pick such a public fight over this? How desperate are they right now? Seems like this is a desperation play that is very likely not to pan out for them. Why lie? Why risk it?" Bob asked no one in particular.

"All good questions Bob. What we need right now are some answers. What we have on this plane are the right people to give us those. Nobody else has you, and we need to protect the three of you as a resource but also tap that knowledge to figure out what we don't know yet. I think we must also assume they have, or had, or are working with Zach. We also need to assume for now that, if Zach knew something they know it too," Tom continued thinking out loud to the team. If there was any doubt about that, it would soon be erased as Tom's pocket began to vibrate from his phones. His attention turned to the headset as he pointed hand signals to the steward to bring up the video screen to his less-than-favorite news network. The updated news clip about China's claims to Thor's Hammer technology contained a short video of key national and party leaders recognizing and praising their weather modification team. And one standout member being recognized in their session, was also recognized by everyone on that plane.

"Well, that changes from an assumption to a known fact now, doesn't it? At least we have a good idea of what they want us to think. They want us to know Zach is working with them, and they want us to know that before they complete their takeover attempt of the UN operations. That means they want us to focus on this revelation. It also means, if they want us looking at this, there is something even more important that they don't want us looking at right now. We need to do both, and we need to do them fast if we are going to keep this whole effort from coming off the rails. Less than two hours until we land, and we better have something before we touch down," Tom encouraged…or demanded. It was often hard to distinguish the two when he was speaking.

Bob and Ann looked at each other in quiet disgust. They had spent a fair amount of time with Zach and knew he had idiosyncrasies and even some character flaws that seemed to go well with the position he held. They believed he was behind the disaster in India, but now they had to put him in a class of despicable reserved for a select few. He was now, maybe had been all along, helping a foreign government undermine his own. He played a role in killing innocent people in the process. And now he was looking to both take credit for the discovery and destroy the reputation of all those around the Thor's Hammer technology and its originators. It now appeared he was personally coming after Bob, Ann and his own countrymen including their Commander in Chief. Zach had gone from "likely" enemy of the state to Enemy of the State #1 with great certainty and visibility for those in the know.

CHAPTER NINE

WHAT ARE YOU TALKING ABOUT?

Good to see you all again, we'll be using this area for the next couple of days. It's not ideal, but it has the least visible access from the outside, and the most limited access from within our small perimeter," Frank explained as he greeted Tom, Bob, Ann, Betty and their security detail leading the way through a solid door with a cypher combination lock on the knob. As they filed into the small but well-equipped work area, he identified the spaces they would be sharing and asked them to take a couple minutes to get oriented, then join up in the briefing area so they could catch up and synchronize their information and next actions. As the new arrivals joined the rest of the UN team, whom they had not seen since their departure, Tom took it upon himself to start the discussion.

"First, I want to thank everyone for all you did in response to the tragic events of the past few days. I know that saying it was difficult is the understatement of the year, but thank you for what you did. Let me also thank you for what you are about to do, and for what you are not going to do. First and foremost, you are not going to blame any of what happened on Professor Mcleod, Ann or Betty. What happened here was not their fault, and we now know why it happened and who caused it. You will also not judge them for not being here the past couple of days to help you deal with all that needed to be done. That was my call, and it was the right one. We needed to get them out of the country for their own safety while we figured out what happened. You needed them gone because you did not need the distraction that having them here would have caused while you were busy with recovery operations. Anyone who has a problem with that brings it up right now, we work through it and move on. But it's right now, or it's not spoken about again. I'll give you a minute if you need to think about it."

After a short pause and a look around the entire room, Tom continued, "OK, hearing none, we will consider both of those topics settled. What remains is describing and putting into motion what we are going to do next. As hopefully you have all heard by now, we believed that our target, Zach, was involved in or conducted a Thor's Hammer wind event within our own event. That's what produced the over one hundred knot wind event. As we were looking into that, the government of China made their claims about the US and UN stealing their technology. They claim we are novices and recklessly endangering the world for money and power to get a political and economic advantage over them. And they will no longer sit by while we do this to them, so they are going to do their own demo here to show everyone how it can be done safely. How we should have done it but couldn't. And right in the middle of their announcement is a video of Zach being recognized for his work with them doing on-demand weather modification." Tom paused, but it was clear by the lack of reactions in the room that he was plowing old ground and everyone in the room was aware of what he'd said thus far.

"We focused a lot of national assets where we were asked to based on our USAF teammates theory of the most likely spot for Zach and team to pull this off. Thank you-guys for taking that initiative because it paid off big. We were able to spot and track a small group of off-road vehicles and some drones that moved into the area you identified a couple of days before our demonstration. This same group then rolled out of their spot just a few hours after the peak wind event. Stopped and spent several more hours at another location, where they seemed to be met by or recovered a balloon of some kind. We were able to isolate some radio chatter from this site, and they were Chinese speakers on secure military frequencies. Analysts were able to follow these vehicles movement across the border into China where they disappeared into a building much too small to house that many vehicles. We have been watching that building since then and have determined that it is likely the entrance to an underground facility."

At that, Bob and Ann looked at each other and rolled their eyes at the same time. Zach and underground facilities sure seemed to go together based on their experiences. Betty sat fascinated as she listened to what Tom had to say and the certainty with which he spoke. He didn't think he knew all this in such a short amount of time; rather he knew this with certainty and continued to speak.

"They are still doing workups on this site, but it appears likely that a few decades of mining operations may have also produced an underground facility on or near the mine site. We think Zach, or a team associated with him were in those vehicles. We also believe that is an underground CCP military facility and that Zach is still there. It is also our working theory that Zach and this same team will be the ones who will be doing the CCP demonstration here in thirty-six hours. The wind event was their dry run, and it worked well. Their main event will be the same place our team used. Our intent is to surveil the entrance to their facility. Track everything that leaves. Get eyes on Zach, do a snatch and grab that will hopefully disrupt or cancel their planned demonstration.

"This delay will buy us time by disrupting their propaganda, enabling us to discredit their campaign to discredit us. Depending on what we learn from Zach once we have him, we can better decide what comes next. In the meantime, we must prepare to monitor their demonstration both remotely and in person. Let's talk about what that looks like and I'll take whatever your questions are at this point," Tom wrapped up and looked around for questions or comments.

Frank was the first of several to ask questions, "Are we going to be part of the snatch and grab, or are we strictly in our UN Thor's Hammer demonstration team roles?"

"Yes," Tom smiled as everyone except the Three Musketeers seemed to understand his response. "Next?"

"What do we think this team is capable of? Do we have an idea of their level of expertise with this technology?" Betty asked, surprising many in the room, including Tom who responded quickly.

"They have not had the devices very long, so it is probably limited to what Zach could teach them in the time he has been missing. If we grab him, we expect that will be a big problem for them going forward. At best we assess that they know as much as Zach was able to pass along, but they can't be too confident in this short of a time without him." Tom looked for the next question.

Captain Lessur raised his hand, and somewhat reluctantly challenged Tom's assessment, "How confident are you in that assessment? I mean, these guys pulled off an event within an event. We haven't even discussed if we can do that, let alone how to do that. How to have two systems concurrently operating to produce different results at the same time. What would that input even look like? They were close enough to see it, and confident enough that they wouldn't get themselves with their own event. And to do it in what looks like their own over-the-border backyard? We picked this place, not them. Yet here they are, and they have us playing defense. We are responding to action right now; not driving the action. I don't want to underestimate him…them.

"They apparently already killed hundreds with their last operation, and with precision. How does that make them only as good as, or not as good as us with something we are still learning as we go? We were looking for Zach and trying to draw him out with these demonstrations, and it looks to me like he just sat back and waited for us to come to him.

"And once we got here, and told him what we were going to do, he just smiled and said, ok come on over and hold my beer."

You could see the ideas starting to take root with those in the room. Bob spoke up next, "You make some good points, Ron. We are certain Zach did the India flooding operation on his own, and now this wind event in India but he is operating from a Chinese bunker, doing state CCP briefings and leading the China effort to take over a UN program? I worked with Zach. So did Ann for longer than I did, and it wasn't that long ago. He would be moving and grooving to cover this much ground in this amount of time. Believe me when I say from experience that a technology like this can land you in front of some very important people in a short amount of time. But do we really think the CCP would go on the global stage with Zach as their lead guy when only a few weeks ago he was our lead guy? For people who play the long game, this would be a short game with high-risk move wouldn't it? How desperate are they for something like this to work, and what are they willing to risk should it fail? If they lose Zach, does it fail? Are their margins that thin on this?"

Tom was not liking where this was going, but he was glad to see they were doing what he asked. These guys were not stuck on what to think, they were practitioners of how to think and that was unfolding in real time in the room. "Why would the CCP risk their credibility on Zach's ability to deliver something for them that they just went out on the world stage and challenged the US and the UN over? Agreed, this does not sound like a risk this group is likely to take. Moreover, if they were willing to take such a risk what conditions would warrant them doing it now?"

"Desperation. They see the US and the UN stepping onto the world stage and doing the people's work. That is a party staple, for the good of the people. If we are already doing it for everyone, why do one and a half billion people need their party?" Ann contributed.

Frank, silent to this point, finally spoke after carefully considering what was so far out of the box that he had to ask the unspeakable. "Ann, while I think that is possible, I think it is also improbable. And since that is where we are possible but improbable, consider this: They are telling the truth. In that scenario, what they are saying and doing makes perfect sense. It works with or without Zach, and that is why they showed him off to us all. He is the distraction just like Tom described, and that works because while we are focused on him, we are not recognizing the red herring that he is to their demonstration. It goes as planned with or without him because they already are dialed in on the whole of it?"

"Frank, that's just not possible. We know Bob and I brought this to the UN, and Bob got it from Doc Auster," Ann countered.

"Yes, we know that. But does anyone know exactly where and how Doc Auster got the Thor's Hammer in the first place? Do we know, or did we assume? Do you know Bob, or do you think you know how Doc got the first one?" Frank was asking, not challenging his friend's version of the story but it was important to cover assumptions to make sure things were what they seemed before moving forward.

"I know he had two. The one I found, and the one he gave Father Gannon. Ann also pointed out while we were at the US facility with Zach that there were differences between the copies I made, and the one Doc made. I don't know if there were differences between the one I had and the one Father Gannon had," Bob paused.

"None that I could tell, but there may have been slight differences I didn't see, but that would have only been in some of the circuitry. I checked everything else," Ann contributed.

It was then Sergeant Andies pulled the pin and tossed a verbal grenade into the conversation. "Doc Auster didn't invent it. He found it. Oh shit, Colonel you are right! Sir, sorry Sir? I mean they don't need Zach because Doc didn't invent it, he figured it out. If the CCP is telling the truth, that means Doc found a device, or found or took their technology and got it the same way Bob did. You said this team with Zach was doing some balloon recovery after the wind event right?" he asked looking more accusingly than inquisitively at Tom.

"Yeah, but what does that have to do with Doc Auster?" Tom asked.

"Doc and Bob collected data for years on that research project, right? That area is all around our military training area. We always have something going on out there. Training and tests and what not. Bob, you guys have sensors all over the forest areas. Lots of wide-open spaces, lots of meteorological sensors, lots of data collected and getting turned over to the state for some long-term study about some insurance lawsuit that only a few people even know about let alone care much about. No offense Bob, Betty." He smiled politely then continued, "All four seasons, lots of variety in conditions including extremes. That's a pretty good cover for a weather modification project and the data is all publicly accessible. It cost them nothing to have us track and report the actual weather, as well as the results of the tests they do to change the weather. The joke has always been, if you don't like the weather now, stick around for a few minutes because it will change. What if they just slipped in changes of their own. I always hear we hide in plain sight, why wouldn't they do the same thing?"

"Doc would have never worked against his own country with the Chinese. He was not a traitor. He was as patriotic as anyone in this room," Betty defended her longtime colleague.

"Sorry to imply that, no offense. I don't mean that he was working with the CCP, but that he found or came across what they were working on. Maybe even what they were testing in his own backyard. I mean that is how Captain Lessur and I found Bob. We have a big area, lots of sensors and we saw something that was happening but should not have been because weather guys looking at weather also see what weather should *not* be there when it shows up. We know what should be happening, and when that is not what happens we tend to be awfully persistent in figuring out why it's not the way it should be. What if that is how Doc came to possess a Thor's Hammer? What if he was out trying to figure out something about the data, or a weather condition that should not have been happening? Good Lord, what if someone, say the Chinese were testing their Thor's Hammer and Doc found it? Weather balloons get used all the time, float along and fall back to the ground.

"These devices are only a little bit bigger than a standard radiosonde. They weigh a lot more, but what if someone was flying one of these and doing airborne testing and it got away from them? They lost it, Doc found it. They *could* be telling the truth then, right?" He paused considering the boundary between the possible and the plausible. He glanced over at Bob, who was considering what this could mean to his version of the past if Andies was even remotely correct. But he quickly recognized that it was not implausible given what Bob did not know about Doc's work, or the devices before he had found them among Doc's belongings.

"That is some thinly stretched thinking, Sergeant," Tom said skeptically. "But I sure like how well them telling the truth fits their action plan thus far. Zach would certainly be a no-risk asset to them and a huge distraction for us in this scenario. This sure would be some shit if Bob's lived truth and the Chinese news release truth were both factually correct from their perspectives. Well, we have a short amount of time so how far do we want to chase this theory folks? And what else do we want to consider?"

"We need to chase this one all the way until we know one way or the other. Doc and Bob are why we all know about this technology. That won't change. Whether Doc Auster invented it, or got it from the Chinese or someone else, that would change his legacy. We owe them both that much, and while we can have two different points on the same timeline, we can't have two different origins for this technology," Betty articulated what they were all thinking. So, they agreed to find what they could and reconvene in six hours to share what they found. Everyone set out to learn and bring back as much as they could about their new working theory.

As they got back together, there were some more revelations that added credence to their idea and none yet that made it impossible. It was Tom that got the ball rolling.

"Since our first meeting about this UN adventure, we've been chasing and watching the most expensive and hard to get parts of Thor's Hammer hoping Zach or someone would try to get the last ones to build a copy device. That was based on the premise that our technology was new and duplicating it for a high dollar sale would need to be fastest to market. So, we took another run at that research from our new perspective, taking a deeper look into some of those component's origins and connections before they were in their current use. Turns out, we found something this time that we didn't see last time.

"One of the more expensive components was built for India's weather satellite program. There are only a couple of those in operation, and a couple of spares in inventory from when they were building the satellites out. We know where these are, and where the last few went including Bob's and the Chinese connection to the companies that bought the remainders. But it turns out, this was a slightly modified version of a similar component that was originally built by another company that was sold a few times, changed some names before the guys selling it now got it. This part also existed under an older and separate patent that is a very slight variation from the one we were watching. The original part was patented several years before ours, but they built and sold about three hundred of these prior to the updated patent that produced the small numbers made and sold afterwards.

"What this could mean, is the pieces we have are the last ones available not the only ones. And more importantly, not the first ones. This would also fit into the scenario we are chasing. If China is indeed telling the truth, they could have an initial operating capability of two to three hundred Thor's Hammers. They may only be using the new patent items for spares and more importantly, to make sure nobody else could duplicate or match their existing capability. No de-facto arms race for this technology because even in a worst-case scenario, three hundred to just a few made with this new component is not a race at all. We are still trying to run down who and where those three hundred went to, but we have already found at least two of the shell companies associated with the last purchases. They also show up in the earlier component's buyers, so we have a connection that I suspect will only get stronger with time."

Tom paused to let the gravity of that sink in and watched the wheels spinning as he looked around at the group.

"If they already had it, why didn't they try to stop us before we got out on the road with it?" Ann asked.

"I'm not sure they didn't try to do just that," Tom said. "Our theory continues to be demonstrably plausible, and that means it's also entirely plausible that Doc's untimely death was not accidental at all. It could have been deliberate and intended to stop whatever he may have considered doing with his discovery. If they knew he had this technology there was risk to their program. The drunk college student testified at his plea deal that he didn't remember getting into his car or anything about the accident that killed Doc. It was his car that hit doc, but he was passed out in it when the cops found them not too far up the road a little while later. But the report said it took a while to get him sober enough to even communicate with him. A few months later the guilt or shame pushed the poor kid to apply a permanent solution to his temporary problem. We can't go back and talk to that kid, and we can't go back and talk to Doc. The loose ends are tied up neatly. That lends more credence to this idea. Anybody have anything that does not?" He sighed and again scanned the group, stopping at Betty who had tears coming down both cheeks.

"If they murdered Doc Auster, and ruined that kid's life, or worse if they killed him too, how could we prove any of that now?" Betty asked not even trying to hide her mix of shock, confusion and anger.

Bob finally inserted himself into the vortex of new considerations. "I am not sure we ever could. But I know that regardless of how he came to possess the Thor's Hammers, Doc wanted to do good with them. That is why we are here. He had them for a while. The recipes were kept in files that are sorted by season and the weather events primarily associated with them. The device he gave Father Gannon was in his possession for a couple of years before Doc's death. So, if we accept those timelines at face value, and lay them over the timeline Tom described for the parts, that would mean the Chinese would have either lost, or had their program compromised at least two or maybe three years ago by what we can tie back to Doc. To get it to a level of sophistication that he could stumble upon a built-out device being used or tested would be another year or so at least in development and mockups. Which would mean the Chinese have had this technology a minimum of four to five years? Does that align with your parts patent and production timeline Tom?" Bob asked, already seeing Tom nodding north and south.

"Yes, we were estimating five to seven years based on that alone. Overlaying this we could match two sources that say the Chinese may have possessed this at least five years ago, perhaps longer. What else can we use to disprove this hard-to-believe theory? So far everything seems to support it's possible," Tom challenged.

"You won't like this, but I am going to say it anyway," Betty added. "The grant that funded the trapline, all the sensors we put up, the University got that grant eight years ago after the lawsuit was settled. That means the network was built and filled with state of the art remotely monitored weather sensors just before then. All of them connected to the web, accessible remotely or in person with onboard data recorders, and all right before your five-to-seven-year estimate. All brand new, state of the art weather sensors spread out across a vast wilderness of uninhabited forests and military ranges making large data sets available remotely and also available to the public for the asking through Freedom of Information Act requests. Since the agreement was a settlement of a federal court decision, access to the data was required since it was a settlement done with taxpayer money. It was all in place just prior to your five-to-seven-year window. Doc was a tenured Professor by then, and he chose to pursue this grant instead of other seemingly better fits. And we won it in open competition. That matches both your timeline and working theory." Betty was not happy to share that important information because it supported the additional theory that Doc could have been working with the Chinese at the time.

Tom nodded, again requesting something contrary to the trending support for their working theory but nothing of consequence emerged. Colonel Lincoln sought some clarity with his questions.

"Assuming the CCP has had some version of this technology for at least five years, why not use it? Why wait until now to claim it's theirs after the UN has already blown the lid off it?" Frank asked the group.

"All due respect Sir, what makes you think they haven't used it?" Sergeant Andies answered. He was as good a strategic thinker as he was a forecaster, perhaps that was why he was such a good forecaster. He knew how to think, not what to think. "Why not use it without letting anyone know they were using it? Isn't that exactly what Professor Mcleod did to get enough money to build his copies? Consider the possibilities. Making money for sure with some well-timed events. Bob did it. How about influencing policy? How much money have we spent on global warming during that same time? Now we all gotta wonder if these two things are related given the timeline we just suggested is highly likely. Every hurricane, flood and tornado in the past five years has the potential to have been a deliberate act intended to expend our treasure, test our responses or just be disruptive under the guise of natural disasters or acts of nature. They may very well have been acts of eco-terrorism. I think the better question for my money is why *would* they admit to having this technology if they did not have to?" He paused, but was on a roll and could not help himself.

"There are only two kinds of change; evolutionary and revolutionary. Their long-term strategy was likely to shape our thinking by accepting what we saw with our own eyes, and understood through our common national experiences. We would never know what we were watching was deliberately scripted stronger storms, warmer temperatures or dryer summers. Conversely, what Bob and Ann and Father Gannon did at the UN was trigger an unplanned disruption of their ongoing evolutionary changes by rolling out to the world a technology that instantly promised a revolutionary change. That single event literally blew up many years of effort and expense. Now they need to salvage their end game by changing strategy, and discrediting the UN effort to get their weather modification technology back within their control. The best way to do that is using their existing arsenal of already fielded systems. That could be why, Colonel. Might not be it at all, but it could be some version of that," Andies concluded.

"Well, that would be a whole new level of WTF!" Tom rolled his eyes knowing full well that the sergeant was far more likely to be some version of right than any version of wrong.

"If this is what we think, what we know is that in about a day these guys who have had and used this technology for at least five years are going to be very nearby. Maybe even right here in about twenty-four hours to show the world how it should be done and why the world should let the CCP lead this effort going forward. What should we do *about that, with that, for that?* Thoughts?" Tom asked, this time it was clear he was asking not demanding.

"We could to the same thing we think they did to us. Program a specific short-term event within theirs. Nothing dangerous, just visible," Ann offered without enthusiasm or serious consideration. She was just uncomfortable with the long silence after Tom asked for some ideas. "It is probably what they would expect and would also be ready to counter. It would be a rookie move, especially with our limited expertise. Producing an event inside their event might just prove their point if we were exposed doing it, so that is a pretty high risk just for a break even with both of us being discredited. We should find something that could be a win, not a draw in the world view," she concluded.

Bob chimed in with the start of something but he wasn't sure where they would end up. "What if we agree with them, and willingly let them lead the way? They must expect us to put up a fight to salvage our image, to try to keep our program alive and stay in the lead of this effort. To do anything else would likely be seen as a big credibility hit. They would not expect us to do it. So maybe that is why we should. We could pull them in close and welcome their help. Learn what they can do by asking them to show us all, out in the open. If we are right, how would they possibly think we are on to them at this point. We have done almost everything wrong that we could possibly do if we're honest. There is no way we do any of what we have done so far if we knew, or even suspected this technology to be old instead of shiny and new." He kept going to wherever this stream of consciousness was taking him.

"We don't have to find and snatch Zach, we invite him to the table to help show us what we don't know. Once we have him here, we can see how much he knows. We can gauge how much he is involved with them, or how much he is not. I know he's pragmatic, maybe we can appeal to him to help us for the right price of course. And that may not be money. We ask to join their team and see what we get to see. I know they won't show us their playbook or all their toys if they have them. But if we are right and they do already have an experienced team of operators at least we can confirm some of our theory and then decide what to do based on what we learn as we go."

Frank agreed, "If we take them up on their offer, I say we call their bluff. I don't think they will see that as a very likely event. At least we won't be doing what they expect us to do, and that might get us some opportunity we otherwise would not get. It also puts us in a dynamic situation where we will need to respond to what we see, act on what is happening without a whole lot of time to react. I like staying on offense, and while our first action in this sequence is offense, after that it's all respond to their response.

"The big question here is do we think the Secretary General, and our President will see it the same way? There has been a shortage of that common vision since we started this effort. Are we going to loop them in and discuss what we think, or are we just going to seek forgiveness instead of approval?"

"I will add that to my action items," Tom said. "I will discuss this with the President and the Secretary General and Mr. Dau." None of whom were in the room but were expecting very positive results from this group as well as being kept up to speed on what to expect next.

"Well, this was not what I expected to be doing today," Tom added. "I shouldn't have to tell you, but I am going to anyway. Everything we said here today stays in this room. And by that, I mean every single scintilla of an idea that the CCP has had this technology long before us goes nowhere except to those in this room, and only while we are in this room. Word of this leaks out, the Chinese will get it and then it's game over. Whatever we want to do will be off the table if they sniff out that we are on them. Is that clear? If it's not, then ask your question now because anyone who leaks this, I don't think God himself will be able to help you out of the shitstorm in which you will find yourself. Hopefully that is as clear as humanly possible?" he demanded, once again he was not asking.

CHAPTER TEN

YOU CAN TAKE IT FROM HERE

G ood morning Mr. President, and everyone else. Please forgive me, but we are very pressed for time, and I will be requesting your direction on this one. It is not something that I believe you are going to want to delegate and, candidly, I am not going to just run with this one." Tom paused and reminded those on the call that the man standing next to him was Colonel Frank Lincoln. They were the only two from their location involved in this discussion.

Tom continued after the President motioned for him to proceed without any of the formalities, "Sir, bottom line up front. We don't have a smoking gun yet, but we do have a high degree of confidence the CCP has had the Thor's Hammer technology for at least five years, likely longer. We believe they have been using it in a covert manner to create or change specific weather events to sway our policy decisions as well as conducting intense direct action weather events designed to inflict damage and expensive recovery operations. As they influence our policy decision, they are doing the opposite for themselves. Sir, they are five years deep into a strategic offensive weather on-demand battle plan. And until yesterday, we were not even aware we were in such a battle or that such a contest even existed," Tom concluded and simply waited for the spears to be hurled in his direction. The short summary literally made Frank wince. To be a field grade officer in the profession of arms serving your nation and not know that nation has been attacked and on the receiving end of an ongoing battleplan for the past five years was both embarrassing and infuriating.

"That is a lot of bottom-line, Tom. Fill in the gaps. This is not an easy story to follow just yet," the President instructed, and Tom obliged. He explained all the group had discussed and concluded earlier in what seemed like the longest day ever. Frank added a few affirming comments, and fifteen minutes later there was a long pause while the ideas and their impacts began to sink in for the President and those sitting in the room with him.

"Put a number on it, Tom. How confident are you on this?" The President asked his National Security Advisor.

"Seventy percent Sir, but I can smell the smoking gun even though we don't have it in our hands yet. It's close enough to smell," he nodded.

"OK. What about you, Colonel? What's your number?" his commander in chief asked. Frank was confident in his response and in his tone.

"Ninety for me Sir," Frank paused, as the response he anticipated came right on cue from Secretary of Defense Fitzgerald.

"Why the delta Frank, where does your twenty percent higher confidence come from?"

"Two things Sir. First, I could see the look on Professor Mcleod's face as we floated and developed this line of thinking. I have worked with Bob several times before, and I could see the wheels turning and everything we were talking about he could fit into what he lived. It was all possible from his perspective and I could see it shook him. Second, is Sun Tzu. He said know the enemy, know yourself; your victory will never be endangered. Know the ground, know the weather; your victory will then be total. Everything we added in fit into a very plausible, even likely, strategy which aligned with their known objectives. The US doesn't work on weather modification technologies, but the Chinese do. Often, we don't see or recognize what we aren't doing ourselves. I believe this is one of those times they are not out to copy our technology, instead we somehow ended up with theirs. That aligns with their need to make a supportable claim about developing this new technology. If they control the narrative, they can be better postured to keep their covert history with this hidden. I'm at ninety, Sir, and staying there. I expect that number to go up and not down as more details are firmed up," Colonel Lincoln said coolly. He was a great practitioner of confidence without arrogance, and capability without cockiness.

"That is what I was afraid of," General Charles added. "Any chance either of you have a recommendation on what to do about it? They are in your backyard with this stuff in a few hours. Is there an opportunity there?"

Tom jumped in to get a civilian voice included with the two senior military officers. "Yes, several in fact. Seems our group's consensus is that we thank them and take them up on their offer. Let them lead. Let them show us what they want us to see, while we are looking around to see what we want to know. This will also, hopefully get us in the same place with Zach. That way we don't need to snatch him from them, for now. And if we do need to get him later, we will know where he is and how to get him. We keep our friends close and our enemies closer. Learn what we can, go on to the next scheduled location for the UN tour and learn what we can."

"That's the best option, really? That's what you want to do?" The President pushed on Tom, who was tired, but he was ready for this.

"Hell no Sir! It's not what I want to do. I want to get all those dudes in a room, close the door and have a big cage match. But that is not what we should do. You already heard what I think we should do," Tom concluded.

"Alright Tom. Then go do it. I want you to check in regularly as this develops. If you are right, we will need to talk through every step of this. And if you're wrong, we will need to do some serious damage control. Either way, the UN is going to be pretty unhappy with us. Do you want to tell them, or do you want me to," The President asked.

"Copy that, and I think it best I talk it out in full candor with Mr. Dau who is on-scene here with us. Let him bring in the Secretary General. He can decide who and how he wants to engage. And knowing him, Sir, he might want to go straight at the CCP and get them to admit or deny. Are you good with that if he does?" Tom wanted to have his bases covered. His boss and almost every other boss had one thing in common; they hate surprises.

"I can live with it either way, Tom," the Chief Executive responded. "He gets to decide for the UN what is the best position to take. We only get to advise. Having said that, you better advise him long and hard about what you want them to do. He has a mind of his own, and when it comes to me, he tends to have a chip on his shoulder the size of Mount Rushmore."

"I will Sir. And, yes, he does. In his mind you earned it, and then some. I will do my best," Tom promised.

"That's why you are there. That's why you are my guy. Now go do what you do. Let me know what you need, and I will do my best to get what or who you need, or I'll find you someone else who can do it better than I can. Most of those people still work for me," the President ended and the line went dead.

"Well, that was interesting and not a lot of fun," Frank offered as Tom considered what just happened, and what now needed to happen.

"Yeah? That was as easy as they get. They have no idea what to do with what we told them, and no comprehension yet of what it really means. We have had a little time for it to sink in, but they are just wrapping their brains around the concept that they have likely been played by a government that has been manipulating the weather for years to get us to be unwitting co-conspirators in our own demise. Next time we talk with them, you can bet they will be spitting nails. Likely worse. So, we better get Mr. Dau and the Secretary General on board and fast," Tom said as they wrapped up the call and departed to rejoin the rest of the team.

"Beyond letting the CCP take the lead, what is your gameplan, Tom?" Frank asked.

"Do I have to do everything, Colonel? Why are you even here Frank? You figure that out with Bob and whomever then let me know what you come up with. I have some other stuff I need to take care of. Meet up in half an hour in the briefing room with everyone and be ready with something. Even if it's the least bad option, bring something we can build from," Tom directed as he continued down the walkway. Colonel Lincoln broke to the right and headed toward the operations room where he was confident that he would find Bob, Ann, Betty and his USAF weather guys.

It only took twenty minutes for Tom to arrive and gesture for Frank to join him near the corner of the room. It was small and nearly every flat surface had computer monitors, radios and other communications systems filling every square inch of space on the tables.

"You're early, Tom," Colonel Lincoln scolded the man he was approaching to see what updates may have been confirmed in the last twenty minutes. Tom smiled, but it wasn't because he was happy about anything.

"Mr. Dau will be here directly. He will be ready to hear what we have to say and bring recommendations to the Secretary General for a decision today. So, we have that lined up. I also confirmed what we suspected about the lineage of these parts and shell companies. They go back to the same timeframes and tie together in and out, back to the original patent holders. That patent was filed six years ago, and that means they had the technology well before that if they decided to actually patent something. They knew they had value and that someday they would need to point to it in some legal or formal way. Looks like we may be pushing them into that position right now, and they will have the goods to back up their claim."

"Well, that's good to know but it's not good news," Frank frowned.

"If you didn't like that, you're certainly not going to like this," Tom continued. "That grant Betty was talking about. Well, the lawsuit settlement required a long-term contaminant deposition study to determine if the charcoal plants were polluting the air and ground downwind. That's the one awarded the University and Doc a grant that was funding their efforts. The same law firm comes up as the patent filer for the first version of those key parts. They represented several of the shell companies. The law firm is linked to all these players. We are still trying to unwrap those guys, but they are the connective tissue, and we know on paper they have several offices in the US. They are a subsidiary of an investment company that among other things also operates a real estate company specializing in larger commercial properties in Taiwan, Singapore and China. I am confident we will have our connection back to some key players in the CCP either past, present or both.

"One more thing. Given all this is panning out to be connected, I think there is likely to be something to the notion that Doc's accident was not an accident. I hit up your and Bob's FBI guy that got onto him in the beginning, Agent Miloc. Read him into what we are thinking now and have him taking another run at what happened to Doc Auster and that night he was run over. That kid just might have been another victim in this instead of a perpetrator. He is going to relook that from start to finish and see if it cracks under this new theory we are working on," Tom paused. "How do you think Bob will handle all that?"

Frank considered the question, then responded "I think Bob will be ok. He told me he worked with Doc, but they weren't that close. The guy kept mostly to himself; they both did. Bob liked Miloc, even let him adopt Doc's dog Buck. But it's Betty that I don't think will handle that very well. She knew Doc for quite a while. You saw her when this whole idea came up. Kudos to her for speaking up, but I don't think she wanted to even think about it let alone speak it into existence."

"Thanks. About Betty, if this starts to unfold like we think, then I'm not sure she is out of the scope of potentially being compromised or complicit. I doubt she is, but we have to consider lots of stuff with all this. She is not much value added out here, and candidly she is one more we need to protect if things go bad. And in that scenario, she is the slowest and weakest in the group so we can only go as fast as she can if we need to get gone in a hurry again, or worse if we gotta fight our way out. What do we need from back home that would require her unique set of skills? Something that does not insult her but passes muster as a strong enough cover that even Bob and Ann won't raise their eyebrows very much if we ask for it."

Frank was quick with his response, as he had already been considering the same thing but for different reasons. "All the records from Doc's house are in their suite back in New York. Bob hired Betty to be his records custodian and whatever else he needed help with during the beginning of the whole UN thing. She should go back and, maybe with the help of Miloc and some of the agency analysts, go through those records again with a fresh set of eyes now that we know more of what we are looking for. That said, we need to keep Bob here, and my preference is Ann stays with Bob instead of going back with Betty but I can make it work either way."

"Good. I agree. Let's let them focus on that idea and where Ann falls into the mix. That will also keep them less focused on the whole Doc thing until everyone is underway. I will hold two seats on the flight out tonight. Betty for sure, another one either for Ann or more room for Betty to stretch out. I do like that lady, gonna hate to see her go. It's like having your mom around looking over your shoulder to make sure you stay in line. I might just miss that," Tom shook his head a little and smiled.

"I didn't know you had a mom. Kinda thought you were just issued to the White House occupant," Frank joked, while trying to read into Tom's unexpected sentiment.

"Seems like that to me, too," Tom agreed. "No, Frank, my mom's been gone a long time. Betty just reminds me that I still need to make her proud. There are some days that can be a very helpful reminder."

"I get that," Frank agreed as the team began to assemble in the room. It was time to turn this dialogue into a working team meeting, and right on cue,

Mr. Dau joined the small group and began greeting the others as they began to take their seats and get started.

After providing a detailed summary for Mr. Dau, and an update on what he had already shared with Colonel Lincoln, Tom was ready for some discussion and the course of action development they all needed for the fast-approaching demonstration. The UN team needed some direction, but they wanted a say in what that would entail. Mr. Dau had been at this for a while, and though he was politically savvy, he was not politically motivated. He could not say the same of the Secretary General,; he was both. Their recommendation needed to consider what would produce a win-win-win.

"We make a press release, but we couch the language saying the UN will gladly accept the CCP's gracious offer to assist us in the mission of safely fielding the on-demand weather technology. We look forward to partnering with someone who may already be familiar with this emerging capability. We are confident that working together can produce a complementary effort that will result in a more efficient and effective fielding of this potentially history changing technology that will benefit us all," Mr. Dau auditioned the idea to those in the group.

"I think this sufficiently puts it all into the gray spaces so we can establish some connections and lines of communication then refine them as we go. Everyone gets to say they are working together but also maintain their original spots without losing face up front. Those losses can be triggered and capitalized on later," Tom agreed as did the rest of the team.

"Good, so Mr. Dau if you will get the thumbs up from the Secretary General, I will pass the same to the President and US senior staff," he paused and observed Mr. Dau nodding in agreement. "Thank you. We will also need you, Professor McLeod, Ann, myself and several others all front and center somewhere to be seen as we observe their demonstration. Hopefully the Indian government can arrange that we are all in the same spot with everyone else. We will need to put full pressure on that being the visual for the cameras. The host nation, the UN delegation, and the CCP demonstration delegation all united in one spot for a combined effort. Without that, the videos and the headlines around the globe will be UN watches as CCP takes over on-demand weather modification efforts in India. That simply won't be good for any of us," he continued.

"Betty, I have a favor to ask of you," Tom put her on the spot.

"What can I do?" she offered.

"I would like you to go back through all the paperwork, records, anything and everything you have from Doc's files, and perhaps even back at the University to see if you can find anything in those documents that supports or refutes what we now think about the early efforts with this technology development and how it got to Doc and Bob. You might see something differently now that you know what you know. But I don't want anyone else knowing this stuff until we need them to. I will have a couple of my guys meet you there to get you what you need, and for you to show them what they will want to examine. I also have Agent Miloc, from the FBI helping on this effort as well. If there is some connection between this and Doc's death, he will find it. He's the same agent…"

Betty interrupted him midsentence, "Yes, I know who he is. And yes, I'll do what you need. I'm just extra baggage out here anyway, and I really don't want to be anywhere near the people who may have done this." She was holding in her fire, but you could see she would not be able to for much longer, so Tom relieved her.

"Thank you. I have a spot for you on a flight out this evening, so you need to be packed up and over to the airfield before too long. You'll be met when you land, so don't worry about the logistics. Just focus on which documents might be helpful, and what else you might need that you don't already have in New York. Appreciate you Betty, thanks for doing this." Tom moved on to the next topic as what just happened began to sink in for both Ann and Bob. As the meeting broke, the three of them huddled up with Frank for their gameplan.

"I'll be fine," Betty insisted. "You two need to stay here and make all of this work. Besides, you will just get in my way back there. Paperwork, records, research? No offense but that's my expertise not yours. You're needed here; I'm needed there. We get more done if we split up, anyone can see that."

Frank supported her logic, adding, "I agree. Ann, that we could really use you here is an understatement. We will want to get our hands on, or at least a good look at their devices. And by we, I mean you. There is also the Zach component of this which is still a huge unknown. You may be integral in that effort as well."

Ann considered their input, which was all rock solid because it was all true. She conceded her initial reluctance, but it was conditional, "OK, I know you're right, Betty. But I will call my dad and have him link up with you in New York. I want you to have some family around to watch out for you while you are surrounded by all those government guys. Plus, he wants to be part of this in some way; he wants to help so this is a win-win."

"I would appreciate that, if he's willing Ann, thanks."

"I will reach out to him and let him know," Ann offered as Frank added a timeline for all of this.

"Let me get the wheels in motion, literally. We will let you know within the hour where he needs to be, and when. Then we can move him and Betty together from her arrival in New York. Simplifies everything for everyone."

Ann agreed and they headed for the door to prepare for Betty's departure and the other events of the day.

Meanwhile, Mr. Dau was on the phone engaged in an animated call with his boss, the UN Secretary General, as he tried to catch him up on these developments and to get his approval for what they hoped to do next. After several tense exchanges, the tone of the call seemed to de-escalate a bit, and Mr. Dau seemed to be calming down as Frank approached him and asked, "How did it go with the Secretary General?"

"Not very good, but we got the go ahead to handle today like we discussed. Beyond that, I'm not so sure we have his support without some more proof about what we believe is going on here," Mr. Dau explained further.

"He is still in damage control mode from our demonstration. He is more inclined to roll over, let them take this over and whatever else goes wrong is on them and not the UN. Taking their help instead and calling it a collaboration is something he is reluctant to do because we take a big risk with little payoff from shared credit. Best we do is get back to where they saved us from ourselves. If we find that they have been using this for years, then he wants the UN to break that story not the United States. He is going to call your President to get his agreement on that point. If not, then our collaboration stops shortly after today's demonstration. He will pull the plug and we will head home to our respective responsibilities which do not include any further Thor's Hammer activities beyond providing specifically requested support to the CCP as they field this capability," he concluded.

Frank was surprised that was where he landed and spoke his mind, "That seems pretty short-sighted of him, if you ask me."

"Well, that is what I thought, but I failed to convince him of it," Mr. Dau conceded. "Let's hope today goes as planned, and they decide having us aboard might be a better option than leaving us in their wake. The press release should be going out as we speak. The government liaisons are assembling for a discussion, and we should know their decisions shortly. This will inform where, when and how we need to assemble for this afternoon's demo."

"You won't be part of those discussions?" Frank asked, his surprise showing more than he intended.

"No. The Secretary General will participate directly. Both a sign of attrition for the past, and a sign of respect and authority for today's offer. I hope it works; otherwise, we will all be on a flight out tomorrow," Mr. Dau summarized what was at stake as Tom entered and approached the pair where they stood.

After Mr. Dau caught Tom up, he filled them in with his most recent information, "The President was alright with our gameplan for now. Although I can't provide any certainty that he will take the Secretary's demands very well, I don't see him pushing back. The UN reputation has suffered more than the US. We are taking flak by association, but the headlines are all about the UN-led effort. I don't see him falling on that sword, not this early in how this will need to unfold."

"That's good to hear. I think we all could use some good news right now. Do you have any more?" Mr. Dau encouraged.

"Nope. That's all I got, and right now I need to check in with my security guys to make sure we are good to go, wherever we end up having to be for this demonstration," Tom said as he stepped off to do just that.

The same issue was being discussed by the group working diligently on making sure the CCP sponsored demonstration of how on-demand weather modification should be done to ensure the safe and effective outcomes of this amazing technology. In addition to the technical details, the viewing areas, seating charts and security plans were all being revised at the last minute because of the late breaking news from the meeting that just ended. Mr. Wu was being briefed on the changes that appeared to be happening in real time as Zach observed patiently from his assigned spot. It seemed his current task was simply to stay out of the way until he needed to input the recipe into the device with enough lead time to ensure the desired conditions would materialize as directed.

"It seems our UN friends are going to make this somewhat sporting at least," Mr. Wu said loudly and with a smile as he waived Zach over to join him. "Good news for you, Mr. Zach. Today you will have a reunion with your former colleagues Professor Mcleod, and it would appear his now fiancée and your former employee, Ann. You know them both, yes?" he asked politely but already knowing the answer of course.

"Certainly, I am acquainted with them both. And how exactly will this reunion come about?" Zach humored his… Well, at this point, he wasn't sure how to describe his relationship with the man.

"After we input the conditions into our on-site device, you and I and others will join the UN team on the observation platform to watch our great technology in action. We will go through a series of simple commands, changes in conditions that will be small but clearly observable and felt by those in attendance. Then we will up the stakes a bit to show that when properly applied by experts, this powerful and violent beast can be tamed and applied with great accuracy and precision. You will be part of our team that demonstrates that to the world. You will also have the opportunity to see the looks on your former colleagues faces, and even rub their noses in it should you choose to do so. Yes, Mr. Zach, today looks like it is going to be an amazing day for us all, and that includes you.

"The UN team has agreed to collaborate with us on bringing this technology to the world in a safe and equitable way. They did not agree to surrender that task entirely to us, nor did we really expect them to, although we had to try. No, they still believe they are our peer when it comes to this, and they do not trust us to do this equitably without them. I can't say I blame them for that. Today we will embarrass them again when we show them that peers we are not when it comes to our knowledge and experience with this weather production. We have much experience and many advances of which they have no idea. You will help us understand what they have learned and what they still do not understand. You're leaving the facility unannounced on that rogue operation in India has left us in a bit of an information gap between what we knew and what we see."

There it was, that was the value he brought. That is what they really needed from him. It was nothing to do with having or using the Thor's Hammers he had with him. He didn't even know what parameters were being affected for the demonstration today, and if they needed him for that it was very late and high risk to not tell him until the last minute. The only explanation for this lack of interest was their own confidence that they didn't need him for the demonstration at all. They did need him for the intel that he was uniquely able to extract from the other team. That could only mean one of two things. They weren't really doing any demonstration today, or they already had everything they needed including the knowledge to be able to pull this off again, without his help. The latter now being a trend could only mean they have had this long enough to be proficient with its use, and so much so that they could do it with little risk on a global media stage. That meant confidence and proficiency, or a stone bluff, or nothing at all. It was at that point that Zach considered the timing of all this, and that perhaps when Bob came to the research facility with his devices and new technology that maybe, just maybe, it wasn't his or maybe it wasn't new. Now that thought gave Zach a lot of things to consider about his past, but it certainly helped these actions in his present appear to make a lot more sense.

"That all sounds like a marvelous way to spend an afternoon. What exactly do you need me to do today?" he asked Mr. Wu, who spent the next few minutes explaining in detail what he considered the best use of Zach's unique talents for this historic day. It wasn't long after, that they loaded into the same vehicles used for their intervention of the UN demonstration, and a much larger convoy headed out to what Zach thought would likely be the same location as they had used for their previous operation. There was something that felt different about this time compared to the last one.

There was more hurry today, more intensity and purpose from those moving about the underground facility. And there were a lot more of them. There were also more vehicles departing the facility than last time, and a good number more joined the convey at various points along the route. Zach also noticed there were several times that some of the vehicles broke off from the larger group. It was unclear from Zach's limited vantage point whether or not they were the same vehicles or just the same type of vehicles but given terrain and speeds they were travelling it seemed most likely to be the latter.

The vehicle that carried Mr. Wu, Zach and several others was much different on the inside but looked the same as the others on the outside. Theirs contained racks of radios, computers and electronic components that were clearly some sort of command vehicle for the rolling group of wheeled diesel trucks. There were a couple of men glued to their seats and their headsets, listening and watching numbers and images flash across the screens in front of them, but the rest of the men in the back of the truck were not particularly engaged in anything except watching their wrists to see about how much time remained before they arrived at their destination. Any occasional conversation among them was brief, matter of fact, and ended abruptly with a scowl or an eyeroll from one or the other. While it appeared everyone was going to the same place, it did not appear they were all on the same page about what was coming next. This gave Zach something to wonder about, and it certainly appeared that he had the time to let his mind wander for a while before they got him to wherever they wanted him for today.

He ran a plethora of scenarios through his mind, with various assumptions and timelines, and potential objectives. It was like an equation with all variables and no constants. So, it could only be solved in terms where each variable was dependent on an unknown constant. The solution could only be expressed in relative terms to each variable. Then Zach realized that he could express one variable with certainty, and that would allow him to better understand the rest of the puzzle. He could say with certainty that Doc Auster had indeed developed the Thor's Hammers and Bob came upon them, and the history that Zach was directly involved in was the true accounting. That would lead to one likely set of events he would encounter for the rest of the day. There was another possible certainty to consider, with the opposite assumption.

What if that Doc was only part of the story? What if the CCP was aware of, or even had the technology and Doc discovered what they had already known about? Using that assumption as a constant at the beginning of the equation would produce an entirely different outcome for today from the same variables in the same equation. That would also mean Zach's day would be something completely different than if the first assumption were applied as true. Either could be true, and Zach had no way to be certain at this point from his position in the unfolding events. But that was just an inconvenience, as Zach did not get to his lofty positions by guessing or not knowing. No, he was used to being in similar positions and learned early on that your odds of succeeding increase dramatically if you hope for the best, plan for the worst and expect the most likely. That said, he was missing some data to help him sufficiently understand that range of possibilities.

It was possible that they both were true he thought. It could be that they both developed their own versions of Thor's Hammer independently but on very different timelines. Possible but not likely. It was also possible, but not likely that both the CCP and Doc Auster got their versions from a third party of which Zach was also unaware. But his two front running theories were the CCP lifted the technology from the research facility which Zach had personally made available to them. He knew that was the most likely, and is what he had in the way of value to the men whom he was riding in the back of the truck. But he could not shake how neatly the recent past and now unfolding events could fit into another scenario where the CCP had this capability for much longer than was possible if they got it from Bob the same time he did at his facility. That equation would likely meet the criteria of plan for the worst, but given everything over the course of the past few days it also seemed to fit into the most likely category as well.

As Zach pondered the concept that the worst case and the most likely case both appeared to be the same if he assumed they had it before Bob and Doc, that little voice reminded him of what didn't quite fit the narrative while he and Mr. Wu were being recognized for their roles in the big wind event that resulted in today's opportunity. At that point something clicked in Zach's mind that provided him both a level of certainty about his situation as well as clarity about what he needed to do next. As he sat back and pondered his options about how to accomplish what he considered needed to be his next actions, the truck began to slow and he could hear the brakes being applied ahead of, beneath, and behind them. It sounded like they were arriving at their destination or a scheduled stop. It was unclear until he heard voices shouting and doors opening. They were at what appeared to be a remote location, but there were also a series of fuel trucks dispensing diesel to the convoy. Troops and men in a variety of civilian attire were stretching, walking around and relieving themselves along the side of the road. Nobody was concerned about traffic from either direction, nor were they concerned about being seen. This was an interim stop for sure, which meant Zach probably had a fair amount of time to ponder the challenge he seemed to be making some progress on.

As he completed the same ongoing tasks as the rest of the passengers and turned toward the truck he had exited a few moments earlier, he was startled when Mr. Wu took him by the arm and provided new instructions.

"No Mr. Zach, our time in the trucks is done for now. We have a more visible task today. We will call it as you say, a white-collar day from here. No longer a blue-collar day for us. That will be for others today. We will be waiting here for a little while first and then we will proceed to the events for the day. Please come with me and we will wait over here for a while." Of course, Zach complied as he wondered what was in store as the convoy began to reload almost all their discharged passengers and roll away down the isolated road. There were only five people remaining in their small group. Zach, Mr. Wu, two of the uniformed men from their truck who both appeared to be general officers of some kind, and another man whom he had not seen before wearing an expensive tailored suit but lacking an overcoat appropriate for the conditions at the roadside.

Watching for traffic from either direction seemed futile, and Zach realized it was when he heard the first sounds of rotors in the distance beating the cool thin air. As the helicopter got closer, the group began to prepare for what they seemed to already know was their transport for the next leg of the journey. They may have known, but Zach did not. And once again, he was slapped with the realization that he was only being told what they wanted him to believe and not what was going to happen. As the helicopter landed, a crewman hopped off and instructed them where to load into the helicopter where he saw the same Provincial Governor from his earlier meeting already seated aboard. The crewman then moved to one of the two remaining trucks, grabbed a hose from the side, turned some valves and then stretched it to begin refueling the helicopter now that its rotors had stopped turning. As soon as he finished, Zach could feel the engines spooling up and they were quickly lifting off and heading toward their destination.

As Zach settled into his seat and adjusted for the ride and the noise of the large helicopter, he looked around at the others seated there. Each man looked somber as they appeared to be contemplating and rehearsing in their heads what they were to do upon arrival. Zach considered for a moment that perhaps, like him, they were wondering what would come next, but he then dismissed the notion of parity. They may very well have been wondering what was going to happen next, but they each knew what was supposed to happen and what they were supposed to do to ensure it did. Zach on the other hand, knew neither of those things. It was becoming increasingly clear that they did not care at all about him, and that it was solely Mr. Wu's responsibility to keep him in check and on task. That was something that would surely come in handy today Zach thought as they headed south.

CHAPTER ELEVEN

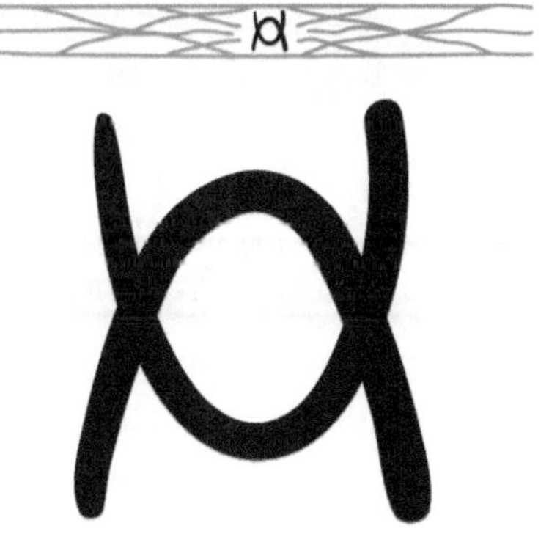

SECOND CHANCES

The helicopter circled downwind and nosed up as it flared and settled down, landing precisely on the designated spot. With rotors turning the passengers disembarked and as soon as they were clear the bird lumbered into the sky and flew toward the horizon, its visual and noise profiles disappearing quickly as those assembled focused more on who had been delivered than what delivered them.

Bob and the others from the UN team watched closely as the passengers exited the helicopter and were both relieved and disappointed when they could see that Zach was among the arriving CCP delegation. That was only one of several airborne entrances for the event today, but there were far fewer in attendance for this one than had been assembled at the same location for the previous event. The host nation was taking no risks for a second disaster should something similar happen out here today. There was a single viewing stand with a main stage and seating for the various national and UN delegations. There were no civilian spectators where the throngs of people had been before, but it seemed there were more press and cameras than before if that was even possible. One thing was for certain; whatever happened today would be covered even better than the events that led to today.

As Zach walked toward the reviewing stand, flanked by Mr. Wu and the others from his helicopter they were joined and escorted by the host nation security details who ushered them to their assigned seating. Much effort went into the protocol for this event to ensure that no important issues were undermined by some seemingly small detail that inadvertently offended someone sufficiently to distract from the reasons they were assembled today. Without any fanfare or warning, the narrator for the event stood, introduced himself and, on behalf of their President, welcomed all the distinguished visitors on hand for the demonstration. And with that, turned over the podium and microphone to the CCP spokesperson who described why they were there and what they would see demonstrated today.

"Today we will show the breadth of conditions that can be altered with our technology. We will begin with a few parameters that you can feel, and end with some you can see. It is important that confidence in our technology be restored after the unfortunate event at this very site which made today necessary. So, that is where we will begin. In a very short time, you will feel the wind shift and come from the east, at precisely eleven knots. It will persist for exactly three minutes and then fall back to light and variable as it is right now." He paused to ensure the cameras had a good view of both the digital readouts from the modern electronic anemometer, as well as the old school spinning three-cup device that mechanically measured the wind speed.

The UN team was not at all happy to hear the words "our technology" repeatedly used. Nor were they very appreciative of the immediate reference to the previous wind disaster, but they took those comments on the chin because they understood what this new group was doing and why they were doing it. The hard part was going to be proving it by exposing their treachery to the world in an indisputable manner. As they waited patiently for the wind to come up, Bob kept his gaze fixed on Zach. He wanted to make eye contact. He needed Zach to see his intensity and react to it. He needed to see if that first look was one of smugness and disdain for his inferior...or, if it was something else. Bob wasn't sure what else that look might be, but he hoped beyond hope that it would be something other than what he expected from someone who had deliberately used Thor's Hammers to cause a disastrous flood that claimed many lives in exchange for money. Bob could feel the wind beginning to come up along with the tensions of those who had also been on-site for the last demonstration. Unlike the previous event, this one behaved flawlessly just as described by the narrator who continued to address the attendees, but seemed to be fixated on the cameras capturing the event.

"As the winds continue to subside as promised, you should already begin to notice a slight cooling of the air. Again, I would call your attention to the digital and mercury thermometers side by side. You will see the temperature drop precisely five degrees in Fahrenheit, or two point eight degrees Celsius. This will begin in one minute, drop down and stay for two minutes, then climb back up to the ambient air temperature. You will both feel and see this on our instruments. And while this temperature change is occurring, our system operators are already programming the inputs for the next condition we will be modifying for you today. But for now, please focus your attentions on the thermometers as they begin to register the cooler air that we promised you." Again, he paused for the cameras as they focused on the decreasing numbers indicating the promised drop in temperature.

While the ambient air temperature was dropping Bob's was rising along with his blood pressure, his gaze remained fixed on Zach who seemed to be glued to what the briefer was saying. The fact that Zach had no idea what was coming next, nor that he had no active role in the demonstration thus far was troubling for Zach but also completely unknown to Bob and the UN team until Captain Lessur asked what should have been an obvious question to nobody in particular, "Who is doing the inputs, and where are their devices? Can you see them, I don't see them."

He was bobbing and weaving to gain a better vantage point of the delegation but they all appeared to be just as much spectators as everyone else. It was right about the time that synapse fired for Bob that Zach turned his head toward the UN team's location and almost as if following a laser, he locked eyes with Professor Mcleod.

Zach's face was stoic, and he did not blink as both he and Bob stood still and silent. The now familiar voice of the CCP narrator came across the speaker, and Bob perceived the slightest of east to west movement of Zach's head as he turned his attention to the speaker resuming his comments. As Bob played the three second encounter over and over in his head, he was increasingly convinced that Zach's look was not one of victory or gloating over his accomplishments. It was precisely mirroring the stoicism of the delegation that surrounded them. His look was exactly that of the CCP member with whom he was seated. There was no emotion, no celebration, nothing. This was all business for them, and they were there to ensure that all went well. They were collectively holding their breath until this was over. The only difference was that Zach, if only for a moment, looked over at the UN team. None of the others did so far. Nor would they at any time during the entire demonstration.

"As I mentioned earlier, the next event is already underway. You will notice some clouds increasing off to the west. You will also notice these are building rapidly, which is not terribly common for this location especially for this time of year. Please notice that, as this cloud grows, the area around it and here for us will remain clear of clouds. This will give you an unobstructed view of the developing rain shower. In several minutes you will be able to see the top of the cloud begin to cap. It will become flat and the rain shaft will be visible as the precipitation falls over the designated area, but we shall remain clear and dry here. This will take another four to five minutes to reach the established level and then I will reveal the last item of our demonstration for today. If you will indulge me a few moments and observe our technology at work in the distance as this rain shower continues to grow just as I described." Again, he paused for the cameras to zoom in and capture the cloud formation behaving just as if it was reading the script and doing what it was told.

And just like before, Bob saw Zach turn his head and look their way. The same stoic look, the same three second unblinking stare, and perhaps most importantly the same almost imperceptible east to west to east twitch before he rejoined the formation of heads and eyes forward. Once may have been a fluke but twice seemed deliberate, or perhaps it was nothing at all.

"I don't see anyone or anything that looks like they are doing what we did with our demonstrations. Nobody is holding or carrying anything that looks like our devices. And nobody looks like they are doing anything other than watching what is happening. They are all 'eyes forward'. They aren't looking over here to even acknowledge our presence, let alone give any indication they want to work with us. Not even talking to us at this point, and I don't see that changing at this rate," Frank stated what everyone else was also seeing and feeling.

"They are operating remotely again," Captain Lessur said calmly. "They have some range calculations, and they must have great confidence in the precision of their operations that we don't have yet. We need to make sure we are looking at this demonstration the same way we did the last one. We need to have everything looking on this spot and expand out in concentric rings until we can see, hear and sense everything they are using. And we'll keep looking until we find it all."

"Finally, someone who gets me." Tom smiled at the urgency in the captain's voice but responded in a calm, quiet tone, "Spot on young man, spot on! Everything we have that listens, sniffs, looks or senses has been focused on this spot since well before we started and will be long after we end here today. Whatever is here, or near here, we will know everything about it and if we don't know it already, we soon will. I need to bring something to this team besides my wit and good looks."

That drew a few smirks and eyerolls from the UN group, but the attempt at humor was appreciated as much as it was needed given the circumstances. And, as if on cue to break the smiles, the narrator began to speak again.

"The rain is beginning in the distance, if you look closely, you can see the outer edge of the rain shaft beginning to form as the precipitation created by our technology begins to fall and quench the parched earth below. This in itself is a feat of tremendous skill and precision. To produce rain on-demand, and with such precision in location, intensity and timing. But I did promise you one more event today, and it is time that I reveal that to you as well. We chose the precise location and intensity of the rain, and when factoring in the location of the sun, and the viewing stand at this precise time of day we can bring you for the next forty seconds the ultimate gift of confidence in our technology and our ability to operate it safely and effectively. Ladies and gentlemen, please look to the east and behold, we bring you hope along with that confidence," and as he stopped speaking, the voices of those in attendance and those operating the cameras all began to rise as they began to find it in their field of view. A rainbow.

As it became increasingly vivid from the changing angle of the sun, the delegation from the CCP began to clap, and the rest of those attending in person followed suit including the UN team. To say it was impressive would be an understatement. The vivid colors showing against the gray sky with the sun at their backs was quite the sight to behold. Say what you will about the motivation behind the event, the theatrics, timing and impact were nothing short of impressive. But while everyone was marveling at the rainbow finale, Zach shot another glance over to the UN team amid the clapping of his delegation. He saw Bob staring right at him. Zach showed the same stoicism, no blinking and another slight but perceptible headshake. He wanted them to see, but hoped no one else would notice. Three looks, all identical, all meaning something. He hoped Bob or someone would notice, and he also hoped they would figure out what it meant. Right now, for everyone else it was all smiles and rainbows as the world watched the unprecedented finale.

"You have to admit that is impressive," Ann said as she stared at the refracted light across the color spectrum that was the rainbow only now beginning to fade. "To do that is one thing, to do that on cue is an epic level up. We were right, they've had this long before they could have gotten it from Bob and Doc."

At that moment the narrator began his closing remarks, "Ladies and gentlemen we hope today's demonstration restores your faith in our technology and the skill in which it can be operated when in the hands of those who understand it, and more importantly know how to use it safely. It is a precision technology that was developed to be used as such. And while it has been revealed to you by the UN before our development and testing were finalized, we are confident that we can work with the UN team to safely complete the development and rigorous testing needed to employ this technology around the world in a safe, orderly and just way.

"That will take time, but with your support and patience, we will be able to bring these benefits to everyone while avoiding a repeat of the catastrophe that unfolded here just a few short days ago. The safety protocols, system overrides, and intense calculations that should be implemented before every use are complex but can be taught and proliferated to those with the skills and the discipline to adhere to them. We will share these with the UN team to assist them and will gladly accept their input regarding when and where to use our technology, as well as, who is advanced and trustworthy enough to operate it on their own. It is our hope that today's events will lead to the healing needed to recover from the past and reignite the hope that this promising technology can bring for all. Thank you very much."

And with that he rejoined the delegation, and they all began to walk toward the short aluminum stairs at the side of the platform. As the media shouted questions at the departing group, the sound of rotors became audible and quickly grew louder as the small group increased their distance from the platform. Less than one hundred meters from the platform the helicopter landed, ingested the men and lifted off for the horizon. Their exit was as impressive as the demonstration. They left the media in a mic-drop moment, taking no questions and providing nothing beyond what was scripted for the narrator. No elaboration, no next steps, no timeline, just the promise to do good and play nice with others including the UN despite what they did. It was well planned, well executed, and well covered by the global media. Calling it a success would be a substantial understatement.

As the UN team watched it all unfold and wrap up around them it was hard to feel anything but a little defeated. Sensing that, Tom smiled and clapped his hand on Frank's shoulder and said, "Damn, that was some seriously deep bullshit we were just privileged enough to see in person. Flash, bang look over here at what we say and ignore what you see us doing right in front of you. Some serious stones on these guys! Wow that was ballsy!" he challenged. "I cannot wait until we get back to start our debrief; let's do it right here. Ann, I think you were spot on earlier as was my new favorite Air Force O-3! They weren't operating from here, nor was this their first rodeo with this thing. A rainbow? For the love of all things holy, what could be better than a rainbow? What else did we learn today class?" This was out of character for Tom from what the team had seen so far but he appeared genuinely excited about what had everyone else down in the mouth until right now.

"They made a commitment to help but didn't promise anything about what that might look like or what kind of timeline they were considering. You could drive a truck through the commitment without details. They could disappear and still claim they did what they promised," Frank offered. "They committed to working with us, but did not define what that would look like either. That puts it in our court if we want to play it that way. We could go on offense with that opening and lean into establishing the timeline and conditions for what we want to learn or do."

"I like that, what else?" Tom encouraged, "There's more; come on now."

Ann added, "Whatever they have at this point is both political and military. They were both mixed into the delegation, and what we saw from the first demonstration it looks like they are comfortable operating in or near here. So, while we don't know how far their capability extends, we do know that they are very capable and comfortable operating in this region."

"Yes, Ann. What else?" Tom pushed.

"We are close to the border, but that doesn't mean the border means anything. Right? I mean a border only exists on a map, especially in this kind of terrain. We had two catastrophic events that we know about that we have attributed to Thor's Hammer, and they were both in India. We find the Chinese operating up here near the border. What if India isn't just an unlucky spot where people go to test their technology. What if they are working with the Chinese on this? Being the 'victim' sure is good cover if you are really in cahoots on an emerging technology that could forever change the global balance of power. They were quick to let this second demonstration take place on the same spot. We must consider the possibility that they might at least know more than they let on. They might even be involved," she posited.

"Damn!" Tom quipped. "That is something we do need to consider and examine. Not where I was leaning, but definitely why we have these sessions. What else?"

"Zach," Bob said and then paused far too long. "I watched Zach the entire time. I don't even remember seeing a rainbow. I just saw him, didn't see anything else. As much as I want to hate him for all of this, and much as I want to blame him for all those deaths…I don't think it was him. Oh, believe me I want to, but I think he was telling me it wasn't him. I want to look at every image, every angle of him that we can find to see if I saw what I think I saw. Let's see if you see the same thing or if I imagined it."

"Bob, what is it you think you saw?" Tom asked.

"Three times, he looked right at me. Just for a moment each time. He was expressionless, he didn't blink not once. And I could swear he just slightly shook his head each time. I think he wanted me to see him see me. He looked just like and did the same thing as everyone around him, except he was indicating he wasn't like them. He wasn't with them willingly. That little almost imperceptible shake was telling me he looks like he is one of them but he is not. He did the same thing three times. It had to be for me to see it."

Ann added, "The Zach I knew, always smirked or winked when he knew he had you. Whether it was a difficult problem someone was struggling with and he knew the answer to, or if he had something he knew you needed and he would give it to you before you asked for it. He always enjoyed being a little or a lot ahead of someone else. It was a game to him, and he enjoyed being better at it than others. He had us; they beat us with that wind event. And the rainbow, at the end. If that was him, I swear he would have rubbed it in our faces. But he didn't and between the wind event and today's show he would have lots of smack to talk if we were back at the research facility. Bob, you might be on to something."

Frank bit his lip and wondered aloud, "Three strikes and you're out."

Tom immediately bit on the reference, and asked Bob, "Are you sure it was three times? Could you have missed one, or maybe gave him extra credit for one because you were so pissed at him?"

"No Tom, I was fixated on him. I couldn't see anything else. Three times, all the same," he declared.

"Damn it, Frank you might be right," Tom considered. "Like Bob said, let's get every angle we can and see if we see it too."

"What does this mean?" Ann asked Tom.

"I don't know if it means anything yet, but it could be Zach's asking us to get him out. Three strikes and you're out, just like in baseball. Zach might have been trying to tell Bob, 'I look like them, I am doing what they are doing but I am really not.' Not blinking normally is a sign of duress. Three times and you're out might just mean get me out. I want to be out, or because I have three strikes I need to be out. Our asshole, Zach, may or not be what we thought. So why would we assume he was what he seemed when nothing else about this entire story seems to be what we thought it was? Now we need to get him so we can find out for sure. The question for us right now is that what we need to do, or is that what they want us to do?" Tom wondered aloud.

Captain Lessur added his perspective next, "If they let us close to him, let us talk to him about this technology it's because they know he is with them. If they won't let us near him, it's because they don't trust him. We already know they don't like and don't trust us. They flew off in a helicopter so trying to get something together in time to snatch him now would be a tall ask. But to get him, we also must consider his traveling companions. They know we can't risk an attempt to get Zach if they can make it look like we were making a play on a CCP Provincial Governor and some generals.

I guess that means they don't want us going after Zach, doesn't it? Maybe we just learned that too?"

"Damn, young man you continue to impress!" Tom said sincerely. "What else, anyone?"

Bob added one more thought. "We need to look again to see that Father Gannon's story checks out, Tom. If everything else is in question, we need to look there too. He had one device and Doc had the other. If they killed Doc because they found out he had their technology or knew their secret, why wouldn't they have found the Hammers and his files and everything else before they killed him? Why not get all the evidence and then unalive him after they had it all, or at least knew what he had and what he did with it? Doc did not strike me as the kind of guy who would hold up very well under any type of interrogation, physical stress, torture, or whatever. I think he would have given them what they wanted if they pressed hard. There is something else that we are not seeing. Maybe Betty will find something, but we need to look all across the beginning not just at the notes and the grant. Something doesn't add up with there being two devices. I didn't know about the other one until Father Gannon told me about it."

"Agreed," Tom added. "Is this fun or what? I told you we couldn't wait to get back to have this conversation. Think of what else we might be missing or assuming that needs challenging after what we saw here today."

"I think we need to take the initiative after today, but we need a judo move next." Mr. Dau, quiet until now added his observation, "These guys impressed everyone today with their control, range and precision. The rainbow was thick icing on an already good cake. We need to jump on their offer and nail them down to some details as soon as possible, right?

"I think we get the Secretary General on the phone, right away. We can ask him to gladly accept all help the CCP has offered and commit to a detailed schedule of information exchanges, trainings and even a few specific employments of weather events that will help resolve ongoing concerns like a lack of rain or some other condition where a practical intervention using this technology in the near term will be considered urgent, but a lack of participation would be considered not aligned with the promises made. I am confident he will go along with that after seeing what we saw here today."

"OK, I like that, too. What else can you think of folks?" Tom paused and looked around the group who all seemed to be processing what they had seen today, and what was revealed and discussed immediately afterward.

"Yeah, me too. That was a lot. Do we still need to do a debrief or do you all have enough to do for a few hours?" The pause was the answer. "Ok I know I have a lot to do in a short amount of time, as it seems you do as well. If you're not taking some of the actions we just covered, be thinking about the likely outcomes and what comes next. I would like to get back together in about four hours to touch base and see where everyone is. That will let the media pot simmer on this event long enough to get a read on what people are thinking and doing. Hopefully, the Secretary General's announcement is out by then, and we have something to talk about from what we were able to see, hear and sniff out during our collections. Conference room in four hours everyone, see you then," Tom said as he and the group began the short walk to the waiting vehicles.

On the way, Tom fell in step with Bob and Ann and quietly asked them, "Gut check. Is Zach the bad guy or is it possible he's scapegoated on this? First thought that comes to your mind, right now."

Ann and Bob responded at the same time, "Both!" as they looked surprised at each other, then at Tom.

"That's exactly what I was afraid of, but thanks. It is what it is," he said as they climbed aboard for the short drive back to their compound.

CHAPTER TWELVE

YOU SAID YOU WOULD DO IT

I t didn't take long for her to pack and get to the airfield. She said her goodbyes to everyone she cared to, and as she sat there with Ann waiting for the crew to allow her to board the aircraft Betty confided, "I am worried about leaving you and Bob here. This is not the normal he is used to being around. I think this guy Zach is in Bob's head, and all these people dying in the earlier flooding and then during the demonstration are just all jumbled together right now, and he feels responsible for all of it. I understand why, but you gotta help him see through that and lay the blame where it belongs. He needs to know that's not on him. I can say it to him, but he won't accept it until you convince him of it. That has to come from you, not me or Frank or Tom or anyone else.

"I will do everything in my power to find something in those files and paperwork back there, and will help whoever shows up for Tom to do the same. But even if we don't find anything, you still need to make him see that it's not on him. Promise me?"

"Of course," Ann promised. "You know as well as anyone that 'making Bob Mcleod do anything' are words that don't really go together. But that is my problem not yours. And while we are making promises and discussing problems, we might as well talk about my dad, too," she smiled.

"Oh dear, I am not worried about Steve he won't be a problem," Betty assured her.

"You misunderstand me, Betty, it's you that I don't want to be a problem. I saw how well you two got along, and I haven't seen my dad that at ease in I can't remember how long. It's been me, the shop and keeping the 'uncles' and their families taken care of for a long time. He always puts himself at the bottom of his take-care-of list. And I know you have been alone for quite a while, too. Now I am not playing match maker here, but I want you to know that if there is something there, I don't want either one of you worrying about what that might mean to me or Bob. You do you, whatever that looks like just promise me that you won't *not* do anything because of me. Or Bob, or me and Bob? Whatever, you know what I mean?" she asked flustered but glad to have said whatever she just said to Betty.

"Yeah Ann, I know what you mean. And thank you for saying it. I am looking forward to seeing your dad again, but don't go blabbing about it to anyone. I have a reputation to maintain." She smiled as she stood up in response to the call for her to walk out to the waiting aircraft that would start her journey back to New York. She gave Ann a big hug, and said, "You focus on what you need to do, and I will take care of things back there. Let's both go do what we do best." And, with that, she followed the ground crewman out the door and onto the tarmac toward the readied aircraft. Ann watched as Betty stepped onto the ramp and walked up into the belly of the military transport where she would take a seat among the small group of passengers and the securely strapped down pallets of cargo.

It didn't take Ann long to rejoin Bob who was busy typing into one of the computers he had been accustomed to having with him most of the time.

"Well, she is on her way. What can I help you with?" Ann asked.

"Honestly, at this point I just need you to tell me that you love me, and you don't think I am crazy. Go ahead and lie to me if you must, but I could really use hearing it. It'd be even better if you meant it, even just a little bit." Bob tried to make light of it, but she could tell there was more truth than joke in his request and she could oblige honestly to both asks.

"OK, Robert Mcleod, I like you a lot and it's ok to be a little crazy," she tried but failed to keep a straight face and he cringed a little. "Wait, wait a minute I know I can do better just give me a second." As she made a second attempt, she walked toward him and put her arms around his neck and looked up at him.

"I do love you, a lot of the time and especially when I don't think you're crazy which is some of the time. But more of the time lately? Does that help, or should I take another run at this?" she asked and kissed his cheek and then smiled again.

"Yes, that really didn't help at all, and I will stop while I can still convince myself that I'm ahead somehow. You really know how to lift a guy's spirits, Ann. Wow! It's quite the superpower you have but are really not good at using." He poked a little fun back at her.

"You know, none of this is your fault?" Her tone changed but her smile and demeanor did not. "You didn't ask for any of this to happen to you, and you sure didn't do any of this to anyone who got hurt over here. That's all on someone else—Zach, the Chinese whoevers, maybe the Indians—who knows right now? We will figure it out. In the meantime, I need you to know it's not on you. And the only way you are going to convince me that you know that is by me hearing you say it…and convince me you mean it." It was clear at this point she was not asking.

"I know this is not on me, Ann. I know it's on them, but that doesn't mean I can stop feeling their pain which was brought on by the device I brought into the light. They are separate but related events. If I hadn't…" Bob stopped in midsentence as Ann cut him off.

"You stop right there! You don't even get to finish that thought let alone that sentence. It doesn't matter here what you did or didn't do. It's not about you, that is your Catholic guilt in overdrive, Bob! What matters, and the only thing that matters here is what *they* did. Those people are dead, and they are dead because of what somebody else did! Not you…them. What they did! Full stop. Done!" She was shouting at him at this point but she was not done yet.

"What you need to do now is make them pay for what they did. You do that by figuring this thing out and finishing what you started. And you don't get to do that alone. *You* can't do that alone; you don't even get to think about or even try to do that alone. *We* do that together. That's what *we* do! You, me, Betty, Frank, Tom and the rest of all the *we* that are out there. *We* hold them responsible for what *they* did! That's what *you* do. *You* bring your best you so *we* can succeed." She paused to regain her composure, let that sink in and wipe the tears from her eyes.

"Thank you. I hear you, pretty sure everyone heard you," he smiled and continued, "but know that I heard you. I will bring my best me. Thank you, and I love you," he said as they hugged the long hug that both of them had needed for a while and had finally found a path to get there. Ann was relieved to hear Bob's words, and happy to have already kept the promise to Betty she had made less than an hour ago. That, she considered, was a promise well kept.

As Bob and Ann entered the briefing room, they were greeted with a flurry. Something big was already happening, and it wasn't going to stop so everyone could bring the two of them up to speed on what they had apparently missed already. Captain Lessur saw them and waived them over as he was talking into a phone and looking at a series of open windows on a large computer monitor on his makeshift desk. He motioned for them to look at the screen, rather the various videos simultaneously running on the screen.

"What's all the commotion Ron?" Ann asked for both of them.

"We got 'em. Most of them anyway, maybe all of them, not sure yet," he told Ann with one hand over the microphone of the phone he held with the other hand. His radio headset occupied the other ear, as he was clearly doing more than one thing right now. They waited patiently until he was able to pause long enough to fill them in on what they were watching, but also what they were missing on the phone and radio calls.

"We have at least six of them, there may have been eight but the first two may already be in. We are reviewing the video to see if or where they were earlier," Captain Lessur began.

"Six or eight what?" Bob asked.

"Balloon teams," he smiled. "Bob they are using balloons for their sensor employments. We have live, full-motion video from some high altitude drone getting the tail end of their recovery ops right now, and we are rolling back the clock on the other sensors to get as much as we can on what and how they did this one.

"It looks like they have an SOP for this that is pretty interesting. What I've seen is the balloons each have a suspended instrument package, one maybe two sensors each, and what must be both power and communications gear. Batteries and radios essentially to talk to and control the devices and the balloons. It looks like a basic but smart tactical plan; low risk because they are using two different types of balloons. The first is a tethered aerostat—basically a small blimp on a cable attached to a winch which, for these guys, is mounted on the back of a military truck. The aerostat goes up a couple thousand feet. It looks like they use that to hold device number one in one spot...

"...and elevation likely increases effective range," Ann finished his sentence.

"Yes, they use that one to create the wind direction and speed needed to get a second device into the position they want for the conditions they are creating. That second balloon is a free-floating helium filled one, with what looks like an electric motor to assist in maneuvering and elevation. This lets them put the free floater where they want it and recover it wherever they want to, because they are controlling the winds with the device on the aerostat. With three teams, they likely used a different one for each of the demonstration items. So, we are still looking for one more team," he concluded.

"That is all good to know, but how does it help us in the near term? We saw a balloon before, now we know how they did this one. They had to know we would be watching, so what else were they doing somewhere else while we were looking at this stuff?" Frank asked from the sideline where he had been standing for over a minute as the group was catching up.

"We know how long it takes them to get one in place. We know what platforms to look at or look for. We know they are working old school," Bob offered.

"We know that is what they want us to believe. Wouldn't that fit nicely into the line of thinking that this is an emerging technology versus one they have had and used operationally for years now. Let me ask you Bob, if you want, or need, long loiter time for these devices to produce the desired conditions would balloons be a good choice? A weatherman's first choice out of convenience or familiarity, or the best choice to do this with?" Frank asked.

Bob's response was clunky but correct, "Balloons are good platforms, especially the aerostat."

"Agreed, but would it be your platform of choice if you could have your pick? And if you could have your pick, what would be the best platform for this not just one that was familiar, convenient, or good enough?" Frank pressed.

But, before Bob could answer, Ann jumped in, "UAVs would be better. Unmanned Aerial Vehicles. And they wouldn't need to be very big to carry or employ the devices we know about. Maneuverable, long loiter time, on-board power; everything a balloon does and more capability, less risk," she offered.

"Put them on a Predator or a Global Hawk and you wouldn't even know they were there. Heck, that's what's giving us what we're watching on our desk right now is basically live video from one or more of those. Damn, and you could *see* what was happening while you are doing it. Yep, count me in with Ann and let's do these from UAVs," the captain cast his vote.

"So, if we stick with our premise that they've had this technology for at least five years, do you think they didn't have enough time to come up with that same idea which only took us five minutes to like better than balloons? And, wouldn't using balloons make it a lot easier to discover than a UAV or RPV?" (Remotely Piloted Vehicle.)

"Yes, Frank it would. But what if using an RPV would have raised more suspicion if it were spotted somewhere a balloon would not? Bob and Ron, what do you guys use back home on your range and your weather study area—balloons with stuff hanging underneath them or drones with stuff stuck all over the sides of them?" Tom asked as he walked into the ongoing conversation.

"Balloons," was Bob's response.

"Same," from Captain Lessur.

"Yep. But we confirmed they used balloons only, for anywhere near this demonstration. We have every aircraft, big and small documented and all the drones are known most of them being ours. That's how we got the balloons while they were still in play. They were easy to find, and maybe they wanted us to see them because none of these were tactical launches. Nobody is hiding anything about the balloons," Tom concluded.

"If this was a new technology for us, we would start on the ground. Maybe consider using some weather balloons to try some airborne tests to increase the range or precision of our devices. So that's what they showed us, that was what they want us to see because it bolsters their current narrative. It's plausible, we watched them do it so we know it is true because we saw it with our own eyes, and our own intelligence systems, and we trust these. We are focused on what we saw and what we are seeing now. It fits, and we have our own proof. So that's what we are going with right now. Thor's Hammers deployed using paired balloons and the expertise and precision to make a rainbow for the cameras. Right now, that makes them better than us but close enough that, with some dedication and effort and some time, we can become just as capable as they are. Especially if we work with them on getting that good, we can do it that much faster right? They aren't that far ahead of us; we can catch up if we focus, can't we?" Tom asked.

"Yes. We have already made good progress in using what we have. I have an extensive recipe list, but all my events and testing have been from fixed ground locations. I'm pretty sure the Zach did some tests where it was moving to see what happened in motion, but Ann and I were gone by then. Shortly after was India, and here we are. With some insights from them, we can save some time and understand what if anything being in motion or elevated does to the performance of Thor's Hammers," Bob responded.

"Good then that is what you will be doing. And we will insist on getting you some time with Zach to help that process along. You will follow that line of reasoning and what looks like the script they have handed us," Tom paused and looked at Frank. "And Frank, you will be his wingman and do whatever you can to convince them this is where our focus is, and that we are all in to collaborate with them. Learn everything we can about what they have and how they do this."

Frank nodded, and then asked what the others were wondering, "So if we are convincing them this is the main effort, that sure sounds like it's not going to be. What is the main effort, and how do I steer them away from whatever that will be, Tom?"

As he smiled, he replied, "Colonel, you will steer them away from it by going all-in like we just talked about. They get Bob and Ann and Mr. Dau. The UN's A-team on this with the full backing of the US military and all that it can bring to this effort. You keep them and us fully engaged in advancing this just like the story is written. This takes us where we need to get, and they will help us get to where they want us to go. They offered to help and we embrace that, we let them and we appreciate them for all of it. And if that's all there is to this, then that gets us right where we need to be and the actions we choose come from that playbook. This course of action is based on what we know, and that is our main effort, but it won't be our only effort.

"Because if we are right, and it looks very much like we are, then we need some dynamic alternate courses of action that we can employ based on what we learn and when we learn it. I will take that and keep running with it, but I am gonna need Captain Lessur or Sergeant Andies. I need some weather skills on my team to cover that gap. Take the best fit for the main effort but you can't have them both," Tom added.

"No offense, Andy, but they will put more credence in our story if we have an officer on the team. They are structured that way, and I am confident they will expect a degreed meteorologist to be our go-to on such a priority effort," Frank explained, and his logic was sound.

"None taken, Colonel, it's precisely that way in our military so that makes perfect sense. Follow the script. I'll get Tom what he needs for whatever it is we are going to be doing," Sergeant Andies responded with no hard feelings. It is what it is, whether that makes it right was a topic for another day with a different purpose. "Do you know what that is going to be yet, Tom?"

"I know what I want to look for, but I don't know exactly how we will know if we find it," he began. "Let's talk through this a little right now, so main effort knows what to be on the lookout for while you are doing your thing. So, we think they have had this for at least five years. We believe Doc and maybe Father Gannon got their devices somehow from the Chinese efforts. Doc's demise is how Bob got involved and in short order he was able to reproduce Thor's Hammer. We discovered that, took it to our best secret R&D facility and that is how Zach got it, then went rogue stole a couple and used them in India. The UN rolls out a global fielding plan, and now we have Zach show up with the CCP as they claim it's their technology. We think they used the Thor's Hammers within our demonstration to undermine our program and take it over. They do their own demonstration using the Thor's Hammers we think they got from Zach, and maybe some copies they were able to do themselves. That is what they have shown us mixed in with a little that we have been able to discover on our own. That is their version and ours, but we have poked a few small holes in this narrative. But what do all these things have in common?" Tom asked the group as they responded in unison.

"It begins and ends with Chinese involvement of some kind," was the theme of the responses, but Tom pushed for more. "What else?"

"Weather?"… "Bob?" … "There is always something more or different than what it first looks like." … "People keep dying around it?" were all answers that came quickly.

"Yes, but what else?" Tom persisted and it was Andies who spoke next.

"Thor's Hammer. This whole story line revolves around the devices. Everything we know is connected to or around the devices. But the devices are simply the delivery method of the technology. We found some of the holes in the story by following a couple of the main parts. That is where we solidified the connection to CCP. If we fixate on Thor's Hammers this main effort makes perfect sense. But if we consider the technology instead of the delivery device, maybe we see a whole different picture. We just did that with the UAV discussion right? What if Thor's Hammer is not what we should be focused on at all? What if we are thinking way too small?

"This technology and the possibilities are new to us, we are considering from our own frames of reference something new. They have had Thor's Hammers for at least five years because that is how long Doc had it. Now we are thinking like Doc was over five years ago? They have a technology plus at least five years to think about it, test it and advance it? Do we really think that if they could do it in the first place that they couldn't do it even better five years later? If they had Thor's Hammers five years ago or longer, then what else do they have now?" he asked the room in general, and the lack of response was telling as the idea was being considered by everyone in the team.

Tom smiled at the sergeant's insights and willingness to challenge what was in front of them all and he voiced that to the group with a single statement directed toward Frank, "Does everyone in the Air Force have NCO's like this? Why do you guys even need to go to work?"

Frank smiled and took the jab in good humor, "Nope, we're blessed with this guy. Just remember he is on loan to you guys. I didn't sign anything letting him go."

Ann brought the conversation back to what was said, not who said it, "That would mean that they could be anywhere, they could look like anything right? I mean we know what ours look like and these are already pretty small. Easy to transport. Low power needs. They put Thor's Hammers on balloons, we used them from trucks, move them with one person. Made a tornado with a single device. Just said we would put them on a RPV and we could literally duct tape this to one and hover or fly it around just like it is now. It is not a stretch at all for me to say we could repackage it as is, ruggedize the shell, put some shackles on it and be ready to fly this thing around in a pretty short period of time. But we haven't messed with any of that because we aren't at all certain about the technology and the science behind how this work. But if we had all that information, we would be in a position to make changes to the packaging, or the components, or the delivery vehicle. You guys are right, we are viewing this from a device-centric lens and they don't have that limitation."

Bob was also pretty far along this train of thought before he spoke up, but now had something new to contribute. "That means we also have to consider that changing the weather with a Thor's Hammer may not be limited to a single event. Think about it, we had one device and we used that to create an event of our choosing. That is our frame of reference for all of this, we discovered and used a device that enabled us to produce a weather event. We demonstrated this at a specific site, at a point in time and made some money, some impressive feats and considered the potential a device like this could do for a place. But what about a lot of them? We considered the potential benefits out in the future, but we never considered what that might look like if it already existed today. What if it did? What if we only have a small piece of a network of devices, and what if they are already in use? What if Thor's Hammer is just one of the tools in a much larger toolbox? In a much larger workshop?

"I mean the weather is a dynamic environment, but it is a closed system if you consider the globe. It is a big system, but it is a closed system. They could have local, even regional networks of these things strung together, nested, or synchronized to do on much larger scales what we have only seriously been considering on an event scale. If we keep looking at events and are amazed by those, we won't see the forest we are in because we are so enamored by the tree. Sorry for mixing my metaphors. This could be how Doc or Father Gannon came to be in possession of one of these, right? Making one from scratch is amazing. Doing it alone and in secret, even more so. Doing all that without funding, really unlikely. But finding one of their experimental devices, a real stroke of luck. Finding one of many in an operational network is more plausible." Bob paused again, and Tom took that opportunity to focus their effort while keeping their thinking wide open.

"You guys are all thinking the right things and questioning the right stuff. I need you to keep doing that, keep thinking that way. But I also need you to do your parts in what we have already decided to pursue without seeing ghosts behind every tree. Look for what does and does not fit. We are going to need to keep each other looped in more regularly as we split our efforts. This stuff is too sensitive to put in emails and calls that can be intercepted, because you know they are working hard to learn what we know, as well as, what we are thinking. Especially if what we are considering right now is even close to being real. Keep all the main effort communications in our normal channels. Anything outside that, we will do in person. Twice a day at a minimum but call a meeting if you find something big that everyone else needs to know. We cannot afford to blow this and believe me when I say I know what I am asking from you. I appreciate what you have done so far, and thanks in advance for what we are going to go out and do next.

"Let's go take them up on their offer to help us. And let's let them help us get what we are asking for and try to see what it is we are looking for," he concluded, policed up his phones, folder, and looked over at Sergeant Andies and said, "Let's go Sergeant, we have a lot to do and you need to change clothes because we have a flight to be on is less than an hour."

Andies smiled as he considered how much fun he was about to have.

After they returned to their quarters, Bob and Ann turned on the small television in time to see the United Nations Secretary General on a video clip with Breaking News scrolling along beneath the loop which seemed to be running on every station right now. The headline read, "United Nations accepts China's offer to take the lead on fielding on-demand weather modification technology as controversy over its origins continue."

This was not the best tag line for the UN, but the Secretary General's comments told the rest of the story for those who bothered to listen instead of just catching the bumper stickers and moving on to the next item, which at this point and time was the same as the one they were switching from.

"We are happy to accept the CCP's gracious offer to partner with the UN in our ongoing effort. Their demonstration today showed us they will certainly bring a lot to the table as we advance the safe and equitable fielding of this newly revealed technology. We are excited to collaborate on the similarities and differences of our experiences and our fielded systems. And, while I am confident we all have room to learn and improve, I am ecstatic to have a new partner in this endeavor so we can do this together. There are still many details to be ironed out, but we have both agreed to begin these efforts as early as tomorrow at the same location where two demonstrations have already occurred.

"We will begin by introducing our technical experts, work out some technology exchange protocols, testing plans and the timing and locations for our next demonstrations which will be conducted as joint operations of our newly combined efforts. I look forward to this new partnership and providing you all additional details as they become available in the coming days. With that, I am happy to take your questions," he offered, although he was not looking forward to answering any of the ones he knew would be on everyone's minds.

"Mr. Secretary, what were your thoughts when earlier today you saw the demonstration? The rainbow, was that something your team was capable of but chose not to do in your previous demonstrations?" asked the closest and loudest of the assembled journalists.

"Yes, the rainbow was indeed impressive. A very complex condition to create for a demonstration that was flawlessly executed. It was wonderful to see this operation conducted with precision and professionalism, and we are looking forward to the same type of collaboration between our teams. Thank you, next question?" he dodged as he pointed to someone deep into the back of the group.

"Can you tell us who will be leading the UN team in this partnership given the disastrous results of the last demonstration?" someone asked in a confrontational tone.

"Yes, and thank you for the question. Our team's composition remains unchanged. We are working internally and in collaboration with host nation and other technical experts to determine, to the extent that can be learned, what went wrong and why. There are many possible factors that may have contributed to those unfortunate conditions developing in such a short amount of time. These investigations will take time and considerable expertise to complete, and we believe we have the best experts in this technology available to assist these efforts and learn what we can from them. They are the best and the brightest, and I have every confidence they can work on these two efforts concurrently. If that proves to not be the case, we will make adjustments that best fit the needs of both efforts within our very deep pool of talented professionals. I have time for one more, then I will need to excuse myself for my next engagement," he warned them.

"Did you know this technology was stolen from China?" came the next question in a manner that was unavoidable from the assembled journalists. With a set jaw and his two eyebrows scrunched into one across his forehead the Secretary General responded curtly.

"I do not accept the premise that the UN, nor any member of the UN's team stole, was aware of, or even suspected anything related to our on-demand weather modification technology being stolen. Nor do I believe in any way, shape or form that the experts working on it had any information available to them that we have not already provided you in the very transparent, and benevolent manner in which we willingly shared this new technology with you. We shared it with you not for any financial gain but for all who might benefit from its expeditious deployment.

"I am aware of the claims to the contrary, and I look forward to working with our new partners to help resolve and reconcile those differing views through our new collaborations. While that is not the purpose of our new partnership, I certainly anticipate that clarity on this topic will be one of the many products of our efforts. Now, if you will all excuse me, I appreciate your attention and your questions and look forward to having more to report in the coming days."

And with that he headed off to wherever it was he needed to be, or wanted everyone else to believe he was going.

"OK then. I guess we know what we will be doing tomorrow," Ann said to Bob. "I suppose I will just have to wait until tomorrow to learn whom from their side we will be meeting with to do all of this. Do you think Zach will be part of their team that works with us? Do you think they will put him with us on day one of this effort?"

"Great questions. If it were me, I wouldn't do it, but I sure hope they do. I would love to ask him a lot of the questions that have been piling up in my head for days now. Time will tell, but I hope we do get the chance to talk with him. Tomorrow, or another day but I don't want to always wonder because we didn't ever get to ask him. Even if he doesn't tell the truth, at least we can see how he reacts. I know the rest of the team feels the same way, but I am glad Betty is not here for this. I am not sure she would be able to keep from taking matters into her own hands if it turns out he had anything to do with Doc's death. For that matter, I am not too sure about myself, but she was closer to him than I ever was. Let's get some rest, it looks like tomorrow is going to be quite a day," he suggested to Ann who was already a couple of steps ahead of him.

"I could use some rest," she agreed, "but I'm not very sleepy. Do you think there might be something you could do about that Professor Mcleod?"

Bob smiled, "I am pretty sure I have something that will help," and with that, he turned out the lights and turned his attention to his fiancé.

CHAPTER THIRTEEN

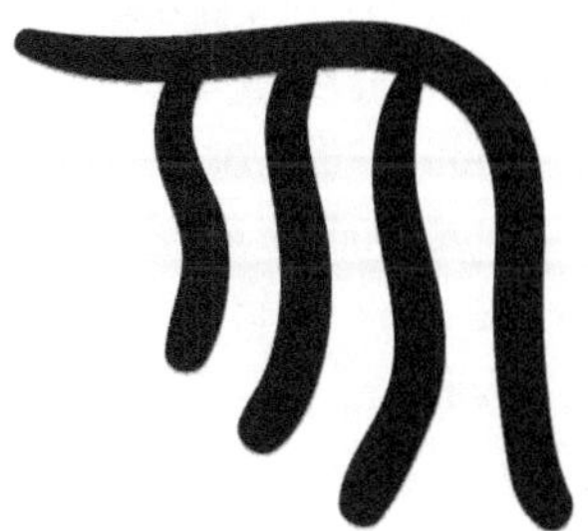

HOMECOMING

I t's great to see you again, Betty," Steve smiled as he greeted her at in the waiting area of the small private terminal in the otherwise bustling commercial airport. She continued walking toward him and gave him a long hug that could have been taken as her being relieved to see a friendly face after a long flight but could also have been perceived as something more. Steve did not concern himself with that right now as his thoughts were focused on an update about Ann and the others, as well as what he and Betty had to take care of for them.

"Now, I thought I was supposed to be the one glad to be back and grateful for a familiar face to greet me. It is really very good to see you too, Steve," she said sincerely as they walked together behind the young men who were there to make sure they were in the right place at the right time. They needed to get back to New York and begin their efforts to find anything in the records and files that would support the UN team's working theory about the origins and timelines of Doc's research and the Thor's Hammers that Bob came to possess.

"How are Ann and Bob? This whole thing has got to be stressful on them, on all of you. I'm sorry Betty, just worried about her but please start with how are *you*? How are you doing with all of this?" Steve's good manners had caught up with his fears and he seemed to be back on track now.

"No apologies, really. You're a good father, she should be your first concern, and I am fine. I had a long flight back and that gave me plenty of time to think about all this and to get my mind right. I'm not supposed to talk about most of what I was sent back to help with, but I have a good gameplan on what I need to look at and where I think I will find it if it exists. I also appreciate them thinking of something for me to do so they could get me out from underfoot over there. It's about to get very real for them, and they don't need an old lady to slow them down or limit their options. They are stronger and more agile with me over here, and they will need to be," she astutely explained with no sense of disappointment or questioning of the rationale she herself assigned to the decisions made.

"You are making it sound a little more dangerous over there than I already imagined it," Steve admitted to her.

"No, I don't mean there is a direct threat that I know of, just that, after the wind event, it was intense and real when they got us out of there. I know that might have played out a little differently if it were just the two of them without the slow old lady to worry about, too. They need better options moving forward; that's all. And besides, the stuff back here is my bread and butter. I know it better than anyone else, and if they tell me what to get or look for then I will run circles around whomever else it might have been. Put everyone in the position to use their strengths. That's smart, and that's what we are doing. That's how I see it; no offense taken. And I don't think they are in more danger right now; probably a little less now that the UN is going to pull the Chinese into working with them, instead of at a distance. They will be in the same places at the same time, with lots of people and media watching as much as they can so I don't expect there to be much physical danger to either of them in that setting," she explained candidly and correctly as far as she and Steve were concerned.

"Thanks for that; it does make me feel better. I am looking forward to a little more information about what you and I will be doing in New York. I'm not a big fan of that city, but whatever you need from me just say the word and I will find a way," he offered.

"Thank you, Steve," as she looked around the holding area where they were waiting to board the small jet that would be their last leg into New York she smiled and added, "Don't worry, we won't be staying in New York very long. I hope you packed light; I am pretty sure we are going to be following some strong leads and I am not sure yet where they will take us. Are you up for following them with me? I would sure appreciate having someone I know I can trust at my side when I do this. We both care about the same people so I know we will be motivated the same way for the same outcomes and that means a lot with what I am expecting to find."

"Like I said, say the word and I will find a way. But I have to warn you, I am going to say my peace about whatever we find. I've never been a blind follower, and can't start now. You are getting more of a partner than you are getting a henchman," he both warned and informed her.

"That's exactly what I need, Steve. It's been a very long time since I had a partner, and I could sure use one right now. Thank you," she smiled, and blushed a little but didn't want to acknowledge or admit to herself that she both heard and liked what he said, and how he said it. And with that the two young men motioned for them to follow out the door and onto the ramp toward the aircraft that was now ready to accept them aboard. They climbed the few short steps into the cabin and settled in as the aircraft was quickly buttoned up and taxiing to the active runway. Before they knew it, they were rolling down the runway gaining speed, and they could hear the landing gear coming up almost as soon as they lifted off and were pressed into the back of their seats during the steep climb-out. These guys were very good, Steve thought wondering just how much more enjoyable flying could be if all the commercial airlines operated as efficiently and effectively as this group.

Steve and Betty were able to talk more freely in the aircraft and lay out some plans for the next couple of days. By the time they landed, they were ready to put those plans into action. They transitioned from the aircraft to a vehicle that drove them, and a new security detail, to the familiar hotel where they had retained their block of rooms that also included the files she had brought up for Bob earlier in this endeavor.

They were not even across the lobby, when the man approached them as they neared the elevator and extended his credentials before the security team grew too concerned.

"Good afternoon, I'm Agent Miloc with the FBI and am here to assist with the ongoing Thor's Hammer effort. Do you mind if I accompany you up to your suite where we can talk?" He looked like he was ready to go, which seemed to fit right into the mood Betty and Steve had ever since landing back in New York.

"What took you so long; we don't have all day," Betty smiled and resumed walking toward the elevator leaving the rest of the group to follow.

Miloc and Steve looked at each other and both shrugged as they fell into step behind her. "I'm Steve," he offered as they walked, and the agent smiled and tried to gain some trust as they shook hands while they walked.

"Yes, I know. You're Ann's father. I told Bob he was out of his league with her, but neither one of them would listen to me," he said.

"Me too, and here we both are," Steve agreed. "At least I know you can see the obvious, maybe we will get something done while we are here," he concluded optimistically as they stepped onto the elevator and rode it up. Once they arrived at the door of her suite, Betty entered the key code, invited them in and offered them to make themselves at home while she excused herself to the rest room to freshen up from her travels. As they awaited her return, Steve and Miloc continued chatting.

"So, you are the same agent from the beginning where Bob and Betty are from? Before he and Ann met right?" Steve was seeking confirmation.

"That's right. I was one of the investigator's looking into Bob's quick change of luck and the addition of a few zeros and another comma to the amounts in his bank account. The IRS and FBI were both looking at him when the military got involved and then it quickly escalated. He went off with the spook squad, I was sent back to do whatever it was I was doing before and told to forget I ever met the good Professor.

"Except, I adopted his recently adopted dog, Buck. Buck was Doc Auster's dog, and Bob kind of got stuck with him as a favor to Father Gannon. I looked after him while Bob was gone, and well it turned into a win-win-win for all of us," Miloc summarized.

"Well, someone who looks out for a dog…and a dog who likes that someone is alright in my book. Dogs seem to be as good or better judges of character than most people. So, I hope your intentions are to help us help Ann and Bob. If not, you are in the wrong place at the wrong time, and we should both be clear on what our purpose is here before we go any further on what we do next? What do you say?" It was unclear whether Steve's words were a statement, a question or a warning. Miloc took them as all of the above, and his response quickly revealed his purpose for being there when they arrived.

"I have been instructed to re-look at the origins of the Thor's Hammer technology to see if any of it changes what we think about how Bob came to have it; or if it changes what everyone thinks about Doc Auster's death, and to specifically look for anything that ties any of that to a list of LLC's, corporations, or individuals that all seem to have links back to communist China and the CCP. While I have to be objective in my investigation, I will have all the resources I need to conduct it and I will follow it wherever the facts lead me. It is my sincere hope, that we can view this as a collaboration to find the truth, which will affirm the innocence of those we all care about while exposing the guilty who are looking to remain hidden, especially if they are hiding behind our friends and family to do so. Does that keep us close enough to a shared objective to work together?" he concluded.

"Yes, Agent Miloc, I can work with that. I think Betty can too, but she will have to give you her own answer. I know better than try to predict with any confidence how a woman will respond to any question," he smiled.

"Well, seems we also have that in common," Miloc smiled, and with that Betty rejoined them in the spacious casual seating area of her suite.

"You know, both of your voices carry. We can save some time and get right to work because we all seem to be on the same page," she smiled, and then continued despite the looks Steve and Miloc were exchanging.

"I have all the boxes with the data from the trap lines over here. I want them all scanned and then sent to Bob and Ann wherever they are. The science people there can look at all the data and see if there are patterns or anomalies. That's their wheelhouse, but there's no way I'm gonna do that from here. Too much and with what I have here it would take too long. So, what I need you to do is get someone to digitize all those records and get them to Tom. Wait, do you know Tom, are you one of Tom's or someone else's?" Betty paused, and waited for the right answer.

"Both. I'm technically somebody else's guy, but until we are done with all of this I report directly to Tom. I don't have to keep the 'somebody else's' informed on anything, as long as, Tom knows where I am and what I am doing," he assured her.

"Does that mean you can do the same things Tom can do, or do you need to go through Tom to get things done. Because I can go to Tom myself and…" Betty was cut off by his response.

"I can't do everything Tom can do, but I can get everything we need until we need him to do what I can't. And yes, I can get a team to take the records and digitize them," he said.

"No, Agent Miloc the records stay here. You need to get some folks here to do that. These records all stay together and they all stay with, or at least are the responsibility and property of Professor Mcleod and not the US government, or any of its alphabet soup agencies. If you can do that, then that is priority one for you." It was becoming very clear who was leading the initial phase of this investigation.

"I can do that, and with your permission I will get that rolling while you are filling me in on my next set of tasks," he said just sarcastically enough to not get in trouble but subtly make his point.

"Sorry not trying to step on toes, we need not spar over who is in charge of what, but I know the things we have and need to get started on to find what we need. That will help inform what you want to see and do next, so just trust me the first hour or so, ok? We are after the same things." She was asking, not telling and Miloc appreciated that.

"What else do I need to get rolling?" he asked.

"We need a flight back home this evening. We need access to the University, its business records and anything and everything associated with the grant that Doc and Bob were working on. I don't have any of that except the technical specs for the weather study. That is really just the data collection plan, the conditions, timing, reporting formats etc. which may become more important in connecting some dots, but it's the rest of it that will provide the early dots that we need to connect to. So, I need you to get us another airplane with seats on it tonight from wherever you get airplanes and we need access to the University records first thing tomorrow. You have three big rocks in your bucket now, do you want some more or is that enough to get you started?" she challenged.

"That's enough for now. Let me make some calls," Miloc said as he was dialing, pacing, listening and talking at the same time.

Steve looked at Betty, "Now I'm a little afraid to ask, but what do you need me to do?"

"You could make us all some tea if you don't mind. I am ready for some tea. And while the water is heating up, you can move the boxes that don't say 'trapline data sets' into the other room so whomever shows up here to digitize all this stuff doesn't get into stuff that's not theirs to see. Put them in the bedroom, they shouldn't be seeing anything in my bedroom. I'll lock that up before we leave this evening. Doesn't mean they won't snoop around, but I will know if they do," she added.

"I can do that." Steve moved into action as Betty was pleased with their start and it did not take long before Steve summoned them both for a hot beverage and an update. "Files moved; tea is ready. What have you two accomplished while I was working hard?" he challenged them. Miloc was good at what he did, and that was on full display today.

"We will fly out of LaGuardia at seven fifteen. That's in motion. And speaking of motions, another one is being drafted as we speak and will be filed and approved in time for tomorrow's activities. I will have a search warrant in hand for anyplace we need to go, and anything we need to see at the University. But we need to try not to use that. We will also have discovery rights to all the grant records and anything related to Doc's work, or Bob's work at the University in preparation for defense in the pending lawsuit against Bob," he smiled.

"What lawsuit?" they both asked almost in unison.

"Ok, awkward moment. The University has sued Bob for theft of real and intellectual property as it relates to on-demand weather modification technology. They claim that Doc Auster, and or Bob worked on or discovered this technology while employed by the University. So, it technically belongs to them, not Bob or Doc. And that they both defrauded the University by claiming to be working on one thing when they were secretly using University resources to work on this side hustle, which incidentally made Bob a very rich man. The University wants either damages or a cut on the money already paid, and that which he might get in the future. There might be another claim or count, but that is the gist of it," Miloc said.

"Didn't know that," Betty scowled. "Durbin is one of the names on that suit, Hugh Durbin?" she said accusingly as Miloc nodded in the affirmative. "That makes perfect sense, and that makes it all the more motivating to find the truth. Durbin has been my boss for a good number of years, same for Doc and Bob. He's an arrogant, entitled asshole. Wouldn't hurt my feelings to get a two-fer out of this effort. If we do find what we think we will to link this grant and maybe even the devices back to the CCP, then this all happened on his watch. Technically it all happened on my watch, too, but he is both responsible and accountable for this program.

And if he was in any way knowingly involved in any of this, and by extension Doc's death then I want his head on a pike," she stated calmly.

"Betty, let's keep this objective and not personal, at least for now," Miloc warned. "If we go in angry and looking to find one thing, we may miss something relevant that we aren't looking for and don't recognize through our anger or vengeance. And I am sensing some of both right now."

"I know, but a lawsuit? That is sour grapes between him and Bob. He never liked Bob, even went out of his way to pick on him. Antagonize him. And honestly, I'm pretty sure it was simple jealousy. Durbin had money, education, a prestigious title and people doing the work for him but that was not enough for him. I think it's because he knew it was all a façade with him, but real with Bob, who did not have all those things but was far more capable, far more motivated; all while still being comfortable in the background. I don't know if any of Durbin's or the University's claims have any merit, but I do know if there is any dirt to be had on this topic there will be traces of it in his pockets or bank accounts. And this lawsuit may mean they have already done some of our digging for us in preparing to file this lawsuit. How much fun would that be to find what we are looking for right out in the open because of his greed and jealousy?" She was getting herself centered back to where Miloc needed her.

"Good, and I agree with you. That's why I want to keep cover over what else we could do if we needed to by focusing on what we can learn through the lawsuit responses. Then it's just us preparing for something they did to us, it won't raise any suspicions about the other theories we are also pursuing. I am confident there are eyes on you since you left India, and we want those eyes seeing us doing what they expect us to do not suspecting we know what they hope we don't," Miloc encouraged them both. "This tea is pretty good, Steve."

"I have many skills. If you two don't need me right now, I'd love to grab a shower and change of clothes before we need to travel again," he said requesting permission to be absent for a little while and wondering what his best option might be. Betty offered that he was welcome to use the shower in her room and pointed him in that direction with the instruction to "Move whatever you need to move, use whatever you need to use, except my towel. Use your own towel, there are clean ones on the shelf above the sink."

"Yes, dear. Thank you dear. Anything else dear?" he said playfully, to which she replied, "Yes, you said shower. That is the only 'S' you have permission to do, not the first 'S', and you don't need a shave so just the third 'S' please," she rallied back in kind.

"Got it, thanks," as he closed the door behind him. An hour later they were at the airport eating what they picked up on the way and were again waiting in the holding area to board a flight. It didn't take long for the aircraft to roll up, they loaded in and were on their way. A few hours later they made a smooth landing, loaded into the waiting car and after a short drive found themselves settling in for a few hours of sleep at Bob's house. This also used to be Doc's house, and they all stayed there together to make the logistics easier for their trip over to the University that morning. Betty was tempted to go to her place, but she didn't want to be a detour along the way and besides, she enjoyed being with Steve and Miloc so why mess up a good thing she reasoned. And as quickly as time can pass, they were rallying in the kitchen over the fresh coffee Steve had made.

"Coffee and tea, those are special talents and I am not jerking your chain. This is good coffee, and the tea was great too. I have never really gotten the hang of making either of these very well despite really loving to consume them both," Miloc complimented his new brew master.

"You're just hoping I will start cooking for you, too," Steve said as he waived his finger back and forth while he shook his head. "I am sorry to disappoint you, but bacon and steaks are the only things I am any good at cooking."

"What else is there really?" Miloc asked as he sipped his coffee. "I don't smell any bacon, so as soon as you both are ready, we can head out. We can eat on the way, or just go to the University."

"I know a place and it's on the way," Betty chimed in as she came down the hallway toward the kitchen. "And it's pretty close to the Administrative Hall which is where we need to check in when we get there. In fact, it is very likely we may run into Dean Durbin. He usually gets a coffee there to get him started before he arrives at his office. Might be fun if he stops in this morning. What do you say?"

"That works for me. We are likely to run into him today anyway so you might as well have your fun early, and in a public place that is off campus. Just promise you won't hurt him physically or I will have to arrest you for assault. That is too much paperwork for a Fed, really that is a local PD action unless I witness it first-hand," he requested.

"Promise, I will be on my best behavior. For as long as I can stand it because I don't want to make a promise that I am not sure I can keep," she hedged.

"Alright that's good enough. Do your best, that's all anyone can ask," he said as he began toward the front door with the others right behind him.

A few minutes later they were settling into a large booth ordering breakfast specials at the place Betty had recommended. As they were finishing their food and had agreed on who was going to be looking at which files and what records, the door opened and in walked Hugh Durbin. As he was heading to the counter to order his coffee, he recognized his now former department secretary sitting with two men he did not recognize. Once he placed his order, he moved toward Betty and acknowledged her.

"Betty, how nice to see you. I was very disappointed for you all with how things went in India, I am glad to see you have returned home safely. I hope you are doing ok, My Dear. And who are your two friends; I don't believe we have met?" he asked as Steve rose up from his seat, Betty responded for all of them.

"This is my friend Steve. And Steve, this is Dr. Hugh Durbin, the Dean of the Atmospheric Science Department and my former boss."

She watched as the two shook hands and sized each other up, neither one blinking.

"Nice to meet you Steve, and who is your other friend," he inquired while still sizing Steve up.

"This is my friend Miloc. Miloc, meet Hugh Durbin," Betty continued.

"My pleasure. And…" Durbin cut him off mid-sentence.

"Miloc? Is that your first or last name?" Durbin asked.

"Both," he smiled and extended his hand, which Durbin was slow to reach up and shake.

"Curious, a man with only one name?" Durbin pressed.

"No, I usually use my title in front of it. Simplifies things and helps manage expectations," he admitted, and Durbin took the hint.

"And what is your title sir?" Durbin asked. And with that, it was on.

"FBI Senior Special Agent," he paused then said with emphasis, "Miloc. But you can call me Senior Special Agent Miloc," he requested without using the word request.

And with that comment, they could see the wheels turning in Durbin's head as he looked over to Betty and asked her, "are you in some kind of trouble Betty? Is there something I can do to help here?"

"No Hugh, I am not in some kind of trouble, but there is something you can do to help," she suggested.

"That is good to hear, I was worried. What is the something I can do to help?" Durbin responded curiously.

"Be on time and prepared for our meeting this morning. We are your 0830 meeting, and I want you to be both prompt and cooperative. We have a lot to get through and we are on a very tight schedule. Now if you will excuse us, we would like to finish our breakfast. We will be seeing you shortly," Betty instructed him, and it didn't sound at all like a request.

All he could think to say or do was turn around to collect his coffee order and leave without a word. That suited Betty just fine. "Well gentlemen I must admit to you that I enjoyed that very much. I may even need a cigarette," she joked.

"I am glad you got that out of your system, even if just a little bit..." Miloc said, "...because you are correct, we have a lot to look through and the sooner we get started the sooner we get done. I need you focused on our tasks not on him, or what he may have done."

"I got this," Betty assured him, and to make sure, she walked over to the counter and paid the bill for their meals and drinks. "Let's go men, we have some discovery to wade through and some Durbin to fry."

And with that, they walked the short distance from the Diner to the University campus, and then on to the Administrative Building where they met the court appointed observer who would accompany them through the University files and records rooms. As they filed into the meeting room, Dean Durbin and several other University staff including the Chancellor were waiting for them to discuss the day's objectives. They were confused regarding the presence of an FBI Senior Special Agent in a discovery file review for a civil case. Miloc explained that he was assigned as personal security for Betty given her role in the UN on-demand weather team and the many threats its members received after the unfortunate event in India. Which made perfect sense to the men in the room. But Miloc could not help himself, so he added a jab of his own for Betty.

"And in addition to security for this young lady, for full disclosure I am also leading a Federal Investigation into the deadly UN event you referred to." He paused as the grin on Dean Durbin's face grew wider as he listened. "If the allegations in your lawsuit against Professor Mcleod prove to be substantiated, and it was your technology which he stole, and subsequently used during the UN demonstrations, then you and the University will likely be both charged with and sued for that event by the governments and families of all those injured or killed. It seems the UN technology team assured everyone involved that the device malfunctioned despite numerous attempts to correct the erroneous conditions as they were materializing. We will be looking into all things around the origins of this technology, the grant that funded the research Doc Auster and Professor Mcleod were conducting, as well as all the individuals and entities involved in the funding and operation of those works. If that technology was developed here, the UN and US will be very happy to be off the hook with the government of India and put you square in everyone's crosshairs. For our sake I hope your lawsuit is legit; for your sake it might be best if we find the facts suggest it was not your technology after all. Anything you might be able to point us to help make that determination would be much appreciated and might shorten our visit with you," he offered for their consideration.

As they quietly talked among themselves, the Chancellor spoke for the group, "Agent Miloc, we do not want any misunderstandings regarding this lawsuit and its purpose. From its inception, it was intended to throw a legal blanket of claim over this new technology while the origins were traced to ensure that any link to the University if warranted through the deep dive into the details revealed that such a claim was demonstrable. The large sum of money Professor Mcleod came into was proximate to the discovery of a device he claims was handed off to him by his friend and boss Doc Auster. Perhaps there were University resources inappropriately used on this technology. We're interested in resolving these uncertainties, and, if appropriate, to be in position to collect any compensation that might be warranted should evidence of any violations be uncovered. To date, we have not discovered any such connections.

"In fact, the prospects of any liability for the misapplication of this same technology was not something we were attempting to buy into. If it would facilitate your investigation, I believe we may be willing to withdraw our claims and drop the existing lawsuit. If any additional information revealed through your effort indicates we are due some compensation resulting from the actions of our former employees regarding the origins of this technology, perhaps a settlement based on those findings need not bother the court. I am confident we could come to some arrangement.

"I imagine this could save us all much time and expense. If it contributes to the investigation, and perhaps to the protection of national security interests I am willing to authorize the immediate withdrawal of the existing lawsuit brought forth by the University, and perhaps even agree to not filing any similar claims in the future. Is that something we might agree on?" The Chancellor postured for closure as Durbin looked on in disbelief, not fully grasping the perilous position the University was facing.

Miloc considered the Chancellor's offer, his position and how the various options might all play out and his response surprised many in the room, "Thank you, sir, for that kind offer, it shows great insight but I am afraid I will have to pass for now. We are here to look at a very specific set of files, contracts and communications and I must insist that we be allowed to do so without delay. You of course are free to drop your suit at any time with a writ to the court as soon as you can get it filed and a judge to act on it and at that point our rights to discovery will be removed. In fact, it may very well be a great idea to do that given what we expect to find today. But I'm afraid I cannot agree to your offer here and now because that would be a binding agreement that would be immediately effective and preclude us from what we are here to do now. That simply will not work for us. So, if there is nothing else, may we proceed? We have a lot to examine this morning and we have a flight to catch so time is of the essence," he politely asked the disappointed Chancellor, who incidentally had been the Dean of the University's Law School before his appointment to his current position three years ago.

"Of course, he replied. What specifically can we assist you and your team with reviewing regarding this case?" he offered while also setting the bounds of what he was willing to show them.

"We are keenly interested in all the correspondence related to the origins of the grant that funded the weather data collection study that Doc Auster oversaw. Everything about and around it. The Notice of Funds Available, the University's grant application, the negotiations, the signed agreements, the reporting criteria, the legal reviews, the lawsuit and settlement that provided the cash, names, dates, addresses, lease agreements, purchase orders from the first whiff of an opportunity to whatever it looks like right now. We will also need all the personnel and employment records of every University employee whose name appears in any of those documents. That is specific. It is focused on this case and only the topic for which your lawsuit addresses. Will that be a problem or am I in a safe operating space from which to begin this morning?" The Senior Special Agent was asking the seasoned professional attorney.

"We have much of that data already assembled from our own preparations and will provide it to you and your team directly. The personnel records will take some time to assemble to get all the names, but we can begin with the key players if you like and fill in the rest as we go?" he agreed.

"That would be wonderful. Can we use the room we are in now, or would you prefer we relocate to where the files are currently?" he asked.

"This room is fine. All of our records are available digitally on our network. We have set up folders that contain the data you are asking about, plus some more that you did not request. They are available for your review as well. There are several computers and printers already set up here. There will be two of our staff members who will be available to assist you in getting started as well as to address any questions or difficulties you might encounter during your efforts. Of course, no offense will be taken if you ask them to leave the room to assure your privacy during your work. Does that meet your objectives for the day Special Agent?" he asked and received an affirmative response from both Miloc and Betty who nodded in unison.

"Very well then, if you will excuse us, we will leave you to your work and we have a writ to the court to write and get delivered." With that, the Chancellor led the small University delegation from the meeting. Durbin shot an over the shoulder glance at Betty who showed great restraint as she was already moving toward a computer to get logged onto the network that she knew well from her decades at this institution of higher learning. She began with her still valid employee credentials and was immediately granted access and the stay-behind technician assisted the others in getting logged in and pointed them all to the neatly arranged files and folders. Betty couldn't help but think to herself how far she had come with just her high school diploma while surrounded by less capable individuals with college degrees stacked on top of more degrees. The words of her late husband rang again in her head just as they did around the dinner table so many times through the years when she brought her work challenges home, "Education does not make people smart, it just makes them educated." She smiled at the memory and was anxious to see if she could find the connections their team expected to be hidden somewhere in the documentation.

After nearly four hours of reading, scanning and asking clarifying questions, Betty asked another one of Miloc and Steve, "Does the name Vidar Technologies show up in any of your documents?"

"No, but I have a Vali Enterprises," Steve added.

"Wait, what? What about Tyr, or Bragi, Hodr, Baldur or Heimdall? Any of those?" Betty pressed.

"Nope not in my stuff," Steve said disappointedly.

"I saw some invoices to Heimdall Manufacturing for some parts. And wait, they were shipped to an address, at 45 Hodr Industrial Center, same local zip code as the other shipments. Why?" Miloc asked.

Betty said, "Never heard of it around here. Just mapped it on my phone and it says location not found. Anyone know what all these names are? They are Thor's siblings, well his half siblings' names. Thor's father Odin's other children in Aesir."

"Did you say Aesir?" Miloc asked intently and Betty affirmed that is what she said.

"The law firm that filed the original suit against the charcoal companies was formed as Aesir, LLP. What is the connection here? If the US component of this operation has Norse mythology names we connect them back to Aesir, and then follow Aesir back to connect it to the other ones we already know about," Miloc added. "So, we assumed Doc had the device and named it Thor's Hammer. But what if we assume Doc discovered the name Thor's Hammer and that is what led him to the device?"

"But we already searched for that name earlier, and thoroughly because we had it," Betty countered.

"What if you weren't looking in the right place, or for the right thing? What if nobody referred to the devices, the Hammer's specifically? What if that is the common item they all understood existed but never spoke or wrote about to help keep them hidden? Where did Thor get his hammer, was he born with it, did he make it himself, steal it, how does the story go?" Steve asked both of them.

Miloc responded, "I have no idea, but the world wide web tells me a dwarf named Sindri forged Mjolnir. And while he was making it, Loki the trickster fire god messed with him by becoming a fly and messing with his concentration which is why the handle is shorter than most other hammers."

"Holy crap! That's it, we aren't looking for Thor's Hammer we are looking for Mjolnir, that is the name of the hammer. How do you spell it?" Steve asked, and Miloc responded from what he was reading. Nobody's searches provided any positive results, and some of the air left the room after the promising connection stalled. Then Steve asked, "How do we pronounce it? Forget the spelling, how do you say the 'Mjol' sound, I can't say it, how do you say it?" he puzzled.

"Another quick web search indicated that Mjolner, in English, was pronounced Miller," Miloc informed the room, "Look for Miller!"

"I have T. Miller's name all over the funding documents of the original grants, and the payments from the grant holder to the University. T. Miller is the grant manager for Aesir LLP!" Betty declared as she jumped from her seat. "If T indicates Thor, then T. Miller is Thor's Mjolner! T. Miller equals Thor's Hammer! Let's follow T. Miller and T. Miller's money!"

"We might just have hit on something, but don't follow any money yet. In fact, we need to stop and take a break. I need to make a call," Miloc directed, but Betty protested.

"Why, we are onto something here we need to run with it," she argued.

"I know, and that is why. T. Miller may be the grant manager for this effort, but I just confirmed that Aesir, LLP also holds several subsidiaries, including the Thyrm Associates. Thyrm Associates employs the lawyer who represented the young man in the DUI case, the one who was driving the car that killed Doc Auster. Does anyone know who Thyrm was? Well, I didn't until just now so I will tell you.

"He was the giant who stole Thor's hammer and tried to trade it for a marriage to Freya. If this naming thing turns out to be real, we may have just connected Thor's Hammer to its source and to Doc's death. I don't want to trip any more cyber alarms than we already may have by getting this far. So, what I need you to do, is go back to your computers and keep looking at files and random things for another hour or two. If you come across any of the names we have talked about already, take a note of where and what, then move on past it without pursuing it. We will collect all the paper later, but don't pursue this on your own anymore. If you come across any other Norse mythology names or connections, same thing. Write it down but don't chase it on your computers.

"We are going to wrap up here in about an hour or hour-and-a-half and then we are going to leave here, go back to the house, pack up, get something to eat and then go to the airport and back to New York tonight. We did good here, but I gotta make some calls and get some experts on this right now. I know in my gut we are right, but if they suspect we are on to something they may take action before I can get all this stuff captured and examined by some of the best cyber forensics guys on the planet. So, you do what I just said, and I am going to go for a walk, and will be back in half an hour to wrap up like we talked about. Clear?" he asked and they both nodded in agreement. And one more thing, "What kind of smoothie do you want? I can't be obvious. I need to be the errand boy for something. There was a place I saw on the way in, looked like they had lots of fruit and stacks of kale."

With that he departed, made the appropriate calls, ordered the smoothies and strolled back to join Betty and Steve. As they drank their concoctions and wrapped up their searches and notes, Betty commented to the men, "Durbin's name is on these documents all the way from beginning to end. He has emails to T. Miller about dollar amounts, scheduled payments and other things. He should know who T. Miller is and how to reach him."

"I know Betty, I know. We did our part. We came here to find what others in our place likely would not have. Now we have teams of analysts and investigators and financial trackers all connecting the dots for us. We told them what to look for, and what to be on the lookout for, now we wait while they do what we need done. Believe it or not, we had the hard part. The rest of this is easier because it's all mechanical and objective. You did the hard part, Betty, you broke the code, made the connections. We will know the truth soon enough, or be able to get to it soon enough. Either way, on whatever timeline, we will get there because of what we did today.

"Now let's walk out of here. Show a little disappointment and frustration for the rest of the day because this was not a very successful endeavor for us. Then we will fly back to New York, get back to your suite and then crack open a bottle of your favorite whatever and celebrate today's breakthrough when we get back. Can you do that for me?" he asked without really asking. Seems that was getting to be a pretty common practice lately.

"Yes, I can do that for you. Thank you, Senior Special Agent Miloc, and thank you, too, Steve. Now let's stop wasting our time here and get on with this. I need something to wash the taste of that nasty kale smoothie out of my mouth," she said in all seriousness.

They wrapped up their activities, policed up their notes, and personal items and thanked their attendants for the minimal assistance they provided throughout the day which was mostly waiting patiently outside the room. They exited the building, walked leisurely to the parking lot where the vehicles and their occupants were either already waiting or converging.

It was only then that Betty realized they had a protective detail looking out for them on campus the entire time. That both assured her and reminded her of just how serious a thing she and her friends were involved in. It seemed surreal, but she knew that if they were correct then the stakes were higher than anything she ever wanted to be mixed up in. Yet here she was.

It was scary, it was exhilarating but it was real. She was glad she found what she found, and even more glad to see Steve and Miloc on either side of her. She was not afraid, she knew they were there for her and they would protect her at any cost, if it ever came to that. She was grateful for that feeling, as it had been absent from her life ever since her husband passed. Now that it had found her again, she decided the comfort it brought her was something she was not willing to do without again. The peace she felt right there as she climbed into the SUV was as refreshing as it was addictive. She finally had it back and had every intention of doing what she could to keep it, and she understood what that meant. She was ready.

CHAPTER FOURTEEN

COLLABORATION

I t was an early start for the UN team as they prepared to host their Chinese counterparts for the first meeting of the newly combined effort to field the on-demand weather technology that each claimed as their own. Colonel Lincoln was the senior military officer on the team, a detail Tom had personally seen to which enabled plenty of room for top cover without a credibility hit for those "above my pay grade" decisions. This allowed time to strategize and conduct behind the scenes discussions and research before getting back to the UN brass or anyone else for that matter. Having a general officer leading the team would make that more difficult, and now with the heavy involvement of the CCP military machine in the discussions the lack of higher-level involvement would certainly become an early protocol issue for their newfound partners.

As the meeting area was readied, it was a little unnerving because there had not been a list of attendees provided to the UN so there was no way to know for sure who would be coming today, and what levels of participation the team should be prepared to engage. As a result, it was all hands at the first meeting to be prepared for any level of engagement. The operational leaders were assembling near the meeting area entrance. Colonel Lincoln, Mr. Dau were the co-leads of the UN effort even though their ranks in their respective organizations were hardly equivalent.

Tom was considered a team member not a team leader despite his nebulously vague title of National Security Advisor. Not everyone on the team, or in the organization knew he was personally advising the President of the United States. Bob was the technical lead and Ann was a key member of this team, as were Captain Lessur and Sergeant Andies, among others. The latter of the two had still not returned from his earlier flight out with Tom, who had also not been seen since their departure the day prior.

And just like any other day at work, the delegation from the CCP team began to file into the meeting room and take seats wherever there were empty ones to be filled. The UN team followed suit as the meeting room began to fill quickly.

Frank and Mr. Dau held their positions near the front row of chairs closest to the podium and waited for the leaders of the entering group to make themselves known to the small group at the front of the attendees. As Bob, Ann, Frank and Mr. Dau scanned the room for their new counterparts, it became clear that they would be the last to enter as they were doing so and the doors closed behind them. The five men made their way toward them as the UN leadership waited to greet them and introduce themselves. Ann could see three of them wearing highly adorned military uniforms, another in a suit of reasonably nice quality, and the other man was Zach.

As they made their introductions, the senior member introduced himself as Major General Chen, followed by two senior colonels, Mr. Wu and Zach. This was their leadership team, and there were about twenty-five others seated in the room in various military uniforms mixed with civilian attired staff. The composition of their team was similar in size and expertise to the UN's team, which did not surprise anyone as they believed they had been studied carefully since the beginning of their operations. The UN team's belief was correct.

Zach's presence had the desired effect of making the introductions and meeting very awkward, particularly for Bob and Ann who both had personal history with him back at the US research facility. The tension was palpable, but the need for collaboration provided the opportunity to gather information about the past and present not just the future. And so, they began as they took their seats at the front and Colonel Lincoln opened the first session.

"Major General Chen, senior colonels, Mr. Dau and other distinguished guests and colleagues, my name is Colonel Lincoln and it is my pleasure to welcome you all to the newly combined CCP-UN effort for on-demand weather modification. We are pleased to have you here, and look forward to working together to bring this amazing technology to the world. We will provide a walking tour of our operations at this location shortly, to allow our staff to introduce themselves and their teams as they show their work centers and current capabilities in support of this effort. But first, I would like to provide Major General Chen the opportunity to address everyone if it would please you to do so, General?" Frank offered the podium to the senior military officer in the room.

"Yes, yes thank you, Colonel," the general accepted graciously and addressed those in the room in well-spoken English.

"It is our pleasure to be here, and to be working with you all on this great technology. We understand it is new and exciting to you and your work fills you with hope and optimism. We too share that hope and optimism about this technology. It will change the world as we know it, that is certain. It is unfortunate that just as with many new technologies, there are both positive and negative advances, and sometimes hard lessons must be learned. We too know that is not an easy thing. It is now our collective mission to do all we can to learn from these successes and failures and apply them in such a way as to advance our shared objectives. We very much look forward to working with you, learning from you, and perhaps teaching some things as well. Thank you all," he concluded smoothly and gestured for Frank to lead the way to whatever he had planned next.

"He is very polished. Smooth, articulate and his English is excellent," Ann whispered to Bob who nodded up and down and simply said, "He sure is. This should be interesting." And with that he fell in behind Mr. Dau and followed them with Ann at his side, to the first work area for their briefing. Zach and Mr. Wu were following behind, and all Bob could think of was how much he did not like having Zach behind him, or, for that matter, anyplace that he could not be seen and continually watched. But that was not to be the case today, and Bob knew he needed to get used to that and get over himself if this was going to work out the way everyone needed it to. They had several main working areas to get through before they got to Bob's team. They were the ones who stored, maintained, tested and employed the Thor's Hammers and he was looking forward to giving that briefing and watching Zach as he did.

After several briefings and a short break, it was time for the group to meet the Technology Team. The previous sessions had gone well, in fact they were collegial across the spectrum of participants. And while Bob hoped for the same here, he was confident that his team's tasks were the most controversial for the merged capability team. He also knew that he would likely be sparring with at least one of the CCP team members regarding the topics and capabilities that he needed to cover today, so he just dove right in and began his briefing.

"My name is Professor Robert Mcleod, but please call me Bob. I am the team leader for the Technology Team. Our primary purpose is to care for and employ the devices that are used to change the weather on-demand. We refer to these devices as Thor's Hammers. Thor is the Norse god of thunder, lighting and storms, and he used a hammer to do his work. Thus, the name." Bob paused to allow for a question or two before he went on but there were none, or nobody willing to ask one yet. Bob figured he didn't have time to waste, so he unlocked the case he had positioned on the portable work table and opened it. He leaned the case forward so the group could get a look and the device firmly seated in the heavy but soft foam padding inside the carbon fiber protective case.

"This is one of our Thor's Hammers. As you can see, it is small and easily portable by one person."

"Is that the one you used in the last demonstration? Is that the one from the high wind event?" The two questions from one of the senior colonels and his tone was not insulting or accusatory, it was in fact almost coldly and objectively a binary question. He was looking for Yes or No, and did not give the impression he needed, or even would entertain a qualified response beyond that which he sought.

"Yes Sir, this is the one that was in use that day," Bob responded and then waited, but there was no follow up from the senior colonel so he continued on with his remarks, explaining how the recipes are entered through an input touch screen.

"What do you think went wrong that day Professor?" asked the other senior colonel as Bob finished his explanation about the input screens. "Could it have been operator error, or a malfunction in the software that took the winds so high?" he posited.

Bob kept his cool and answered in a very matter of fact tone. "We are still looking into the events of that tragic day, Sir. At this point we are not sure what happened, but our investigation will be thorough and fair," he replied in truth, although he did omit a few important details about how he hoped that was going to happen. And then it happened.

Zach's question was a quick follow up to the colonel's thought. "If you aren't sure what happened, could a possible explanation be that perhaps something did not happen, and that is what caused the unfortunate event?"

"Of course, yes, that is also possible," Bob conceded the awkward point.

"It has been my experience that when something of this magnitude goes wrong, it is most frequently because something did not occur when it should have. Finding the source of what did happen is often revealed by first understanding what did not happen. Perhaps focusing there might be helpful to your understanding of that event," Zach concluded his experience-based insights.

"Thank you, Sir, I appreciate the advice," Bob said and then continued with his discussion about the devices themselves. The rest of the presentation went well, but only scratched the surface of what needed to be covered in much more detail with specific members of the teams. But Bob was replaying Zach's words over and over in his head. He wanted to believe there was a message hidden in plain sight, and that it was along the same lines as what Bob had perceived during the live demonstration. It could also be that was their intention, to plant the seeds of doubt regarding Zach's presence and participation in the CCP operations. It was working, Bob was not sure what to think or what to do next to provide any clarity. So, he decided to go for it, after all he had always heard that fortune favors the bold.

"How long have you been working on this technology?" Bob asked Major General Chen, who had certainly been prepped with canned responses to the most controversial issue likely to come to the group.

"Not too much longer than you and your team Professor. As we were completing some critical milestones of our own, we were quite surprised to see you and the UN disclosing a very similar capability to the press. That was very disappointing for us," he paused with a sigh.

"Yes, I can only imagine," Bob replied, as the general had not quantified his response and it certainly could be interpreted in more than one way. As Bob was thinking to himself, I bet you were disappointed to see us in the press with your covert program and technology in hand to eliminate any plausible denial of its existence. I bet that was disappointing, so let's find out how disappointing it really was.

"And you, Zach, how long have you been working on this technology with your CCP counterparts?" Bob tested his own theory about him. After a brief pause, his response was transparent.

"I was only recently brought onto the weather modification effort, but have been working on the CCP advanced technology team for many years. You will find them quite talented, and very resourceful. I am confident that our collective efforts will be very productive. You have my commitment to contributing whatever I can to that success," he promised Bob and the others in the room.

Well, it seemed everyone in the room was telling the truth but with a meaning far different than the words meant at face value. Did Zach just admit to working with the Chinese while he was at the US classified research and development center? Did he just tell us to look at that and see that he has been providing US technology to them? If so, and he has only been on the weather effort for a short time, that would certainly fit the scenario Tom and the others were pursuing. It would also fit the meaning of Bob's observations of Zach's behavior during the demo. They may have picked him up and are forcing his participation. That seems to be a real possibility. Zach may not be working for the CCP, it could very well be that he is being held by the CCP. And it could be both. If he was a double agent for them, he could very well be a double agent for us. That needed to be sorted out. Sure would be nice if Tom got back soon Bob considered as Ann was wrapping up her response to the most recent question to the team.

As if Bob had wished him into the room, he saw Tom walking across the back of the group and having a brief conversation with Frank. As quickly as he appeared, Tom was gone again. There was no indication whether it was good news or bad that Tom had delivered to the colonel. That update would likely have to wait for the debrief which was to occur immediately after the CCP team's departure. Today, in fact the next few days were labeled as orientation for the two teams. This was an initial period to meet collectively and individually as needed to gain a common understanding of what each side could contribute to the agreed upon objectives. The next step after orientation was planning, and this included assigning roles as well as resource allocation. Not only did this cover equipment, funding, key and support capabilities but also people. It made sense that Zach would be assigned to the technology team, but with Bob and Ann leading that effort for the UN it was unclear if their counterparts would put him in close proximity to them if Bob's hunch was right. Rather than wait to see, Bob took the proverbial bull by the horns and made a bold but uncoordinated move as their workplace briefing was wrapping up.

"Major General Chen, Sir, I was thinking about what Mr. Zach said earlier. It was sage advice. We are still not one hundred percent certain what went wrong with our demonstration. We don't know yet what did not work properly and to advance, we really need to understand that. If I could focus on that, it may assist our collaboration moving forward. I would appreciate your consideration to having Mr. Zach lead the technology team efforts. I mean the precision that was needed to accurately put the rain shower in position to project a rainbow for the audience was admirable. My team and I should be able to close the knowledge gap quickly, and with his unique experiences with both of our programs I can think of no one better qualified to lead this portion of our efforts than him. Would you please indulge my request, Sir? I believe it is by far the best option. No disrespect intended for other members of your team, Sir," Bob concluded as he could see Mr. Wu fidgeting uncomfortably as the Professor made his request.

"That is certainly an option we will consider given your rationale Professor. You may not be aware that Mr. Wu has been our lead on this effort since its inception. You might say he has a role very similar to the one you fill on the UN team. It may be true that he does not have the same familiarity with your device as Mr. Zach but he is a brilliant scientist and a quick study. We will give your request serious deliberation as we proceed making our recommendations and assignments," he assured Bob as he took a few steps toward Colonel Lincoln and began the walk to the next work center briefing.

That was the discussion Bob expected to hear if indeed Zach was an untrusted agent or a captive participant. Had he been in position where the CCP team was leveraging him into a US technology as the rest of the world is seeing with their own eyes, they would have jumped at the chance to take the lead on the technology team where he would have access to virtually everything about the UN technology, but they did not. One reason they might not is because Zack does not know what to steer our team away from as we move forward. That, or they do not trust him to steer us clear from critical facts or capabilities as they relate to the CCP version of on-demand weather modification.

That would mean Mr. Wu is the one who does. And that means we need to learn as much about Mr. Wu as we can in the shortest amount of time possible. Bob was comforted in the idea that Frank was probably updating Tom as much as the other way around. Bob smiled as he had gotten smart enough to know that once their leadership team was introduced, there were intelligence professionals hard at work collecting, analyzing and producing for us every detail that could be known about these men. Whether they used their real names or not, there was still facial recognition and DNA databases that were likely already being used to verify whatever results were already in. Water bottles, coffee cups or pens used to sign in; all provide sufficient opportunities to get everyone soon enough if they were lagging behind their teammates. Bob and Ann followed the group to the next session, but Bob's mind was on the debrief more than the business at hand which was not an ideal situation.

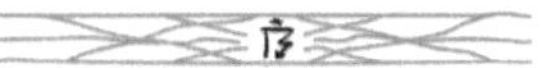

After their day at the University, and the uneventful travel back to New York, the three entered Betty's suite at the hotel to do some form of private celebration. After finding what they hoped were a series of connections to the evolution of the Thor's Hammer and the Chinese shell corporations, Betty, Steve and Miloc were looking forward to a drink and an opportunity to discuss and shake off the very long day. As they entered her suite, Betty was surprised to see some portable tables set up with computers, scanners and other equipment all being fully engaged by a group of very young and very caffeinated men and women. Some were in sports jerseys, some in khaki pants and polo shirts, others wore jeans and t-shirts. All were busy typing on their computers, talking into their headsets, or texting in their cell phones, but it was clear they were all business. This group assembled in her room was one comprised of the best and brightest the nation had to offer, and who had offered to serve her interests within one of her most secretive agencies.

They barely looked up to see who had entered their new makeshift operations area, and once they saw an older woman, her gentleman friend and an obvious Fed they went back to their work without delay.

"Well, I guess we don't need to check in for an update from Tom, but I did text him and let him know we were back. Betty, this might not be a quiet or restful place for you tonight as I don't believe they will be leaving until they are completely finished with their work. Do you think we could use some of the extra rooms Bob has on this floor for a night or two? That is what he got them for isn't it?" Miloc asked.

"I am already checked into one of them when I got here, so we have at least one," Steve offered.

"We can check with the front desk to get keys to the other one, and maybe there are already keys in Bob and Ann's suite. I know I didn't have a key to any of the other rooms except the one we used to store the files and they took the bed out of that one for us when we arrived," Betty added as Miloc spoke into his radio to have one of the security team check with the desk for them.

"That works for now. Betty, would you grab whatever you need for the night and tomorrow from your room and we will head down the hall to Steve's room?" Miloc asked.

"I have everything I need in the bag I have with me," she smiled confidently. "Let's go. And if you don't have something to make a drink in your room, we better have them bring something up with the keys."

"Oh, no worries there. I have your drink options covered," Steve smiled as he led the way down the hall toward the room fiddling around in his pocket to find the paper containing the keypad combination. They settled into a comfortable spot and Steve filled the role of bartender making each their drink of choice before he joined them. As they sat and tried to relax, they recounted the events of the day, discussing what that might mean and what they hoped the team just down the hall would successfully uncover. As the drinks and comfortable seats began to work their magic, Miloc frowned a bit and responded into his radio microphone after what appeared to be bad news arrived through his earpiece. "OK, no worries bring up the codes to theirs then," he directed, and then turned to Steve and Betty. "There is only one additional room, so I asked them to bring the key to Bob and Ann's suite, so you could stay there, Betty. It is the most comfortable and I am sure they won't mind you using it a day or two while they are gone. I'd like to be close to the team in your room and to you both, so if it's all the same I will take the empty room down the hall. Then Steve doesn't have to shuffle anything?"

"Fine by me," Steve agreed.

"If you wouldn't mind, I am really not comfortable staying in their rooms while they are gone. And if I'm being totally honest, I am still seeing ghosts behind every tree after all that has happened. Steve, would you be ok if I stayed here with you for tonight? It's comforting for me knowing you are close by. In my mind I know everything will be fine, but feeling that way is something I have not yet achieved," she confessed.

"Fine by me," Steve agreed, again.

"You two do you two, whatever you prefer. Just so I know where to find you both if I need to locate you in a hurry. Well, with that new development, if there is nothing else you need from me then I am going to call it a night. It has been a long day, well a long week really. See you both in the morning," he said as he headed for the door, but was intercepted by Betty who stopped him, and gave him an appreciative hug.

"Thank you for everything. You're good at what you do, and you are a good man. We are all lucky to have you as a friend, and I believe Doc put us together for this very reason. I know he is helping us from wherever he is right now. I can feel it. Let's finish this as soon as we can," she said.

He smiled, and nodded as he closed the door behind him leaving her and Steve alone to settle in for the night. Betty walked back toward her drink, picked it up and finished it then set the empty glass down on the table next to Steve's. Without hesitation, she sat in his lap, put her arms around his neck, told him "Thank you for everything." Then she kissed him on the lips and kept kissing him hoping he would kiss her too. He did not disappoint, as the pair helped each other rekindle feelings suppressed for years since their spouses had passed years before.

Day one of orientation ended with a mostly collegial exchange of information and ideas of where each team was on the ability spectrum of the key areas for their respective programs and an agreed upon start time of 0800 for tomorrow. The UN team debrief was a smaller group than usual as there were some key discussions and decisions that needed action. The location was also different for what Bob perceived as security and perhaps electronic surveillance concerns. They moved their discussion to Tom's small, isolated office that was also a mobile SCIF and one of the areas not made available to the CCP delegation on today's tour. Tom, Mr. Dau, Frank, Bob, Ann and Captain Lessur were the only ones in attendance which indicated this information was to be as closely held as any they had yet discussed.

Tom began the discussion with his usually candid BLUF (Bottom Line Up Front) statement. "I have a lot to share, and candidly I am still processing much of it myself and it is still dynamic with new information coming in as it's learned. The CCP was correct when they claimed we had their technology. They developed and fielded a weather modification technology almost ten years ago. The Thor's Hammers we possess were not invented by, developed by, nor built by Doc Auster. That is a lot to unpack so let's begin there, but that's not all, so strap in for more as we go."

Looking around the room, Tom was interested in the body language and the responses from those in the room, but he was most focused on Bob. Afterall, he was central to the story they were told and why they were where they were today. If there was a connection between Bob and the CCP it had not been made yet, until today. And that connection was Zach. It was not that Tom really suspected Bob of anything given the journey he had taken, but Bob was the one with a five-billion-dollar bank account courtesy of Thor's Hammer so he was certainly at the top of every "watch for" list that was being run by every national entity that Tom could engage to get to the bottom of all this.

"Betty, Steve and Miloc from the Bureau came through. They leveraged the University's lawsuit against Bob to access all their records as a discovery exercise to prepare your defense. Smart. They looked at the origins of the grant, the lawsuit, and funding, etc. and made some connections between some of the names on those documents. Then we tried to connect them back to the companies that we already knew about. It did not take very long to connect many of them together and tie them back to a couple of key entities within the CCP. Sparing you the details for now, suffice to say that the weather data Doc and Bob were collecting and analyzing for the purposes of determining downwind levels from deposition of industrial uses was a cover and not the primary interest of those funding the weather data collection efforts under that grant."

Bob's face visually contorted, and he asked Tom, "What was the primary purpose of this long-term study?"

"It was the testing, then operation of the Thor's Hammer on-demand weather modification regional network, Bob. It was one of several areas covered with special weather sensors that observed both the standard environmental conditions, plus a couple more the CCP needed to be able to monitor. But these efforts were not limited to standard equipment on the typical national weather observing systems. They hid their research, their operations and their monitoring systems in plain sight and funded them all through a series of lawsuit settlements like the one that drove your project and the grant funds they provided for it."

"Tom, you said regional network, what does that mean?" Bob asked hoping against hope that Tom misspoke.

"Thor's Hammer was the name given to their early devices, and they deployed a number of devices in each region to get area coverage and area impacts. They were not just for one site. And there were multiple areas in play at any given time. We know of at least five in the US alone, and are uncovering others in different places OCONUS. We believe Doc, not sure yet how, but that Doc discovered and obtained one of the devices from your home region. We also believe that the small differences between the device you got from Doc and the one that Father Gannon had were because they were from different regions, or they were different versions of the ones used in your region. Could be either reason works out to the same result. Have to give Betty and the boys credit for connecting the names. The network in your region were all Norse in origin and relation, but the other regions were each based on different mythologies or legends. Once we got a theme to follow, and knew what we were looking for, our nation's best sniffers did the rest.

"But credit for the rest of this breakthrough goes to Sergeant Andies. You guys are never getting that dude back from me without a fight. Sorry I know I promised to give him back, but that's one promise I may have to go back on. He looked at the data sets Betty sent from New York and started seeing something happening at sites that did not make sense for what was happening in the region. And then claimed something about most of the region not making perfect sense with what was going on upstream or some kind of weather speak. He started looking at charts and graphs and pictures, got pissed off, got happy, got pissed off again and a day or so without sleep and a couple gallons of coffee he had it figured out. He showed us, and then the whole thing began to come into view."

Captain Lessur, was pleased to know his sergeant was key to the solution, but more shocked at the implications of the discovery. "Tom, I am going to want him back, eventually. But what you are telling us is the CCP has been manipulating the weather in the United States for years now, and without us knowing they were doing it? That is hard to fathom."

"Ya' think?" Tom said sarcastically. "Well, Andies convinced me, and the three other meteorologists now read into this program are all verifying everything he has claimed so far. It's already confirmed, and they are steadfastly failing at disproving any of Andies' claims."

"They won't find any flaws in his work, I am confident of that," Bob added. "This all fits together and it is frightening. Moreover, knowing what you just told us, everything the Major General and his team have said today is technically true and correct. From their lens it means one thing, but from ours given what they want us to keep believing it means something completely different. It's been that way the whole time. They can say one thing truthfully and produce a result entirely different than what we want or expect based on our reality as we understand it. That's brilliant and simple in its complexity," Bob added.

"That can also mean that the whole time we are looking at Zach for the whole flooding disaster in India, he may have had nothing to do with it. Same with the high wind event. Do we know if this region of India is one of the regions they were already operating in?" Bob asked.

"Now you are doing more than coming along for the ride, Bob," Tom added. "We have not found anything that ties this area to one of the regional operations areas yet. That doesn't mean it wasn't one. But what we did find up here after we re-analyzed all of our sensor collections was more than just those balloon ops we found earlier, or more appropriately that they showed us. Thor's Hammers are all we knew about, so they kept us chasing the rudimentary approaches and we took that bait. Bit hard on it. But when we looked back at both events, each one had a similar anomaly. A search and rescue mission for a missing aircraft. A late arrival for an overdue flight plan, both of which turned out to be nothing other than a flight plan error and the planes and those onboard were accounted for, appropriately chastised and sent on their way.

"In both of these cases the host nation used some long loiter UAVs to conduct a grid pattern search for the overdue aircraft. And in both cases these UAVs originated from the same airfield, which should not be a surprise…until you hear that the airfield and the platforms were both from just across the border and responded to an emergency assistance call which allowed them to safely and legally cross the border without incident. These UAVs have some unique flight and electronic signatures that are not found on other aerial surveillance platforms. We have ascertained that these are airborne versions of the same technology that has been deployed to conduct weather modification operations. And we have confirmed the presence of at least forty of these exact platforms deployed to Chinese airfields in a number of countries.

"We are also sure that at least one of their aircraft carriers has three of these exact UAVs assigned. While we are confirming, I am confident there will be others if not all of the others that have the same capability. That means they have an in-place operational ability to do regional on-demand weather modification, including in some or all of our own country. And the ability to project that same threat from the air and the sea."

"Shit, holy shit," Colonel Lincoln said as the gravity of that capability gap between the two nations sank in.

"Hang on to your hat, Frank. It gets worse," Tom added. "So, we now know, with certainty that they have a mature, operational regional capability that can be employed from the ground, or projected via air or maritime assets. It exists in different configurations, including the man-portable version which we are familiar with. Right now, they are not using it as a power projection weapon. They don't have to, yet. It's still a secret to the world. But they are using it as an economic weapon to systematically increase their financial holdings by impacting others, then buying the pieces for pennies on the dollar. Our financial guys are working as fast as they can to uncover the details by doing postmortems on the greatest losses in the past ten years.

"So, what we need right now is to buy all these folks some time to do what they do. The best way to do that is to keep everyone's eyes and ears focused on this team and the new collaboration. Keep our friends close, and our enemies closer shall we say. What is the best way to do that?" Tom stopped for now and looked around the room.

"We schedule the next demonstration for three days from now in some different location," Ann suggested. "We announce it, and we start packing up. We know they can operate here; they have done it twice. Let's take them somewhere it won't be as easy for them. They probably want us to sit here and be paralyzed by an analysis they know won't produce any results beyond what they want us to see. Let's continue our orientation by showing them how we pack up and leave, and how we unpack and set up when we get somewhere new. Let's go do a demonstration on some neutral ground. Let's make them show us how they pack up, what they move, and how they set it up when they get there. We announced this spot a week before we got here, that gave them plenty of time. We have already blown our previously announced UN tour locations and dates. Let's pick one that is both highly visible for the press, and one that we can monitor easily with whatever we need to look at them with."

"That's why we do these things, Ann. I like that idea. Thoughts?" Tom pressed, and Mr. Dau suggested Australia. "Why Australia?"

"It's a long way from China. They are a US and UN friendly nation. And they are in the Southern Hemisphere. Do we know how this technology works down there, or if it does? They may need to reveal an entirely different capability to work down under. It may all be the same stuff, I don't know, but the distance along with the relative isolation means we will have lots of time to see who is coming," he explained.

"OK, I buy all that," Tom said. "Any other suggestions or downsides to Australia? Seeing none, then Australia it is."

"Tom, earlier you said there was more. What did you mean?" Mr. Dau asked.

"Oh, yeah, that. Well now that we have a gameplan that we all bought into, I need you to stick around for another half hour or so and pitch it to our bosses," Tom, explained as he was typing or texting into one of his phones. "Get ready. We are on in three minutes with all the principles at UN and the White House." And with that the video teleconferencing computer and monitors came to life as the encrypted systems began their extensive digital handshakes that enabled such secure communications to occur without fear of being intercepted by those who sought to listen but were not invited.

There were blocks of the screen that showed the room they were in, one showing the UN headquarters with the Secretary General and a small number of his staff, the White House portion showed the situation room which was crammed with uniformed personnel from different services including General Charles and SECDEF Fitzgerald, as well as several other well-dressed men and women whose faces were quite familiar to anyone who paid attention to politics these days. The last square on the screen was labeled as the US Embassy, India and the Ambassador, his Chief of Station and military liaison were the only three visible in that room. Once all were signed in, and the encryption confirmed panel was lit, they were ready to begin and the President of the United States strode to his desk in the Oval Office, took his seat and began speaking as he did so.

"Hello everyone. Mr. Secretary General, Secretary Fitzgerald, Ambassador, Dutch and the rest of you out there, thank you for coming together on short notice to discuss this matter. Where do we want to begin?" he asked to measure the room, and those on the call.

It was Secretary of Defense Fitzgerald who responded first, "Mr. President, I can say that, since we last spoke, we have received nothing but confirmations that this capability is real, and that it is operational, and that it has been for quite some time. I don't think now is the time or place yet to hash out how that can be true without us knowing, especially on our own soil but that appears to be our new reality. It is employable by foot, by ground, air and seaborne vehicles. And they are good at both using it, and hiding when they are using it.

"We are currently examining ways and systems we possess that might be effective in monitoring or countering their use of Thor's Hammers, but we don't know the extent or electronic signatures of what other variations of the same technology are already out there or in development. We are not blind to their systems, but it will take a while to figure out what we are looking for, and what it looks like when we see it. They have been hiding it all in plain sight for so long that we really need to question the voracity of everything we have been collecting on for years to see if it really is tied to what we think it's tied to."

"Well, that's encouraging Fitz," the President said sarcastically. "Tom, what can you add from out there? How did day one with these guys go?"

"Sir, day one went much like we expected. We showed them ours, they talked about but didn't show us theirs. Some jockeying for position, but all very collegial. We are as confident as we can be this early in our examinations that while they have an advanced regional capability, they are only, or primarily using it for economic gains, that can then be translated into soft power gains. They are working hard to keep this off the books and behind the scenes, and, until Doc Auster and Professor Mcleod, they appear to have been wildly successful," Tom paused, and the President took the opportunity as it was presented.

"What do you want to do out there, while we are burning up brains and computers back here?" he asked.

"We want to get the defense off the field, Sir, and send in the offense. Specifically, the consensus here is that we consummate our new partnership with the CCP by announcing our next demonstration. We want to do it in Australia in three days, and we want to announce it tonight." Again, Tom paused to see if that idea was dead on arrival or if there was an appetite to discuss the why behind the notion.

"Explain," the President entertained the notion, and Tom provided almost word for word the rationale Ann had provided him only moments earlier. The President looked around the room and at the screen, then asked nobody in particular.

"If anyone has a better idea, I want to hear it now. If anyone thinks this is a shit idea, I want to hear why right now too. We can't afford to screw this up so speak up if you're not good with this for any reason," he invited. Bob reluctantly seized the opportunity, despite the plan on the table being Ann's idea.

"Mr. President, I am all for taking this course of action. But I would be remiss if I didn't bring up for consideration the notion of Zach, and his role in all of this." Bob paused, taking a page from Tom's playbook, before putting his thoughts out there despite the invitation from the commander in chief to do so.

"OK, Professor what about Zach has your knickers in a knot?" He was calibrating Bob's confidence and resolve in whatever concern he was about to share.

"Seems that with all we have learned in the last day or so, that we need to question a lot of things that just don't seem to be what we thought they were. Especially me sir, this is a lot for me to process being square in the middle of it all. But I am now doubtful that Zach had any role in this beyond stealing the devices with the intention of selling them to the highest bidder. I think he may have been selling our secrets to the CCP, and he probably was looking to sell this to them or someone else but I don't think he is helping them undermine our UN efforts by choice. They may be blackmailing, threatening, or otherwise coercing him to play along until he can make the leap from them back to us. I am pretty sure he is looking to have us help him get out from under the CCP. He might be in a position to help us in a number of ways. He could be an asset," Bob offered for consideration.

"So what?" the President shot back. "He sold our secrets to them, joined up with them, and you think we should invite him back? Of course, he wants to come back over to our side, he knows they consider him untrustworthy. Once a traitor always a traitor. They aren't going to show him anything meaningful and they will use him as a propaganda tool as long as he is valuable to them. When he no longer is, they will disappear him. He is a loose end that needs to be tied up, and that is the case for both them and us. The sooner they take care of that, the better for all of us. Double agents cannot have singular loyalties." He was ready to move on, but Bob persisted.

"I must disagree, Mr. President. Double agents do have, and only have singular loyalties. They are loyal to themselves. They are in it for themselves, and if they are threatened will do what it takes to mitigate that threat and survive. His singular loyalty is to himself, and you said yourself they are going to disappear him. If we can control that, we can leverage him to give us what we want in order to get him out before they do. And I think we can do that in Australia while we are there for the next demonstration if we stick to the timeline Tom laid out."

"I'm not sure if you are trying to convince me to go with or avoid this Australia recommendation, but candidly I know Zach will get what's coming to him. The only question is the timeline. OK, if nobody has any other objections, let's go with the Australia plan. Tom, Frank you guys need to be on you're A-game. If this starts to go bad, I need to know the same minute you do.

"Mr. Secretary General and Mr. Dau, are you both on board with this idea? Can you meet the timeline, and what do you need from us that you don't already have?" he asked.

Mr. Dau nodded in approval without saying anything, as he left the verbal response to his boss who took the opportunity.

"Yes, Mr. President. I can see that path may produce the short-term outcomes we seek, while we refine the longer-term objectives. I will make the announcement this evening to ensure there is some room for plausible denial from Mr. Dau and the team on the ground there. It will be portrayed as an overly enthusiastic directive from the UN Headquarters to show the world how well this new collaboration is working and what a great idea it was for the Chinese to make such a gracious offer. I think we have all we need for the time being," the Secretary General assured the President.

"Sounds like you do, I can't wait to see this press release and the video that goes with it," the President chided the Secretary General.

"OK, well I guess this was a productive meeting. We all have a lot to do. Thanks for your time, now let's go figure out the rest of this mess," he concluded and stood up behind the desk and the screens all went blank.

He walked over to his two senior military advisors and asked, pointedly, "Is there anything we have in our vast arsenals that can counter this if they decide to use it as weapon against us? What do we use on them if they turn this on us?" The concern was beyond hypothetical.

"We don't have anything on scale to match them right now. I mean we would need to fight fire with fire, and counter whatever bad weather event they send our way with the opposite kind of weather. We talked about that before but that is a reactive posture, and all we have to do that with are a couple of Thor's' Hammers against their in-place regional arsenals," Secretary Fitzgerald offered little new to the discussion.

General Charles added, "We could try to locate and isolate what they have fielded. Take out the computers controlling them, shoot down, disable, capture their fielded systems in place to limit their effectiveness. But for that to work it would have to be a coordinated attack on all of them at the exact same time. Anything we miss could be used to counterattack because, well, we would have attacked them first. Right now, they are just using this stuff to get rich without full disclosure. That's a crime maybe, but we would be starting a shooting war. And they have the ultimate weapons of mass destruction to shoot back with. I don't like that course of action at all, Sir," Dutch concluded.

"The other thing we can do is try to catch up or pass them. If we can get, or steal what they already have, that would help even the playing field. Shoot them with their own gun so to speak. I don't know how long it takes to build these things but we better hurry up and start, because we are in an arms race that started years ago and nobody told us we were in it. That is how you lose races, not win them."

The President nodded in agreement with his Chairman and looked to the Secretary of Defense for any other ideas. "This leaves us in a bad position, we are playing catch up just to try to get even. How can we get ahead? What can we do to get an upper hand on them while they are still unaware that we know what they have been doing?"

With that question, the SECDEF spoke what he was not yet ready to explain, "If they are doing regional operations, and are doing it from carriers, and UAVs then the next step for them or us is to be able to do it globally. I mean those are our realms of operation, local-regional-global. So, let's put these damned things on orbit and get global capability from space before they can do regional attacks on us. We can counter globally from space-based systems if we have a capability up there."

"I like where you are going with this, Fitz," the President smiled. "I guess you and Dutch have your next homework assignment. Go figure out how to get some of this on-orbit but control it from down here. Not sure how you are going to do that, but that's why we pay you the big bucks and give you all that neat shit to play with."

It was few hours later that the headline on all the new channels included the announcement that the UN and CCP on-demand weather team would be conducting their first joint demonstration in three days near Darwin Australia. That widely publicized announcement made for a very turbulent second day of orientation for the burgeoning team as both the UN and CCP members complained bitterly about the ill-informed blindside from their headquarters back in New York. Nothing brings people together like a common foe or unpleasant task directed by seemingly detached leaders far away from where the real work is being done. And this was just one of those occasions, much to the delight of Tom, Frank and the few others in the know.

CHAPTER FIFTEEN

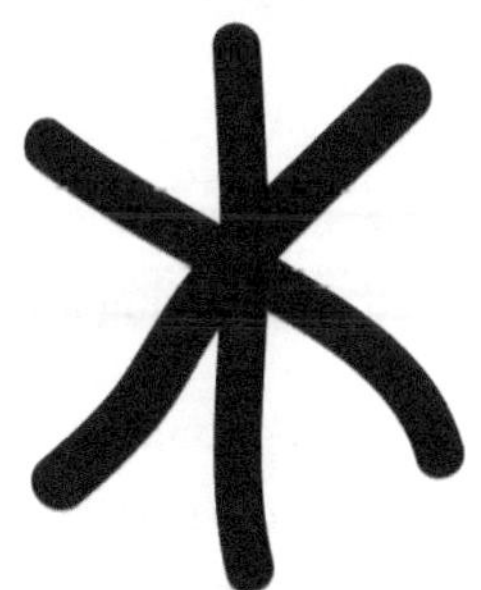

DOWN UNDER

I t is inexcusable," Major General Chen fumed in the small room with his UN counterparts. "Decisions of this magnitude should not be made unilaterally when all of the resources involved are not contributed by a single entity. This is not how collaboration is done."

To the extent they could, without overtly undermining the UN Secretary General who had personally made the announcement earlier from halfway around the world in New York, the on-site leadership of the UN team agreed in principle with the upset major general as they were discussing the announcement.

"Yes Sir, as military men that would not typically be how we would make such decisions regarding our troop deployments. The United States has committed to support the UN led effort, and while we too were caught off guard by the Secretary General's announcement, I can assure you that myself and my contemporaries in theater and at the Pentagon will do all within our power to live up to the commitments made by our senior leaders. I have already directed our group to begin dismantling and packing up our supplies and equipment in order to have any hope of meeting the very short timeline to get to Darwin in time to coordinate and set up for a demonstration there," Colonel Lincoln explained very carefully, then added an offer to assist his senior military colleague.

"If there is something we can do to assist you and your team's preparation we will provide whatever we have at our disposal. If you have an idea of how many people and pallet positions you will require, I can begin by securing the needed airlift so we can coordinate the logistics for the flights. My country has promised both airlift and security for the UN mission, and by extension that of course includes your team, supplies and equipment. With a headcount, I will get my team on securing the required logistics, transportation, food and lodging arrangements."

"That is both gracious and professional of you, Colonel, but please stop the posturing. We both know you and your President are as unhappy about this Secretary General grandstanding with the sole purpose of elevating his own relevance above those who are out here cleaning up a mess of his making. Mr. Dau, I trust that you were equally unaware of this directive, but I must ask if that is the case, or did you know it was coming?" he asked the lead UN official.

"Sir, I am not offended by your question, and I can assure you that Colonel Lincoln and I both learned of this change in plans at the same time. I had no advance notice, and if I were to be totally candid when I saw it on the news that was my notification that we were going to Darwin. Not a very good look for me, but we all work for someone and mine is not to judge my boss's methods or timing," Mr. Dau said truthfully, but it also conveyed a completely different meaning to the person who was hearing it. He was appreciating the advantage that getting into a position to do that regularly might provide, and wondered if the major general was able to shift gears back and forth between what he was meaning when he said something and what the person hearing it would take it to mean. That must be maddening, living in two worlds at the same time.

"Yes, well very self-serving and poor form. Undermining your own staff is not the best way to start off a partnership and build trust. Makes one wonder what he is willing to do to us if this is how he treats his own." The general introduced the concept and let it lie there for their consideration before he continued, "What do you envision being our staff and equipment needs for this demonstration, and how does this impact our discussions on being able to work together with any confidence or proper safety protocols on such little time? "

"Indeed, that will be difficult. We can do some tabletop collaboration on the aircraft enroute if you care to, but I am skeptical that will be enough to become proficient. While I am reluctant to ask, and would not do so if Professor Mcleod were present, would having your team conduct the entire demonstration in Darwin be something that you would consider? This would allow Bob to focus on what went wrong earlier. He has been under tremendous stress since that tragedy, and I fear the pressure of pulling a demonstration together on such short notice may very well be more than he can withstand right now. You guys did such an impressive job with the one here, rainbow and all, that will be tough to equal let alone top," Frank queried and waited patiently for his request to be sufficiently mulled over by Major General Chen.

"I believe that would be a prudent option, Colonel, but I am not sure the aggressive timeline is conducive to a successful event. The travel time alone eats away more than half of the hours between now and then and we are still discussing how to depart from here," he cautioned them both.

"What if I can get us an additional twenty-four hours?" Mr. Dau tried to sway the general's opinion. "Would that be enough time if Frank can get you the aircraft you need, and the logistics? I think I know a way to stretch the clock, and it might also provide a little payback to my boss so next time he considers doing something like this he consults with me…us, first?"

"That may be enough time for me to make the required arrangements, but only if it comes with a lesson learned by the Secretary General. What did you have in mind that might accomplish this Mr. Dau?" After a brief explanation, and a gentleman's agreement the three men went their separate ways to commence fulfilling their portions of the agreement.

Major General Chen began assembling the men, equipment and supplies needed to conduct the demonstration with the UN team observing but not directly participating except as training opportunities presented during the preparations and the event itself. Colonel Lincoln requisitioned another four military transports for the effort as some of the operational systems the CCP team would need are vehicle mounted and already in the region for the recently completed demonstration. And Mr. Dau had already drafted the short mea culpa statement the Secretary General would personally deliver to the press correcting the date which he had read incorrectly from the prepared remarks earlier. With his sincerest apologies for the careless error, what he meant to say was the demonstration will be in four days in Darwin. He was terribly sorry for the error, and any confusion or inconvenience his mis-reading may have caused. That was enough 'payback' to satisfy the three deployed leaders, and to bring them a little closer together for having gotten it as a team. This collaboration stuff was not as hard as people made it seem.

As the last of the loading was complete, and they were just a few hours from the rally time to begin loading for the long flight a familiar face joined the group. Sergeant Andies was in uniform, laden with a loaded rucksack and carrying another with his personal items, civilian clothes and other necessities for the next leg of their mission. He was glad to see the smiles on the familiar faces that were already assembled, as they were wondering if he would be making the trip with them or working on whatever Tom had him doing for them. Nobody was happier to see him than Captain Lessur. First and foremost, there was no longer the looming confrontation with Tom to get his right-hand man back. Also, the weather work on-site here was challenging when fully staffed but almost untenable when a key team member like Andies was missing from the lineup. The captain was relieved to know he would be along for whatever came next in Australia.

They exchanged greetings and lighthearted jabs about being AWOL and coming back just after all the work was done. Almost as quickly as it began, the lighthearted atmosphere was sucked from the assembly area as the buses carrying their CCP counterparts rolled into the loading area and began to discharge their occupants and cargo. There were about four CCP team members to every UN member, and the sheer volume of people and cargo was a bit unexpected. It seemed the vast majority of those unloading wore their country's military uniform and it lived up to the description, they were uniform. They all looked exactly the same except the various rank insignia, you could barely tell one uniformed member from the other in their crisp new attire. They were making a show of it, and why not, Captain Lessur thought. They want us looking everywhere but where we should be looking to see what they don't want us to know. It seemed the gamesmanship never ended, but it was easier to see when one understood. And Captain Lessur counted himself fortunate to be among the few who could look beneath the bluster and showmanship and posturing and know what this mission to Australia was really all about.

With this many people, even as they were spread across the large military transports it would prove to be a long, crowded flight to Australia. Each aircraft was augmented fully with a second crew to ensure they could swap out as needed with several scheduled mid-air refuelings to enable them to reach their destination without enroute stops. There were not many creature comforts available on such long flights, but it did provide ample opportunities to catch up on your reading, videos, or anything else you could do on a computer with a headset. Conversations, especially private ones were nearly impossible inside one of these airships when in-flight, the noise was substantial and hard to ignore or overcome. It did however have its own rhythm, that both lulled you to sleep and then jolted you back awake with a cadence that made no sense except to the aircraft herself. Somehow, she knew when you needed to rest and when you needed to be awake. And so, it was on this aircraft when Bob was bounced from a nap by some turbulence that just happened to occur as Mr. Wu was checking on some cargo strapped to the floor of the aircraft. There was nothing remarkable about the cargo case that drew his recurring attention, but Mr. Wu had visited this same box several times during the flight thus far and they were only four hours into the long trip. Bob made careful note of the markings on the box and the number painted on the exterior and reminded himself to keep an eye out for others similarly marked.

While he hoped to see Zach before their departure, neither Bob nor Ann had put eyes on him. It was even more disappointing to see that Mr. Wu was on their same aircraft but they had not seen Zach whom they reasoned would likely be traveling together given their roles in the CCP effort. But they also recognized that the more distance between Bob, Ann and Zach the less risk there was for some unauthorized disclosure between the former colleagues reunited by circumstance rather than by choice.

Tom and Frank travelled together, but on a different aircraft than Bob and Ann. They decided to split the main team up to have more eyes in more places, but needed the quick access to resources in one place to synchronize and initiate actions in near real time from the robust communications center in the cockpit of the remarkable aircraft that could literally fly itself from point to point if need be. Zach was not on their aircraft either, in fact his name was not listed on the manifest for any of the aircraft carrying the team of teams to the land down under. That was both unfortunate, and telling, when overlaid with what was emerging as the new true on-demand weather modification program.

As Frank and Tom connected their headset to the communications console, the radio operator gave them a thumbs up that the secure satellite communications link was up and they were both connected and encrypted for their incoming call.

"Go for Tom," he said into the kiss mic that rested on his top lip.

"Hope you are having a great flight, Tom," the voice said smugly, "I have a few things you need to hear so pay attention. Who else is on?" the voice asked.

"Colonel Frank Lincoln," he spoke his own name into his mic as he did not recognize the voice in his headset.

"Hi Frank, it's Dutch Charles. Listen you guys, here are a few things you don't know yet but need to be aware of," he paused to compensate for the slight delay for what you say to get to where it is being heard. It's magic doing this encrypted while in-flight, but it's not without its warts.

"Zach is not on your military flights, but they are flying him there themselves along with some cargo that is also not on your loads. Look for him and whatever boxes he has with him. It looks like he will get there after you guys do because they don't have tankers lined up to get you there like we do. Got that one?" he asked.

"Copy, look for Zach plus extra cargo to arrive after we do," Frank confirmed.

"Next item, we have high confidence there is *not*, repeat **not** an operational network of Thor's Hammers in Australia. They will be using whatever they bring with them, or get from a pre-staged asset. There are no Chinese carrier groups close enough to get them what they need before the demonstration begins, but there is always an air option or like I said, pre-staged assets. Most likely, something important is coming on the plane with Zach…who may also be on the plane because he is another something important for them. Got that one?" he asked.

"Copy. High confidence no operational network in play. Look for what comes in or has been pre-staged to conduct demo. Again, see Zach," Frank summarized.

"Good. Next item, expect the UN Secretary General to show up in person and unannounced for the demonstration. This is intended to disrupt them not us. The Chinese will scramble to get someone of stature there as well, this will keep them off balance. Might help you see something while they are occupied with impressing some party big shot. Got that one?" again, he paused and waited for confirmation.

"Copy. Secretary General surprise DV—look for opportunities," Frank said.

"Good, next item." This was a longer pause than the others, "They confirmed the DUI driver in Doc Auster's hit and run was not behind the wheel until after the accident. FBI, forensics, local cops all in the same rooms put it together and of all things a doorbell camera from a vacant house had video of someone pulling the kid from the passenger seat into the driver's seat then running off. They are pretty sure they ID'd the guy as an investigator for the law firm representing all these lawsuits.

Doc's death was not an accident, Frank. Tom, your guys found it and they can prove it. Got that one."

"Copy. Doc murdered by CCP. Smoking gun recovered," Frank affirmed.

"Sorry. Next item," followed by another pause. "Maintain the belief that we have a new technology. Do not, repeat **not** indicate that we are on to them or even suspect they possess a more advanced version of the devices from Professor Mcleod. We need that level of tactical deception for as long as we can keep it. Got that one?"

"Copy. Basic capability only, maintain Tac-D," Frank confirmed.

"Good, Last item," Dutch began, "every press outlet that can get to Darwin will be there. You cannot buy a seat on a commercial flight for the next week and a half. You have a global stage gentleman, put on a good show because everyone who is not there in person will be watching courtesy of those who are able to get there. Got that one?"

"Copy. Press coverage out the wazoo. Last item from you, two from us," Frank confirmed as he saw Tom holding up two fingers.

"Go for two from you," Dutch confirmed and Tom's voice followed immediately behind the general's, "Item one, we are going to need some eyes and ears on Zach from his arrival on. He and his gear, we need to know where they go, who they talk to, what they say and how they disperse. Got that one?"

"Copy. Eyes and ears on Zach and gear. This is not our first rodeo boys, we got you covered on that already," the Chairman confirmed.

"Item two," Tom paused, "if you are so smart then why haven't you been able to convince the President to promote this colonel to brigadier general before you cause an international incident with Major General Chen? He's already pissed off, and you keep making that Chinese two star talk to a US colonel like they are peers or something. It's embarrassing for him and us, you made your point. Besides that, I'd say Frank has earned it.

How many other O-6's are you talking directly to today to personally make sure they have what they need Dutch? Got that one?"

"Copy, item two. You're right but Brigadier General Lincoln; one star is the best I can do for now. That's already done. Congratulations Frank. Tom has some stars in his pocket for you. Put them on right after we end the call. We'll do the formalities when you get back. Safe travels gentlemen. Out here," and the line went dead.

Frank was dumbfounded at that last exchange, at least until he noticed Tom's outstretched arm and the shiny five-pointed stars in his hand. "Congratulations Brigadier General Lincoln. Now please put these on because as of a few seconds ago, you are out of uniform. That's not a good way to start off, General," Tom smiled and turned his hand over and dropped the pair of stars into Frank's open hand.

"Thank you, Tom, thank you very much," Frank said with much gratitude as the shock was still fresh and lingering.

"Don't thank me, I'm just the delivery man. That was all Dutch and Fitz. They know what they have in you, and they trust you. This is them letting you feel that and making sure others do too. You're the right man in the right place at the right time, Frank. We're all lucky to have you on this, especially Mcleod. This could have gone very bad for him, just like it did for Doc but for you and your team. He may not see it yet, but you guys have already saved his ass once, and now we are all off to Australia to do it again," Tom rolled his eyes. "He's lucky to have such a good wingman."

"All the same," Frank insisted, "thank you, Tom. Speaking of Bob, as soon as possible after we land, we need to get the entire team linked up and on the same page. We will likely have some other news items besides these to convey since we will have spent the better part of a full day getting there before it's all said and done."

"That's still the plan, just like we briefed before we left. Please don't let me handing you that star be the first step in your cognitive decline, General." Tom's halfhearted humor received the appropriate halfhearted middle finger response, with the appropriate caveat of "…with all due respect to the National Security Advisor, this is all I can muster at this time." They both unhooked their headsets and headed back to the main body of the large transport where they could both see and be seen by the others on their flight.

The rest of the flight was filled with checking details, getting updates, snacks, and power naps until the landing gear touched down on the long concrete runway and the large transport taxied to the assigned parking area. This happened four more times in the next half hour as all the US airlift arrived in close interval. Passengers and cargo were all marshalled to and held in a secure area for customs, paperwork and transloading pax and gear onto a convoy of trucks and buses assembled to move them to their operations and billeting areas. As the group was assembling into their respective teams for the well-organized ground movement, Captain Lessur popped to attention and rendered the appropriate salute as Frank approached the loosely assembled technology team with Tom in tow, "Colonel Lincoln, Sir," he greeted, and then noticed the eagles were not in their assigned position and had been replaced by one-star brigadier general's rank insignia.

"Excuse me, Sir. General Lincoln, Sir! That must have been some flight Sir! Congratulations, not sure what I missed but that looks good on you, Sir, if I may say so," the captain recovered a bit awkwardly but proudly for his commander.

"Thanks, Ron, and yes it was some flight. How about you and yours? Everyone make it ok, everyone good?" Frank got right back to business, after all they had lots to do now that they were on the ground.

"All good, General, all good, Sir," he confirmed loudly as they were joined by Bob, Ann and several others.

"General? Did you call him General?" Ann asked quickly and with a big grin, which got even bigger when she saw the star on his uniform tab and gave him a big hug to affirm her approval of whatever she missed on the way here. "That's great Frank. Can I still call you Frank? What's the protocol here, I don't really know what the rules are on this so someone please help me out here," she stopped talking hoping someone would throw her a lifeline.

"Frank is just fine, and thank you, Ann," he assured her.

"That's great, General! Congratulations, Frank!" Bob added receiving a scowl in return with a brash, "That's Brigadier General Lincoln, Professor, I said she could call me Frank, that doesn't mean you can." But he couldn't keep a straight face long enough to make anyone uncomfortable except Bob for a split second before they all laughed loud enough to draw attention from those around them. Before very long the news had spread to the entire team of teams, and the first order of business had become congratulating the newly promoted officer while they were marshalling and loading the transports. The real work would begin shortly, and victories needed to be celebrated briefly but promptly lest the work sweeps away the opportunities, and the celebrations never regain their relevance, falling into the infinite bin of missed opportunities. It only takes a moment to mark a moment was a lesson too many people failed to learn early enough, if they learned it all.

The small team assembled for their pre-brief half an hour prior to the main briefing. Tom, Mr. Dau, Brigadier General Lincoln, Bob, Ann and, at this point, Captain Lessur and Sergeant Andies who were so integral to the operations that it was simpler to include them up front than to answer their insightful question later. After exchanging the latest information and guidance from the US and UN higher headquarters, the group decided their working strategy was still sufficient to go into the next phase. They confirmed next steps and wished each other luck as they broke to join their teams for the main briefing where much of the same information and guidance would be passed to the larger group for action but without some key rationale or details as to why these were the actions selected or by whom.

As the teams began to congregate in the designated rally areas from their billets, work areas or chow lines Bob saw Zach and Mr. Wu approaching the technology team's designated area in the main briefing. All told there were a little over two hundred fifty total and two thirds of the group wore Chinese military uniforms but it was still easy to spot Zach and Mr. Wu in the crowd given their builds and attire. Bob hoped those tasked with eyeballing Zach and his equipment had been successful in their tasks, but he had his own to concentrate on right now. As they approached the group, Bob made a bee line to the two approaching men.

"Gentlemen, I trust your flight was not too unpleasant and that you have been able to settle in just a little prior to the briefing. I do have several items I need to discuss prior to this main meeting getting started if you will indulge me for a moment," Bob asked and continued before they could disengage or defer his request. "This whole southern hemisphere thing really has me spooked. I kept worrying more and more the entire flight because I have no idea if that matters to how Thor's Hammers work, given the rotations are opposite down here from those in the Northern Hemisphere. I mean do we have to compensate for that with our input? Does it know if our lat/lon is below the equator and does it account for that on its own, or do I need to put a minus in front of the wind direction when we are down here? All these things on the flight over kept me from having any sleep or comfort enroute. Do you guys have an idea how this will work down here compared to north of the equator?"

"Professor Mcleod," Mr. Wu responded, "My good Sir, rest assured we know all about our technology and how it works. We will bring you along to slowly increase your knowledge and also your comfort level with it. In the meantime, that is why we are here. That is why we are helping you learn and leading this effort for you. We will help you understand how it works best, and help you see the true value in this technology. These devices are not dependent on a grid system or the location relative to the equator. They work on proximity to the device in a radius around it not a gridded reference. It will be fine here, just like the rainbow we did in India. We will not let such unpleasantries as your wind event occur on our watch," he assured Bob, who immediately thought he was getting somewhere so he persisted.

"Thank you that is good to hear, but how can we be sure? As you can imagine, I am still a little gun-shy about using our devices here given the, as you refer to them, unpleasantries we encountered in India. That was the Northern hemisphere where we had used them in the past and we had an unfortunate outcome. We need the confidence restored, but of course I am concerned about the risk. How would you recommend we mitigate that risk, as we have a very short amount of time before our demo here?" Bob appealed to his expertise hoping he would share, and praying he would overshare.

"Professor, given the timeline we don't have sufficient time to conduct a large-scale test, but we can do some small-scale events to be sure the confidence in your system at this location is warranted. Would that help put your mind at ease?" Mr. Wu offered, and Zach stood by silently observing the exchange to see where it would go.

"That would be wonderful; what do you suggest?" Bob asked, hoping he was not overdoing his feigned concern.

"Now is good, it should only take a few minutes and we can finish before the main briefing begins. We will simply do the system test sequence and internal calibration check. That is the best and safest way to check the operations of the device are properly functioning," Wu said, without really recognizing that what was so obvious to him was not to those with him. "Your device is available, yes?"

"Of course, it's right over here," Bob assured him and led the way, unlocking the transit case and removing the Thor's Hammer and handing it to the expert conducting the training. Bob, Captain Lessur, Ann, and Zach were all paying very close attention to what came next.

Mr. Wu explained as he held the device where all could observe his expertise in action and began to explain what was happening as he proceeded, "First, while it is still powering up, we go into the system auxiliary mode, you press this and type in a-u-x in the English keypad. It is different in Chinese. I never understood why it is not A-w-k for awk-sillery. English is a hard language, so many inconsistencies in its letters and sounds. Very hard to learn for me, but I would say I am doing ok, yes?" he explained.

"You are, you're doing great," Bob stroked his ego and continued to appear eager to learn more from the man. "Yes, of course but what settings do we need to double check to be safe, surely not all the options are necessary? That would take some time, and our briefing is starting soon." Bob was bluffing knowledge that was logical, but he did not know. Poker seemed to be a useful hobby right now, although he hadn't played much.

"We don't need to do the software version review or security updates, nor do we need to do any of the component connection checks. They don't matter to our effort; they are whatever they are and we aren't here to do updates. All we need to do are the internal, component comm checks, the external comms checks, and the calibration checks. Those take only a few minutes." He paused, then his body language revealed his realization that he said something that he did not intend to reveal. While he recognized exactly what that was, he gave no indication that he recognized the slip up about the external communications ability.

"Ok, so can you do that, or do you want me to? Time for the briefing is only ten minutes from now," Bob stayed on task.

"I can, it will be faster," Mr. Wu resumed very glad to keep moving forward, further away from what he hoped was no big deal now. "Calibration will do a quick temperature and dew point change up 1.2 degrees and down 1.4 degrees, then back to ambient, a pressure up one millibar and down two, then back to ambient, and that pressure change will also induce a wind speed change of up 2.3 knots, and a wind shift at ninety-degree increments from due north, east, south, and west at the same 2.3 knots. When all these are accurate within four decimal points of precision, it is calibrated and the system will go from aux into the main menu for entering the recipes. Only three minutes to go; see?" he asked as he began the check.

"I hope it works down here like it did in the Northern Hemisphere," Bob said staring at the calibration screen as the display indicated the measurements as it proceeded through its calibration check but his mind was focused on Wu's revelation of the, until now, unknown aux mode as well as his use of the word recipe. Again, it seemed Doc had been given credit for something he likely discovered and documented, or perhaps learned the hard way. Much faster than he hoped, Bob smiled as confidence seemed to return to the Professor, "Yes!!! Green light. The function check and calibration are good. That is excellent, all my worry for nothing it would seem. Thor's Hammer will work fine in the southern hemisphere; we need not worry now. Thank you, Mr. Wu. I can now use it with great confidence for the demonstration," Bob thanked him.

"You are welcome, Professor, I am glad your confidence is restored, despite it being slightly misplaced," he said almost apologetically. "Perhaps there is a misunderstanding? I was informed by Major General Chen that I would be operating the Thor's Hammer for the demonstration, and that you and your team would be observing and training under my guidance. Similar to what we are doing this very moment. In time, we will transition to some solo tests, then supervised operations, and then solo operations once your training and testing have been demonstrated sufficiently and documented. It is not personal, rather the opposite, it is the same training regimen we use for our own operators," he assured Bob.

They all heard it, and Mr. Wu in his effort to establish a teacher-student construct with Bob failed to recognize the blinding flash of the obvious to all present except himself as he continued. Established training regimen for all their operators?

"Given your education and experience already, I don't expect this to take more than a few more demonstrations before you are certified ready and able to do some on your own again," he assured Bob, and looked around at the rest of the group who were almost invisible to him as he focused on making the desired connections with his American contemporary for the UN effort. "I believe we can have all of your team ready in a very short amount of time after your training is complete Professor Mcleod," he assured them all as he looked at Bob when he spoke.

"That would be ideal," Bob said appreciatively, "and for now we should put this back in secure storage and join the main briefing before all the seating is taken. I don't want to be standing the entire time Brigadier General Lincoln is speaking," Bob joked as he tried to shift the focus to the next items.

"Brigadier general?" Mr. Wu asked. "A promotion for the colonel? I am certain he was wearing eagles when we departed."

"Yes, a well-deserved promotion. He will be wearing stars when you see him in a few minutes. He is a fine officer," Captain Lessur assured Mr. Wu as he and Zach exchanged surprised glances as the group all headed to the briefing.

The entire team assembled was an interesting sight to the UN delegation, but they went over all the typical items including a safety briefing, billeting, chow, transportation, work area accommodations, timelines, host nation contacts and there were very few questions. The UN team had all done this more than once before, and the CCP team either had also done this before or were instructed to save their questions for an internal forum with their own folks later in the day. Immediately after the main briefing broke up, the UN delegation leads shuffled into the small SCIF for another senior leader discussion and update. This one proved to offer even bigger news than the last one.

Bob could not contain himself and began to speak before everyone was settled in. "We learned three very important things from Mr. Wu today. Thor's Hammers have an auxiliary mode, that is useful to know about. He explained to us what it contains, and we tested and calibrated ours. You will be happy to know it works fine in the southern hemisphere. We also confirmed that it is a proximity device with a limited but unconfirmed operating radius. It has an external communications module, which means it can either be accessed and or controlled remotely and/or it can talk with other systems. These things can be networked, nested, and work together to cover a region or a path, routed together in a string or whatever. He used the word recipes for the input. He also confirmed that they have a formal training and certification program for operators of their devices. That means they must have instructors, and a curriculum which means documentation. There is documentation to be found, they can't do it all ad hoc and if they document it, they keep it somewhere and that means it can be found. We need to learn where to look and what to look for because it will be a treasure trove of information and a huge time savings as well," Bob paused.

"That's more than three things Bob, but that's ok. Great work!" Tom added. "You forgot to mention that Zach was with him; he was right? My guys are also following the equipment that came over with him, it did not follow him to link up with us here."

"Yes, Zach was with us the whole time but he never said a word. Also, I forgot to mention, on the flight over Mr. Wu checked on one of the cruise boxes a couple of times. Just the one was all he seemed interested in, but there were a couple others that had the same markings. They looked like, this." Bob showed Tom a picture of the container on his phone.

"Ok, thanks Bob. We also learned a few things that you should know that I am reluctant to reveal right now, but it may help as we go forward so I am going to apologize in advance for dropping this news on you in this way."

Tom paused, then put his hand on Bob's shoulder as he continued, "We have proof that Doc was not killed by the drunk kid because he was not driving the car when it hit Doc. We know it was an investigator working for the law firm that represents all of these Thor's sibling entities. Doc was a threat to their operation and they killed him, Bob. We don't know for certain exactly which 'they' yet, but we know it was connected. I am sorry, but we need to be extra cautious because they have already killed to protect this technology. And be assured, we have a security detail on Betty and Steve in New York, or wherever they are traveling to. Plus, your favorite Fed Miloc is with them, too. They are in good hands, but we all need to be on our A-game out here as well. We are playing with fire, Folks."

"What about Gannon? Why Doc but not Father Gannon? Somebody needs to let him know too, he needs to be looked out for as well," Bob said urgently.

"Yeah, well we aren't going to tell him anything about this. He is sidelined for a reason remember? But we have been on him the entire time, and will remain so. He is safe, and will stay that way," Tom affirmed for Ann and the Professor. "I am sorry Bob, but Doc discovered what they were doing and they killed him to keep him from revealing it. But for you and Betty they would have gotten away with it. You did good."

"But the secret got out anyway. They killed him for nothing because Thor's Hammer is out anyway," Bob said, frustrated and angry at the news.

"What if it wasn't all about what he knew, what if it was more about what he didn't know yet?" Captain Lessur asked out loud. "We've been looking at this with tons of resources and found their networks. But they don't know that yet. Doc didn't have those kinds of resources. He possessed, one maybe two devices. Killing him may have been to keep him from finding the other networks they have up and running. Again, one device is amazing, and that was the extent of our story until very recently," Lessur reasoned but Andies had another angle.

"I think you are right, but it was the way Doc went about it. I think he may have embarrassed them by tricking them into showing it to him. His notes and the data are sparse, but the random sets of charts in his records are only from random days, but all are days where there were regional modification operations occurring. Doc didn't know how to control or change the weather but it seems he suspected someone else was. He didn't have to control the weather because he already controlled the weather data. They were using his data collection to verify their regional operations, so he polluted the data set to make them see what he wanted them to see not what was actually happening. He manually altered two stations at the beginning of the trap line at least twenty times that I could find.

"I don't know if this is what happened, but others are finishing off my theory while I'm here with you guys for this dog and pony show.

"He made it look like the planned events were starting late and farther away than they should for a number of events, and he kept doing it. Same problem, same locations. Eventually he was in the right place when they came out to physically check on the device to see if it was functioning properly, if it was calibrated correctly. That is how Doc got his hands on the actual device. He who controls the data controls the narrative right? Well, the next time they come to check on it and it's gone and then another one is gone too? They were able to figure out pretty easily that he was the problem. I suppose they were confident that you were not in cahoots with him which is why they didn't go after you at the same time, Bob. Having you both un-alived at the same time would have raised some eyebrows and they didn't need to take that risk. By the time you figured it out and started using it, you had too many eyes on you too fast for them to act without having the Feds, Military and everyone else on them too. The whole UN thing is their improvised Plan C," Andies concluded.

"Damn, Andies. I was going to ease him into it," Tom rolled his eyes. "Sorry Bob, but we're near certain. Just dotting I's and crossing T's at this point. That's how it went down."

Ann was dumbfounded as she looked at Bob who was processing what he just learned. "So how does this new information impact what we have to do next? We have a demonstration in a day, do we do anything different? Is there anything we can do to make this right, I mean Doc was murdered, and that means that kid who was blamed for it probably was too. Even if he did kill himself, it was over guilt for something he didn't actually do. Someone needs to pay; we need to make this right."

"We do what Doc did," Bob stammered. "The devices are everyone's focus because it's all new to us, the press, the world. Everyone but them. We are here to demonstrate a device, to show what it can do. What we don't know is if our Thor's Hammers are old versions, new ones, the only ones, or what the other ones can do. They have airborne versions we have not seen; they have maritime versions too. We have something, but we don't know what we don't have yet. We already have one UN disastrous event where people died and now the CCP is here to save us and help the world. That's their narrative, and we are playing along. We take that and flip the script again. Tomorrow's demo needs to be a total failure and we need to make it fail."

"Where are you going with this Bob?" Frank asked concerned but not opposed to this line of thinking.

"The devices are just a means to an end. They are vital, but the controllers and synchronizers who integrate the inputs are the brains of the operation, the devices are the brawn. We need to see, and get our hands on the brains. I bet that is what Mr. Wu was so concerned with on the way out here. He is transporting the controllers, and Zach and his guys were bringing out the regional devices because there aren't any down here for them to use already. They are probably staging them as we speak. Mr. Wu explained to all of us that he is the one who will control the device for this demo. My hunch is that is because this device is either a decoy and they will be using their regional system to keep things aligned in order to do another complex demonstration which cannot be done with just one device. They use this one as a token player in the whole thing just so it looks like they are masters of a device when in fact it is a larger more capable system that is producing broader and more intense results. They are masters, and we are novices, rinse and repeat at each demonstration. They stay in control and we and the world are none the wiser while they continue making money and power moves on scale but at an accelerated pace. We need to disrupt that."

"That's sick Bob!" Sergeant Andies smiled. "Sick! They will have to go into damage control mode and we will be watching with everything we have. Once we see where they are, we can swoop in and snatch them up and get them red-handed. Tom, we are gonna need a couple more teams before the demo starts. How fast can you get them here, unless they are already here?"

"Tap the brakes boys, what exactly are you proposing?" Tom needed some clarification, which Bob willingly provided.

"If we go by the CCP and Major General Chen's script, then Mr. Wu is going to be controlling the inputs to our Thor's Hammer. Those inputs will be relevant to the overall conditions because he knows we will be watching and he will be showing us what and how to properly use this device. But those conditions will already have been calculated and considered in the regional inputs that are really governing the demonstration area. It is very similar to how they did the wind event within our demonstration. Multiple devices can either counter or complement each other's outcomes," Bob paused.

"So what?" Tom asked as Bob continued.

"So, we have to spook them by reporting conditions that are not what they expect. Like Doc did. We fudge the data to make them think something is going wrong, that what they expect is *not* what is occurring. They will have to go into assessment mode of the various systems. The more systems we know about before we start, the better our odds of getting them to react to our false reporting. When they troubleshoot their systems, we find them, track them and go get them. If we do this right, we can graduate from a single device to a regional network by the end of our time in Australia. The CCP might know we are on to them when we do this, but we will know what they have and we will have what they know."

"Sounds great, but exactly *how* do we do all this in less than a day?" Mr. Dau finally chimed in.

"Zach," Ann said flatly. "We get Zach to help us, and we can save a lot of time and mitigate a lot of risk. Having him report the discrepancies will add credibility to them and the need for an urgent response. Taking the bait from us might be a longshot, but taking the same bait from both Zach and Mr. Wu? Now that is the kind of punch we need to get the response we are hoping for right?"

"Probably a good point Ann, but how do we get Zach on board?" Frank asked her politely.

"I have an idea on how we might do that," she smiled. After listening to her idea and talking through a series of branches and sequels about how to bring this all about in what was essentially a twenty-hour period they began to see a path to their objective. After Tom summarized for everyone to ensure they all knew their actions, timelines and expectations the group agreed to go for it and began to break up before their next briefing in ten hours. At this meeting they would communicate their actions and results and decide whether this plan was a go or a no-go.

As they began to walk together back to their team room, Ann added for Bob, "I really am sorry that Doc had to pay the price for all of this. I know that will be hard for Betty to hear, as well. But I have to say that I am both sad and thankful. Without all this, you and I would likely have never met, and we would never have gotten together. I am also glad that the US government in all its forms got to you before the CCP did. Again, that might be selfish, but I am glad we are together. I am glad we can work together to make this right," Ann said as she held his hand and matched him stride for stride.

Bob looked at her and smiled as he said, "Me too, Ann, me too. Now let's make sure they don't get away with it."

CHAPTER SIXTEEN

OWN THE DATA

The day began early for everyone as the preparation for the important demonstration had to be transformed from ideas into live events conducted in an orchestrated timeline that very afternoon. At the first meeting of the morning, Major General Chen suggested the team do the exact same demonstration that they had done in India earlier. He reasoned that the same condition changes and creating the distant rain shower in a precise location where none otherwise would be occurring and that it be precisely positioned to create a rainbow in plain view for the assembled crowd would impress everyone here just as it did then. Additionally, it would prove that India was not just a fluke, as this time they would announce it in advance. And finally, it would show everyone that the CCP team could operate the technology safely in either hemisphere. It was a well-rehearsed and solidly reasoned recommendation which was equally well received by his peers and the host nation's attendees who were coordinating the demonstration on their soil.

Bob looked at Ann and smiled as he said, "That simplifies things for us. We know what parameters we need to adjust. Now we need to intercept Zach before this session breaks up but I have not seen him yet; have you?"

"No, and if I were them, I don't know that I would have him anywhere near the preparations today. I would trot him out just in time for the demonstration, in plain view for the cameras then walk him back out with the big shots," Ann said. "So, big shot it is," she said and almost on que, the UN Secretary General walked into the room and headed toward the front of the briefing area where Major General Chen was wrapping up his comments. A little surprised to see him amongst the operations team, the general politely adhered to protocol and introduced him to those in attendance and turned over the presenter's platform so he could address the group.

"Thank you, Major General Chen, it is a pleasure to finally meet you in person," the Secretary General said as he shook the man's hand and turned to make sure there was sufficient opportunity for a few pictures from his entourage before he continued talking.

"Let me say how much I appreciate you, personally, and your team assisting in this worthy UN work. It is important that we not only ensure this new technology is proliferated fairly and safely, but that we all understand its potential impacts whether they be positive or negative. In our efforts to help some, we must avoid any unintended consequences that may cause harm to others. We are in unchartered territory here, and it is comforting to know that you are willing to share your expertise and resources to achieve those objectives.

"I understand we are in for another rainbow treat this afternoon. That is something I am very excited about seeing in person. It was impressive to see it on television when your team did that in India, very impressive indeed. I can only imagine how magnificent it will be to see in person this afternoon. Very exciting. But I must also apologize in advance to you and your team because my travel windows for earlier commitments will require me to depart directly from the demonstration to get to the airport in time to make my departure for my next engagement. I won't be able to celebrate with you after today's event, but I will make sure to get around to thank everyone in person before the demo. I want to personally thank everyone and will try not to get in the way. Thank you again; it is great to be among you all as we do this very worthy work."

And, with that, he walked over to the seating area and took a seat so that the rest of the briefing and preparations could continue as needed despite, or with the additional pressure of, the UN leader's attendance. Once everyone was clear on the objectives, communications, timelines and plans up to and during the event, they were released to go make it happen. With that, the Secretary General began his thank you tour with Major General Chen, Brigadier General Lincoln, their Australian counterpart, Mr. Dau and the Australian Ambassador to the UN. They exchanged the necessary diplomatic pleasantries and listened to how the teams were organized and located for the events before, during and after the demonstration. The press area was clearly defined, but there was no confusion about the fact they were, and would be, everywhere today not just confined to the designated media areas.

The security plan was equally well informed and briefed. Once all were comfortable with the good work of the integrated team in preparation for this afternoon's world-wide event, they began to walk toward the team areas. The first one was the logistics team which had again quite impressively pulled together the needed resources, equipment and facilities on very short notice in a relatively isolated area of the globe. As they began their transition toward the technology team, Bob gave his group a head's up to be ready for the distinguished visitors or "DVs" who were on their way over. It was then he saw Mr. Wu making his way toward Bob with Zach in tow. It was clear that they did not want to miss the opportunity for a photo op or a few words from the DVs with their CCP-American expert standing with Mr. Wu and General Chen providing their expertise for this improved team effort that clearly no longer needed Professor Mcleod; the man in charge during the debacle that was the UN's solo effort in India.

As the two men joined Bob, Ann and Captain Lessur at the entrance of the Technology Team's work area Mr. Wu greeted the team with a polite, "Hello. Good morning, everyone." Zach smiled and nodded without saying a word as he flanked Mr. Wu. As they stood there watching the DV's slowly making their way toward them, Tom walked up and took a position slightly behind but next to Zack who blocked Mr. Wu's view of the new arrival to the group. As he slid into position, Tom pushed a small piece of paper into Zach's pocket making sure he could feel the contact as he said softly to him, "Read it later. Listen for what he wants; not what he asks."

And, with that, Tom continued past the team leadership and greeted the DV's as they made their entrance. He apologized for not joining them earlier, but assured them he would be available to assist them as needed for the remainder of their tour and through the live demonstration. It seemed a bit arrogant to some that the senior US delegate was late and presumed that it really mattered to anyone that he was. With that, they made their way in, and Bob introduced himself as the UN's team lead and then introduced Mr. Wu as the CCP's team lead.

The Secretary General, good to his word, did the same as he did with the logistics team. He asked the name of each individual, where they were from, what their role was here and then personally thanked them for their contribution. He smiled as he began with Ann, and warmly greeted her making sure the group knew they were already well acquainted.

"Ann, so good to see you again. This work seems to suit you, as you are as lovely as ever, perhaps more so today despite the challenging schedule we have you on," he gushed over her, as he thanked her and listened as she briefly described her role for this effort. She wrapped up her comments as the Secretary General moved next to Zach and gave him an inquisitive look as he extended his hand.

"I believe we have met somewhere before, Sir, but I cannot recall where? Your face is very familiar to me, but I am sorry I don't remember your name; please forgive me, you are?" he asked apologetically as Zach considered Tom's words in his ear before he responded to the question.

"Good morning, Mr. Secretary. I am afraid you are mistaking me for someone that I am not. We have not met in person before today, I can assure you that I would remember if we had. My name is Zach," he said politely, only answering the question he was asked in order to neither ignore the Secretary General's question nor break the rules Mr. Wu had explained in great detail to him.

"My mistake then," the Secretary said graciously, "and what then is your role here Zach?"

"My role is to assist the UN's technicians and the CCP's technicians in achieving the desired outcomes when they employ the Thor's Hammers during the demonstrations," he said truthfully and deliberately.

"So, you have experience using the technology then? I thought I had met all the US experts already during my work with Bob and Ann?" he said curiously.

"That is likely very true sir, as I am no expert. But I do have extensive experience transitioning many technologies for both the US and CCP. My CCP customers thought my unique expertise could provide valuable contributions to their effort. They invited me to assist them and, of course, I could not refuse the opportunity since I was between projects at the time. I hope I can help bring this UN effort along to meet its objective," he smiled.

"Very good then Zach. I hope so, it was nice to meet you," the Secretary General said and moved along to greet Captain Lessur and meet the rest of the operations team. One by one, he did the same for every member of each team just like he said he would. This kept lots of eyes on him and the DV's as they did so, which was the intent. The meeting and greeting were good for morale, but the one conversation that it was designed to conceal already happened and had produced the desired result. Hiding a stolen car in a full parking lot seemed to work for car thieves, and it also seemed to be working for concealing conversations. Zach's responses indicated that he understood Tom's instructions, and they upheld the team's working theory that Zach was not wholly what he seemed. That he was neither working willingly with the CCP nor was he responsible for what had happened previously. At this point, there was still great optimism that the note in his pocket may very well be the most important piece of paper of any produced to date for this effort.

Frank was again doing and orchestrating most of the heavy lifting for today's demonstration. The man was able to see multiple activities on their own timelines and synchronize them into an impressive culmination of efforts at the same place and time to produce something impressive to behold. It was remarkably similar to an orchestra conductor, Mr. Dau thought to himself as he impatiently waited for Tom to re-appear with the group after another in a series of unexplained and unannounced departures throughout the afternoon. As the DV's were assembling in the viewing area for the demonstration which was set to begin in less than half an hour almost everyone was hoping they would see a flawless demonstration as they had in India, with the earlier promised rainbow. The few that were not, were hoping for something even better; a failed event for the right reasons would mean a tactical failure but a strategic victory. It was unclear to Mr. Dau whether Tom's absence should be perceived as a sign of confidence or concern. It was Mr. Dau's nature to see it as both and be ready for whatever happened next.

The media were already in place and broadcasting for hours in advance of the event. They had staked out various vantage points for what they thought might get them the best shots of the speaker's stage and both the rain shower and its rainbow when they appeared. There was a surprising number of people in attendance given the relatively small population of Darwin. This included a good number of aboriginal community members who were concerned about others modifying the weather in or near their ancestral regions with little or no consultation with them.

The technology team was making last minute reviews of the equipment and readying for what seemed like a fairly mechanical "re-do" of the last event. Just do what we did last time. Except for the UN members of the team, who were not included in the "we" that did that last demonstration. It was all new to them, and so they were eager to watch and see in action what the CCP team had explained and showed them many times in the run-up training and dry runs prior to the live event. Near the main operations area, the technology team huddled around the computer displays showing the numerous readouts of the network of portable weather sensors the UN team employed throughout the demonstration area. This included two portable doppler weather radars: one primary and one spare. There was also a variety of radio and network communications systems that shared power sources, antennae farms and other technical commonalities with the weather systems that were co-located to ensure operations and troubleshooting any system anomalies could be examined and resolved in the context of impacts to other systems. This helped assess things like whether a lost signal was confined to a specific system or perhaps the result of a power source failure impacting several systems concurrently. The Thor's Hammer was located nearby and surrounded by a special security team with very advanced perimeter defense systems and a direct path in and out of the technology team's work area.

"It is time. We will input the recipes into the Thor's Hammer now to begin the sequences we briefed. The temperature changes, the wind direction and speed changes and then the rain shower to the northeast of the viewing area. Shall we, Professor?" Mr. Wu invited Bob to join him as some of their team members followed and some remained behind with the task of monitoring the readouts.

"Yes. Let us go create another chapter in the legacy of Thor's Hammer Mr. Wu," Bob agreed as they walked toward the small machine that had brought them all to this place at this time. As Mr. Wu entered the various recipes, he explained what he was entering and how to enter each keystroke for the planned events. After completing the rain shower location and intensity inputs, he wrapped up and said, "All that remains now is to monitor the results and enjoy the show. The fruits of our labor will soon be revealed."

With that, he closed the panel that protects the input pad and looked around as Bob asked, "That was to create the rain shower, but you did not explain or show how you selected the location for your input. How are we to understand how and when the rainbow will appear relative to the location of the sun? That you did not discuss with us. It was my understanding that was to be part of this training," Bob challenged.

"Yes, Professor. That was calculated prior to our coming out. Today's lesson is input of the recipes and confirmation of the input on the device to ensure that it is accurately programmed with the prescribed input. The calculations you refer to are advanced and require substantial amounts of sophisticated computations and that training can come later," he assured them.

Bob persisted, "But how can it be that complicated? It's basic trigonometry, no? Angles, distance, radiance, some suspended aerosol particle refraction, maybe? What else is there? This is fledgling technology; it can't be too advanced that we won't understand it. We are all well-educated and experienced scientists—bachelor's, master's and doctorate degrees. I am sure we will be able to follow along, Mr. Wu."

"Of course, Professor. Please forgive my arrogance, as I did not mean to offend anyone especially my own teammates. I will be sure to include that discussion at your convenience as our training continues. Right now, though, we are on a clock and there are many waiting on our return and thumbs up for them to begin. We should not keep the other teams nor the attendees waiting, don't you agree?" he apologized and suggested they stay on the designated timeline for their execution checklist events.

"Thank you, Mr. Wu that will be helpful. And yes, we should not hold up today's events for something we can do at our own leisure," Bob agreed as they continued their short walk back to the operations area and gave the radio call indicating to everyone on the net that the inputs had been made and the timeline for the various atmospheric changes had been initiated. It was showtime.

The cameras flashed, the questions flew, and the cheers and jeers began as the UN Secretary General, himself, started up the event from the microphone-laden podium. He went to great lengths to thank the CCP, the Chinese delegation and the people of China for joining the UN effort to bring on-demand weather modification to the world. He stated again his confidence and trust that their new combined team approach was leveraging the strengths of all involved to make this revolution in technology safer and faster to field for the benefit of all. This was music to the ears of the assembled crowd and to those watching around the world hoping to see for themselves actions to support the words. There was great hope spread far and wide but still veiled in skepticism after the disastrous wind event. Was the rainbow a fluke, or was it repeatable and worthy of putting one bad event behind them with renewed faith fueled by a developing partnership? It was time to find out.

The Secretary General turned the podium over to Major General Chen who was flanked by Mr. Dau. The duo would co-host and narrate all of the events of the day. Frank and everyone else would be elbow deep in communicating and ensuring what the two were explaining was actually happening and updating them as they did so. As they were explaining the first modification they would experience, the small temperature changes first up then down, the technology team was busy monitoring and updating. Sergeant Andies was the first to call out the anomaly.

"Hey Captain...Professor. The temps are coming up on sensors 3, 4 and 5 but they are climbing past five degrees and still going? Is that what you put in?" Andies asked for confirmation.

"No, Sergeant. They should not be coming up that high, double check them," Bob replied. "Mr. Wu, could you join us please?" Bob asked calmly and the man finished his conversation with one of the radio operators and joined the professor.

"Still climbing Professor. They are now up seven degrees Fahrenheit. And now sensors 8 and 9 have dropped three degrees, they are going in different directions, but they are out of sequence, and both are almost six minutes ahead of what you told me. Did you change the event sequence or the timing from this morning's briefing sheet?" Andies asked now concerned at what he was seeing.

"No. Nothing changed. Mr. Wu, is this what happened last time? This is not what we were expecting to see," Bob asked calmly.

"I am sure it is ok. Just adjusting to the new environment, or perhaps the sensors are not functioning properly? Are you sure they were set up and connected correctly?" Mr. Wu queried accusingly.

"Everything was ops checked repeatedly. I did the sensor placement with your team myself. They were perfect three hours ago during the dry run and nothing has changed since then. They are holding steady while the stage sensors are reading what you said it would be, but the sensors just beyond the media area and those on the northeast in the surrounding area are nowhere near what they should be," Andies reported.

"See, we're feeling what it should be. It surely is your sensor malfunction," Mr. Wu assured the sergeant. "Captain Lessur, those should be checked out after the demonstration is completed. We cannot afford to be distracted by erroneous data at critical times like this."

"Agreed. Mr. Wu," Captain Lessur confirmed as he shot a glance at his sergeant and noticed Zach standing near one of the CCP radio operators.

Sergeant Andies, reported to the group again, "Winds on sensors 4, 6, 8 and 10 are from the east at ten knots. But sensors 5, 7, 9 and 11 are from the west at 14 knots. What the hell is going on? That can't be right, that is not how wind works, especially with them being that close together. Professor, what the hell is happening? This is not supposed to be doing this?"

"Mr. Wu, can you help us understand this anomaly? We cannot afford another disaster here while everyone is watching," Bob pressed him urgently.

"What does the viewing area sensor read?" Mr. Wu asked. "Is it indicating the winds as we input them?"

"Yes," Bob reported with some audible relief in his voice.

"Good," Mr. Wu sounded a bit relieved, as well, as he glanced over at Zach who was still standing next to the man speaking Chinese and typing frantically into his keypad. Zach shrugged his shoulders and raised his eyebrows in slight confusion and curiosity, and he offered nothing more to alarm or console Mr. Wu.

"Professor, you should come look at this," Captain Lessur alerted Bob loud enough for all to hear. The screen displaying the returns from the portable doppler weather radars both indicated a developing rain shower was beginning to form as expected, but there was a problem. It was in the wrong place. "You told me the rain shower would be to the southwest, this shower is to the northeast. It's not moving, nor will it move to the southwest with this upper-level flow. It's in the wrong place, Bob! Rainbows are a result of refraction as light passes through tiny rain droplets, then reflects off the back of the interior of the droplet. The sun must be behind us as we look at the rainbow. For a morning bow in this hemisphere, at this time of year, that means the shower must be southwest of us. This is not going to work. What the hell guys? What is happening here?!" the captain demanded from nobody in particular.

As Bob and Mr. Wu examined the screen and Captain Lessur operated the controls, they confirmed the return echoes were not at all where they expected them to originate. While it was early in the development of the planned shower, it indicated a catastrophic outcome for the promised repeat rainbow. That was an outcome Mr. Wu could not tolerate as he knew his superiors would not either. He strode quickly toward Zach who was nodding up and down with a concerned look on his face.

As Mr. Wu approached, Zach moved toward him, took his arm and informed him quietly, "They are seeing it, too. It is in the wrong place. They reported the winds were all messed up. Something is not right, and we in here are not the only ones who are seeing it. What should we do?" Zach asked. "This cannot fail, you know what they will do to both of us and your family if it does."

With that Mr. Wu told the radio operator to get up from his station and Mr. Wu replaced him and began both typing and talking as quickly as he could. Captain Lessur and Sergeant Andies took turns reporting on the growth and location of the rain shower and the wildly erratic surface wind directions and speeds from the various sensors. With each report, they would raise their voices with concern directed at both Professor Mcleod and Mr. Wu who together led the combined technology team.

"Why is this happening you guys? What do we need to do? We cannot have another tragedy. This is not making any sense. Tell us why this is going on." There was increasing and mounting pressure on the two to respond to the events unfolding around them. The clock was ticking and they had not made any updates or changes to Thor's Hammer to modify the trajectory of the programmed events that so many were assembled to witness. It seemed like Mr. Wu had been at that station for a very long time when Bob finally called him out in front of everyone.

"What are you doing over there, we need you over here and we need you over here now. We need to change something, or this is going to be a total embarrassment, a total failure. We made a rain shower, that's great but we put it in the wrong place and the narration script is wrong. The rainbow won't happen from here, can you fix this or not?" Bob demanded, but Mr. Wu stayed firmly in his seat, fixated on the terminal in front of him and the conversations in his headset.

"We are running out of time Mr. Wu, are you going to help us or not? This whole thing is coming apart over here," Bob pressed and Zach tapped Mr. Wu on the shoulder and pointed to his watch, gave a puzzled look then pointed to Bob again. His response was a glare that communicated he was not to be interrupted again, and Zach relayed the message to the panicking UN group,

"Just a few more minutes, I believe Mr. Wu is currently doing what it is you are asking about. Let's give him a few more minutes please, we don't want to mess this up do we?" Zach defended Mr. Wu's lack of response while concurrently communicating to the UN team that the results they were really after were occurring in real time.

"OK, but we are running out of time to either announce a change or eat a very unfortunate outcome of a less than successful demonstration,"

Captain Lessur announced. "Indecision is its own decision, and we are about to pass the point of no return on this."

And after the captain's warning, almost on que the team could hear the crowd begin cheering as the faint rainbow began to darken into bright vivid colors as Mr. Dau and Major General Chen stood proudly and accepted the cheers on behalf of the UN and their assembled team. The demonstration had delivered as promised, and the world saw through the lenses of the media what could be done when great minds combined to collaborate on a worthy goal. The Secretary General joined the two front and center, stood between them and grabbed hands and then raised them above their heads in victory as the rainbow showed brightly behind them. A smashing success for the demonstration team and the restoration of the faith in the UN effort to bring the technology safely to operations.

Mr. Wu emerged from his station angry and disappointed that he was missing out on the success and celebration because of the incompetence of his UN colleagues.

"I am very disappointed in the performance of this team. Your data was horribly inaccurate and your ability to interpret it appalling. I have never seen such an unprofessional and inaccurate operation. This is unacceptable and we need to hold accountable those whose incompetence nearly cost us the failure of this demonstration. They will be removed and replaced immediately with members of my own team. Failures such as those seen here today will not be tolerated, Professor Mcleod. You have assembled the equivalent of a meteorological clown car here today," he fumed as he stormed off toward the celebrating senior leaders to join in their jubilation.

"I guess that means I get to go home early?" Sergeant Andies grinned and said loudly as he tried to draw everyone's attention toward him while he watched Tom take Zach by the arm and walk him briskly out the other way.

"Me too, Andies. This is all on me. This was my responsibility, and we will have to see what happened here. That rain shower is actually where it should be, to the northeast not the southwest. Are you sure you had the antennae oriented on the radar mast correctly Captain Lessur?" Bob asked.

"I thought you did that Professor?" he responded with a grin. "You're the team leader. That was an important task, so I figured you would want to do that yourself and not trust it to some lowly Air Force captain."

"I don't remember that discussion, but maybe that would be a good place to start our after-action review. Right now, we have a demonstration to wrap up, don't we?" Bob asked.

"Yes, there are still a good number of things to complete before we are done here," he was reminded.

As Tom led Zach quickly down the passageway into the awaiting vehicle, they were quiet until the three vehicles sped off, then Zach broke the silence with a question.

"Where are we going?" Zach asked, and accepted Tom's limited response.

"*We* aren't going anywhere. *You*, are getting on a plane that will take you to a safe, secure, and very isolated place that I am sure you will enjoy, and do you know how I know you will enjoy it?" Tom asked.

"How do you know I will enjoy it?" Zach followed the script.

Tom continued, "First, because there won't be any of your CCP associates there. Second, you will get to decide your own fate. You will be debriefed, and get to tell your story, which we will of course verify or discredit so please don't waste our time. Third, you won't have to worry about any of this weather modification technology at all. Full stop, nothing more to do with this. You can pursue your favorite hobby as long as it's not this one. The more helpful you are to us, the better you will get to be at something else. Have a safe trip Zach, and choose your fate wisely. I am sure I will get the chance to check up on you before too long. I hope it's all still good with you when I see you again," Tom said sternly as the vehicle rolled to a stop near the small aircraft parked on the long stretch of road.

The doors opened, Zach was removed from the vehicle and loaded into the small jet that immediately began rolling down the roadway and lifted off to points unknown to anyone except Tom and the crew flying his airplane. The vehicles flipped around and headed back toward the demonstration area. Tom rejoined the technology team before Mr. Wu returned from his elbow rubbing with the DV's celebrating their success.

"It's good to see them so happy," Tom said as he joined Bob, Ann and the Air Force weather guys.

"Yes, it is. Where is Frank? I thought he was with you," Ann asked Tom, who replied vaguely. "He is still busy, will be for a while but I will see him when he's done," Tom predicted as he congratulated the team and walked off. "Great work today, you guys really suck! You made Mr. Wu freak out over nothing, shame on you."

As Brigadier General Lincoln saw the President's National Security Advisor joining the large group which had been incrementally assembling at the closed hangar on the remote Australian military airfield, he closed the distance between them quickly, smiling as he did so and began to fill him in.

"We have them all here, except one. It is in hand, and enroute, should be here within the hour," Frank began.

"Really? That's better than I expected but that's great news!" Tom said, genuinely impressed at the outcome of the day's events. "You guys got them all? You sure?"

"We got everyone who was on the net, at least everyone with a call sign, everyone who transmitted. If they had anyone only monitoring or in receive only, like on standby or something we didn't get them. But if they were active today, and I think everyone checked in so I am confident we got them all. There were seven remotely piloted vehicles and the control node was a vehicle mounted system, maybe twenty clicks from the main demonstration site. Every station that Mr. Wu contacted to check on their data, or their system sensors we were able to identify and find. We tracked them, and then, once the last airborne system was on the ground, we hit them all at the same time," Frank explained.

"We have the airborne platforms, their devices and communications suites from each of the regional nodes they used down here. The command node was all self-contained in one vehicle. It's already loaded and tied down in the plane. Once the last one gets here, we will load it with the rest and get them all out of dodge. Should be wheel's up and on our way in less than forty-five mikes," Frank concluded.

"All our eggs in one basket? Isn't it a little risky putting everything on one plane, what if something happens to it?" Tom questioned.

"Not all. One is on the same flight that took Zach out. We may need it to verify his story, plus it may speed things up on the next phase if they are in the same place at the same time. And like you said, eggs and baskets and all," Frank clarified.

"Good, that's good. What about the rest of the team? You know Major General Chen, his senior colonels and Mr. Wu are all gonna be in the hot seat for this soon enough despite their outwardly successful demonstration. I don't see the UN team coming out of this intact, we need to make sure the kids don't get hurt in the divorce." Tom was thinking as he was talking, "This all came together pretty fast."

"Yes, and we have our Aussie teammates to thank for the extra strike teams. Good news is nobody was seriously injured, the CCP teams were all civilian looking so they blended in, but not many were armed given the gun laws down here. Those who were, all appeared smart enough to recognize they were going to be on the losing end of whatever action they took if it looked like anything other than compliance. We will have to see if the general, his colonels and Mr. Wu want to disappear from here or go home and answer to their party leadership for what just happened on their watch. It won't surprise me if we get some advanced technical assistance to help out with our new systems. Seems the smartest of the options but that will be your problem soon enough. We will need to get back there pretty soon or you and I won't be able to rejoin the team at all," Frank cautioned as the last of the newly acquired systems rolled into the hanger and was immediately transloaded into the transport.

Shortly after that, the ramp closed, the hangar door opened and the aircraft was towed outside, where power was applied, and the engines started. A few moments later it began to taxi then rolled onto the runway took off and slowly disappeared into the sky with its precious cargo bound for who knows where?

As the senior group assembled back at the UN operations area for the demonstration debrief, they were a couple of minutes late starting. This was due to Brigadier General Lincoln's uncharacteristic tardiness, for which he apologized to the group as he began the debrief.

"Sorry I am late everyone. It could not be helped and I am happy to share the reason why with all of you. I just got off a call with the President of the United States, The Prime Minister of Australia and the UN Secretary General and each of them asked me to extend their personal appreciation for the exceptional work each of you did today. They conveyed their thanks for an immensely successful demonstration, that is being received positively around the world. So, that is what I am doing right now. You have their personal message of gratitude, and I would also like to extend my own to accompany the messages I am carrying for them. Great work today, everyone. Mission accomplished, and we could not have done it without the professionalism of each and every one of you as individuals who worked together as a team to accomplish a common objective. Please give yourselves a round of applause!" Frank encouraged and the group willingly complied, except for the couple of senior leaders of the CCP delegation who were notably not in attendance.

After the large debrief, the small UN team assembled in the makeshift SCIF for their Thor's Hammer and Thor's Journeymen updates, which Tom immediately summarized for those in the small room.

"Great work everyone. Ann, I gotta say maybe you need to consider a career change and an upgrade in man-choice. I think you are sandbagging, seriously. It all worked," he smiled as he continued. "The data spoof freaked Wu out. He got on their network and contacted the command node who did check ins with everyone. They reported in and out with the temps, winds, and rain and we were able to identify and track all their players digital comms. We got teams in place and simultaneous hits produced their devices, computers, even the command vehicle itself. We got Zach's help selling it to Wu and he is already on his way somewhere we can help him decide what to do next.

"General Chen, his two senior colonels and Mr. Wu are all getting their asses handed to them right now. As soon as their bosses are done doing that our friends will get a visit from some of my other friends who are concerned about their well-being if they return home. My other friends may be in a position to provide them some alternate travel plans if they are interested. The rest of the team, and the world got to see a successful demonstration, and we get to wait and see what the UN decides to do for their next demonstration." Tom paused and looked around the room at the smiling faces.

"There are few items that still need to be decided. Next assignments are on the table, right now and I would like to know your preferences. I am being deadly serious with this question. Do you want to stay on with the current UN effort to show the world how Thor's Hammer promises to improve the quality of life for as many as possible...which is the overt and public effort that must continue.

"Or, do you want to be part of the team that needs to very quickly understand the current regional and integrated operation of the systems we just acquired? They suspect we know, and they are going to suspect the Aussies, or the UN, or the US or all of us are responsible for the disappearance of their deployed systems. Even if we can convincingly blame this on their own guys, they will suspect we know. But no matter how that goes, the CCP is going to step up their own timeline or take even more drastic action. We are going to need to understand the regional application of this technology and then level up at nearly the same time.

"We need to get this capability on orbit so we can control this on a global scale to disable or at least counter their other fielded regional systems.

"And we don't have much time to pull all this off. You are all the best we have at this, but you can't be in two places at once. And we cannot be competing for your attention or be distracted by other priorities. So, the President asked me to consider your preferences then come up with a plan that does not put anyone doing something they would be opposed to doing. That's the good news. The bad news is I gotta get him the plan fast. Which means if you already know what you want to do, I would appreciate your letting me know right now," Tom concluded, and looked around the room at the team in hopes someone would willingly respond to his offer.

"Count me in on getting this on orbit. If it's anything like I just got to do with your group, I'd love to keep down that path, Tom. That is if the offer includes active-duty Air Force guys?" Sergeant Andies requested, and without delay Captain Lessur also presented his own hopes.

"Me too. No offense to anyone but that is much more in my wheelhouse than this. As enjoyable as this has been so far, that sounds like a great fit for me."

Tom willingly accepted both men's request, "SECDEF assured me we could put you guys anywhere you wanted to be. You earned a say in what comes next for you. Thanks, you're in."

Mr. Dau chimed in next, "Well someone's gotta pick up your slack if you're both leaving. I might as well keep doing it since I've gotten pretty good at it while you were here. Not much of a change really, so if it's all the same I will stick with the UN effort. Besides, I like to get out of the stuffy headquarters building whenever I can." His sense of humor was dry, but appreciated and he was clearly well suited for what he was already doing.

"I am afraid my decision has been made for me, so I will pass on the discussion if you don't mind," Frank offered as the only two now remaining were Ann and Bob.

"And what was that decision that was made for you, Frank? Can you share that with us?" Ann asked.

"If you like, yes, I suppose I can since I was not expressly told not to disclose it." He paused, as Ann persisted with a look of impatience, "I will be assisting with the technology transfer and spaceborne development."

"Thank you, Frank. And since I am talking already, I will tell you all that wherever Bob wants to go, that's where I want to be." She looked at him, smiled and continued, "This is not a copout or pressure on you to make me happy. I got into this because of you, I stayed in it for you, and I want to move ahead with you. That simple, I don't have a preference on what role. My preference is solely based on who I'm with, and that's with you."

"OK then," Bob took a deep breath, looked around and then back at Ann. "You and I should finish what we started. Let's get this out there where it can help everyone. Let's get this where Doc couldn't. Let's all work to make this right. Ann and I will keep with Mr. Dau and the UN effort. If we do this right, and work together everyone wins."

"Everyone still ok with their choices, or does anyone want to adjust now that we have all spoken our minds? You should also know it will be my job to keep all you cats herded in the same direction," Tom added.

"Hearing none, I guess we now have an outline of what comes next. Let's get packed up and loaded onto the aircraft tomorrow. We have a lot to do, and we can't do much of it until we get back to New York. Yes, New York. Apparently, that is the latest update from UN as the Secretary General was departing from the airport after today's demonstration. Two rainbows, that was enough to get everyone's confidence to a level where we can plan how to take this to the next level. The world is behind this effort. No pressure you guys. See you at the airport, I still have some things I need to wrap up and I know you all still have lots to do. Let's get it done," Tom said as he left the room, and those in it with much to consider.

EPILOGUE

Taking a play from their new UN teammates' playbook, Bob and his teammates manipulated their weather data to deceive Mr. Wu, inducing him to take actions to achieve a desired outcome. This less than honest manipulation of data produced a disastrous outcome for the CCP's on-demand weather modification program. With the total loss/capture of their deployed operational airborne systems and ground control nodes, it was now clear to the powers that be that their covert capability was, or soon would be exposed. As they attempt to find out what happened and who was responsible, there will also be time sensitive strategic decisions to be made regarding their other regional systems. Will they play defense or offense with their remaining asymmetric advantage while they still can?

Professor Mcleod said of Zach, that double agents have singular loyalties; loyalty to themselves. It remains to be seen whether Zach will help or hinder the newly underway US efforts to understand the existing fielded systems, and to counter them with the hasty launch of an on-orbit global capability. Will he help the CCP, the US or just himself? Tom said he would get to choose his own fate, but what will that look like in a world of on-demand weather? What will any of our fates look like in a world where governments, organizations, groups and individuals all have the ability to control or change the weather? When they agree on what that looks like, it could be great but how will disagreements or aggression be resolved? And by whom?

They say with experience comes wisdom for those who choose to see it. The team that successfully executed operations as *Thor's Journeymen* will continue that work and expand it to address the new challenges of countering a mature in-place capability. The existence of covertly operational air and surface systems already controlling the weather on a regional scale in key locations around the world is a clear and present danger. It is also an exciting opportunity to leap into new applications of this technology that is now known to be anything but new. See how Professor Mcleod and the team from *Thor's Journeymen* take their efforts to a whole new level in *Thor's Craftsmen*, the exciting conclusion of this trilogy.

Symbology

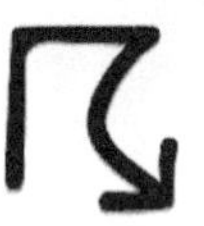 Thunderstorm, discovery

 Protection, shield, sanctuary

 Wet fog

 Zodiacal light

 Lightning

 Magic, mystery, feminine

 Heat, visibility reduced by smoke

 Dawn, break-through, awareness

 Disruption, confession, loss, change

 Heavy thunderstorm with snow

 Growth, beginnings, liberation

 Joy, success, peace, fellowship

 Fusion

 Revelation, knowledge, creativity, inspiration

 Decompose

 Power, authority, strength

 Reduction of gold to powder through heat

 Endurance, lasting energy

 Mirage

 Space, the stars, safe travels

Thor's Journeymen shows us how on-demand weather modification is the same as any other tool. In the right hands and used for the right purpose, it can provide amazing benefits. Alternatively, in the wrong hands or used for the wrong purpose, it can produce devastating results; sometimes intended, and sometimes unintended.

Professor Mcleod and his team prove that controlling the weather data can be almost as powerful as controlling the weather itself. Employing a deceptive information operation at a pivotal point in time enabled them to turn the tables on those working to undermine their well-intended efforts. If we look with intellectual honesty, we may regularly see this in our own lives, organizations and governments.

Importantly, they also learn the dangers of intended public information denial via clandestine operations. We must remain vigilant in our understanding that other nations may very well secretly possess and employ undisclosed technological advantages against our own. We must resist a national arrogance that presumes that, if the US doesn't have it or know about it, then it must not exist.

The real impacts of denying the potential threats of a technology we do not possess can be catastrophic. In *Thor's Journeymen* that technology is on-demand weather modification, but the hidden truth is discovered in time to do something about it. In *Thor's Craftsmen*, you will learn the rest of their accomplishments. Let's hope Bob Mcleod's fictional success mirrors our own in the years to come.